## It was a hell of a mess

Blake emerged from the cockpit and shook his head. "They had a small charge rigged under the instrument panel, Captain. Between that and the hand grenade, there's not much left. The plane cannot be flown or taxied. If we want to move it, it will have to be towed."

"No other explosives? Remember, they threatened to destroy the plane completely."

Blake nodded. "That's right, Captain. The charge in the cockpit was far too small to destroy the plane ... Unless they were bluffing, there must be another bomb with a much bigger charge. We'd better check the luggage racks and the baggage compartment."

He paused for a moment. "There's one other thing, Captain. We may have overlooked something. Maybe you should ask General Sykes to evacuate the airport."

Tower stared at Blake blankly. "Why should I do that?"

"Nothing says it has to be a conventional bomb, Captain. It may be a nuclear weapon."

**Also available in this series:**

WAR MACHINE
ZERO HOUR

PATRICK F. ROGERS

# OMEGA
## TARGET ZONE

A GOLD EAGLE BOOK FROM
# WORLDWIDE.

TORONTO • NEW YORK • LONDON
AMSTERDAM • PARIS • SYDNEY • HAMBURG
STOCKHOLM • ATHENS • TOKYO • MILAN
MADRID • WARSAW • BUDAPEST • AUCKLAND

First edition October 1993

ISBN 0-373-63209-6

Special thanks and acknowledgment to
Patrick F. Rogers for his contribution to this work.

TARGET ZONE

"The first stage of battle is the location and
identification of the enemy."
—Frank Barnaby, *The Automated Battlefield.*

# 1

Captain Ibrahim Amer had never fired his guns in anger before. He found the prospect of firing on the enemies of Egypt exciting rather than frightening. The fact that his twin DEFA 30 mm cannon were loaded and that there were live Matra air-to-air missiles under his wings did not trouble him at all. Amer checked his cockpit displays as he and his wingman flew steadily south over the Red Sea. His sleek Mirage 2000EM was performing perfectly. Amer was a happy man. He loved to fly anything with wings, but to fly the newest fighter in the Egyptian air force leading a real mission was all that he could ask.

He looked at his navigation display. He was close to the planned intercept area. If Egyptian Intelligence was right, the terrorist plane should be there now. He pressed a switch, and the Thomson-CSF radar in the Mirage's nose began to scan the air ahead. Almost immediately his radar display indicated half a dozen targets in the area, but only one was on the right course and speed, flying across the Red Sea toward Sudan. Amer spoke quickly into his microphone.

"Arrow Control, this is Arrow Leader. Radar contact. Target course and speed are correct. I am ready to intercept on your order."

"Arrow Leader, Arrow Control. Do you have visual contact?"

Amer sighed. He didn't like the Egyptian air force's policy of operating its fighters under strict ground control. Still, that didn't matter. The general hadn't consulted him on the matter. "Negative, Arrow Control. I do not have visual contact. There is a cloud layer ahead. He is staying under it. Instructions?"

"Stand by, Arrow Leader."

Captain Amer seethed quietly. Something seemed to happen to the best and boldest fighter pilots when they were assigned as ground controllers. They became cautious and bureaucratic, afraid to take responsibility. He hoped it never happened to him. He glanced at his mission clock irritably. He did not have unlimited fuel. What were they doing down there, drinking tea?

"Arrow Leader, Arrow Control. Proceed with your mission. Make visual contact and identify your target before taking action. Remember, you must force the target down if possible. We want to capture the terrorists and the weapons they are smuggling. Shoot down the target only as a last resort. Do you understand?"

At last! He felt like giving a victory salute. A decision, an actual decision! The unknown colonel was a prince of ground controllers. Quick now, before someone down there changed their mind. "Arrow Two, follow me."

Amer pushed forward on his stick and put the Mirage into a shallow dive toward the clouds ahead. He was closing on the target at six hundred miles per hour. He checked his radar display and saw that the target was maintaining its course and speed. Its crew showed no sign that they knew they had been detected. Good, he would give them a real surprise, a welcome they would never forget.

The two Egyptian Mirages dived into the clouds. For a few seconds Amer's canopy was shrouded in gray mist. Then the two Mirages flashed out into the clear air below the clouds. He should be able to see the target now. Yes, straight ahead, he saw a speck in the distance. The terrorist plane was lumbering along at three hundred miles per hour, and the Mirages were closing rapidly. Amer checked his weapons. He was in easy missile range, but he would use his missiles only as a last resort. His orders were to force the target down, not destroy it. He pushed the weapons-selector switch to guns and pushed the safety off.

The target seemed to grow larger and larger in his canopy. Now he could make out details. It was a four-engined, high-winged monoplane. The big shape was familiar; it was a Lockheed C-130. The Egyptian air force operated them, but there were no Egyptian C-130s in the area. As Amer shot past the target, he could see the markings on its fuselage clearly, the red-and-white-and-black-and-green insignia of the Royal Jordanian Air Force. He doubted that. He pulled his Mirage into a hard left turn and came up behind the C-130. Its crew showed no reaction, but unless they were asleep or blind, they knew he was there.

Amer smiled grimly. It was time for some friendly conversation. He switched the Mirage's radio to the international emergency frequency. The C-130 should be monitoring that. He pushed the transmit button. "Unidentified C-130. You have been intercepted by the Egyptian air force. Acknowledge."

There was no reply. Amer repeated his message in English and again in Arabic, but there was still no answer. It was time to communicate in a language that every one understands. He placed the gun-sight symbol in the heads-up display a hundred feet in front of the C-130's nose. He pulled the trigger, and the Mirage 2000 vibrated as its twin 30 mm cannon spouted flickering tongues of bright orange flame. A stream of yellow tracers streaked in front of the C-130s cockpit. It was only a one-second burst, but it was impressive shooting. It carried a message that was easily enough understood in any language. Almost instantly Amer heard a voice on his radio. It was an angry voice.

"This is the pilot of the Royal Jordanian Air Force C-130. We are in international airspace. Why in the name of God are you firing at us?"

"To attract your attention, Captain. You did not respond to my message. You will change course to 196 degrees and fly to an Egyptian airfield. You will land there and be searched. Turn left now. If you do not do so at once, I will shoot you down."

"You are making a mistake. I am a Royal Jordanian Air Force aircraft in international airspace. I am carrying medical supplies to the Sudan. My plane is of no interest to the Egyptian air force. You have no authority to force me down."

Amer smiled grimly. "Perhaps all that is true, but my government's information is different. We believe you are carrying weapons to be used against the Republic of Egypt. You will change course, land and be searched or be shot down. As for my authority—" Amer centered the aiming symbol in his

heads-up display on the C-130's left outboard engine, and
squeezed his trigger again. A dozen 30 mm shells streaked toward the C-130. Amer saw a series of flickering yellow flashes
as they struck and detonated. Smoke began to pour out of one
of the C-130's engines, and its propeller stopped rotating. Amer
felt a pardonable sense of pride. That was damned good
shooting.

"Thirty-millimeter cannon ammunition is expensive. I do not
believe in wasting it. The next burst goes into your fuselage.
Change course immediately!"

For a moment there was silence. Then the C-130's pilot replied, his voice hoarse with rage. "Do not fire again. This is an
act of war, but I have no weapons. I cannot fight Mirages. I will
follow you and I will land. But I warn you, my government will
protest! The government of the Sudan will protest. In God's
name, you will pay for this!"

Amer shrugged. The threat didn't frighten him. Whatever
cargo the C-130 was carrying, he had followed his orders precisely and the target had been identified by ground control.
"Turn left to a course of 196 degrees. Maintain speed and altitude. Do not try to escape. If you try to escape, I will shoot
you down." He watched carefully as the C-130 turned and began to fly toward the Egyptian coast.

The Intelligence officer who had briefed him had warned that
the terrorists they were dealing with were dangerous men, capable of almost anything if trapped. He couldn't imagine what
a damaged C-130 could do to two Mirage 2000s, but he intended to take no chances. He stayed alert, maintained his distance and kept the limping C-130 in his sights.

Time crawled by. Amer didn't like flying slowly at low altitude. The only real threat he could anticipate was a patrol of
Sudanese fighters. They had MiG-23s. The Mirage 2000 was a
better plane, but if he were suddenly attacked by surprise, he
might be dead before he had a chance to prove it. Egyptian
surveillance radar should warn him if unidentified fighters were
in the area, but he didn't like to bet his life on that. He would
be happy when the C-130 had landed.

He looked ahead. The coastline should be in sight by now.
Yes, there it was, a dull brown line stretching across the hori-

zon. He checked his navigation display. It said he was on course. That was good, since it wouldn't improve his chances for promotion if he forced the C-130 to land at the wrong airfield. Amer ordered his wingman to guard the C-130 and swept ahead. The whine of his SNEMCA M53P-2 engine deepened as the plane accelerated smoothly to six hundred miles per hour.

He could see the airfield ahead. It looked right, but it was best to be sure. Amer pointed the Mirage's nose at the runway and dived, leveled off at five hundred feet and howled across the runway. The base wasn't manned, but he could see several Mi-8 Hip transport helicopters lined up on one side of the runway and men in desert camouflage uniforms carefully dispersed around them. He could see the red-and-white-and-black Egyptian insignia on the helicopters' sides. A wave of relief swept over him. God is great! The commandos were in place.

He put the Mirage into a victory roll and spoke into his microphone. "Blue Leader, this is Arrow Leader. Mission successful. Our guest is on the way. Are you prepared to welcome him?"

"Arrow Leader. Blue Leader here. Congratulations, you have done well. We are ready. We will give our guest a warm welcome indeed."

Amer smiled. He was sure that was true, because even the most desperate terrorists were no match for a company of elite Egyptian commandos. His part in the mission was almost done. His wingman would make sure the C-130 landed. Amer wanted some altitude. He couldn't stop worrying about Sudanese MiGs. He pulled back on his stick, and the Mirage shot upward like a homesick angel. He leveled off at ten thousand feet. Below, the C-130 was turning on its final approach. His wingman was following carefully, guns ready. That was good, but Amer didn't think they would be needed. The terrorists were landing tamely, and he was slightly disappointed. He had never met any fanatics before, but he had imagined they were desperate men, ready to die rather than surrender. He hadn't expected they would give up so easily.

The C-130 touched down and began to roll along the dusty runway toward the waiting commandos. It is over, Amer said to himself. Time to think about going home. Suddenly he heard the voice of the C-130's pilot in his headset. The man was no longer angry, but there was something about the way he spoke that made Amer uneasy. He banked to keep the runway in sight.

"Mirage Leader, I would like to ask you a question. There is something I would like to know. Are you a pious man? Do you truly believe in God?"

Amer answered almost without thinking. He was not a religious fanatic, but certainly he believed. "God is great! I am a true believer," he said quickly, almost without thinking. His attention was concentrated on the C-130 below. Something was going to happen; he could feel it. Automatically he pushed his throttle forward and went to full power.

"Good," the C-130 pilot said calmly. "It is well that you are a true believer. We shall all go to God together. Fire the weapon, Ahmed."

Amer stared at the runway and the two planes far below. For a few seconds nothing seemed to happen, but human senses are slow. The weapon had already fired. The display lights on the instrument panel flickered as an immensely powerful pulse of electromagnetic radiation traveling at the speed of light swept through the Mirage. The Mirage's aluminum fuselage was as transparent as glass to the X-ray and gamma radiation that formed the pulse. Random bursts of current surged through the fighter plane's electronic systems. If it had been a commercial aircraft, it would have died instantly as its electrical nervous system burned out, but the Mirage 2000's French designers had built it to survive over the nuclear battlefields of World War III. They knew their business. Surge supressors flashed into action automatically, and shielding and electronic hardening protected the vital electronic components.

Amer knew nothing of this. The electromagnetic pulse was invisible and the Mirage had been struck and survived before a human being could have known or reacted. The first thing he saw was an intensely bright yellow-white point of light where the C-130 had been a fraction of a second before. Then the plane was gone. Not blasted to bits or shattered to tiny fragments, but literally reduced to its component atoms. The point of light expanded rapidly into a glowing ball of intensely bright light. For a fraction of a second a small piece of the sun seemed to have appeared on the earth's surface. The cockpit was illuminated by an incredibly bright flash of light and heat. Only the protective visor of his flight helmet saved him from being blinded by the flash, and even with the visor's protection his eyes were dazzled and the cockpit seemed to be filled with floating green spots.

Amer began to turn hard left and fired his afterburner—anything to get away from the close approximation of hell that had appeared below him. Then a giant hand seemed to strike the Mirage, hurling it through the air like a feather trapped in a hurricane. The blast wave had struck. The world seemed to be revolving insanely around Amer as the aircraft cartwheeled over and over. The plane's structure groaned and creaked as the g forces and the aerodynamic loads built up. Dazed and half-blinded, Amer fought his controls in a desperate effort to save his plane. He was flying more by instinct than by conscious thought, but he was a fighter pilot and a good one. Somehow he managed to get the Mirage under control and into straight and level flight.

He tried to check his displays, but he was still half-blinded by the flash. All he could tell was that everything seemed to be working. God is great, but God alone knew how Amer would get back to his base and land. His radio was chattering. It was his ground control.

"Arrow Leader, Arrow Leader, this is Arrow Control. We have lost contact with Blue Leader. He does not reply. What in the name of God is happening?"

Amer glanced back at the airfield. He knew what he would see. Even his dazzled eyes couldn't miss the huge brown-and-white mushroom-shaped cloud that was swelling ominously upward into the sky. His nerves were tingling and his skin felt flushed, as if he had been in the desert sun too long. Perhaps he was a dead man. He shrugged. He would live or die as God willed, but he knew his duty. Live or die, he must report.

"Arrow Control, listen carefully. The airfield is gone! The commandos are dead! They are all dead! It was a nuclear weapon."

The colonel in ground control forgot his radio procedures. He was almost shouting into his microphone. "What? A nuclear weapon? In the name of God, Amer, are you sure?"

Amer was beginning to feel strange. He didn't know if he were dying, but he might have very little time. "Listen to me, Colonel. As God is my witness, it was a nuclear weapon. The airfield is destroyed. You must notify high command.

MAJOR WAYNE BAKER was having a boring evening. Commanding the United States nerve center for strategic-attack warning wasn't nearly so interesting since the break-up of the Soviet Union. He looked at the display boards. Nothing was happening. Space command's network of orbiting early-warning satellites were operating with predictable efficiency, maintaining continuous, unblinking surveillance of the earth's surface. Baker smiled. Whatever you can say against computers, they don't get bored! There was really nothing for him to do unless something happened. Since the odds were overwhelmingly high that anything that happened would mean trouble, he was content to remain bored for the rest of his shift.

Baker yawned and glanced at his watch. Four more hours to go until his shift was over. He needed to stand up and stretch his legs. Perhaps he would have another cup of coffee. Air Force coffee wasn't the best in the world, but it would keep him awake. Suddenly an alarm sounded. It wasn't a particularly loud noise, but its frequency had been carefully selected to be almost impossible to ignore. Baker no longer needed coffee, and he was no longer bored. His system was flooded with adrenaline.

Instantly his eyes swept across the satellite command-and-control consoles. A red light was blinking on the display board of one of the eastern hemisphere birds. Number Three, 22,300 miles above the earth's surface, was reporting. It had detected something in its field of view, which included western Russia and the Ukraine. Several hundred ex-Soviet intercontinental ballistic missiles were still based there. Was it a missile launch? Sergeant Conroy was already on Console Three, and Baker waited tensely for Conroy's report, his hand poised on the command phone. If something significant had actually happened, he must inform the general immediately, but he had to be sure. Computers have been known to malfunction before, and General Reeves was not amused by false reports.

"NUDET, Major, northeastern Africa, Number Four confirms." Baker no longer hesitated. He picked up the phone and pushed the button. One satellite might conceivably malfunction, but the odds that two satellites would report the same false data simultaneously were vanishingly small. The phone rang twice, and Reeves was on the line, sounding reasonably alert. He was used to being called in the middle of the night; it was part of his job.

"Major Baker, duty officer, First Space Surveillance Wing sir. Flash NUDET report. Nuclear detonation." He glanced at the figures coming up on his display as the computers processed the data from the satellite sensors. "Single detonation, yield approximately twenty kilotons, surface or near-surface burst. Location, southwestern Egypt, near the Red Sea, dual satellite confirmation."

Baker could hear Reeves take a deep breath. This was not an attack on the continental United States, but it was sure as hell a crisis. The United States government did not take unknown nuclear explosions lightly. Baker waited for the question he knew he was going to hear.

"Are you certain, Major?"

It was Baker's turn to take a deep breath. "Yes, sir," he said calmly. "We have green boards on both satellites. There is no indication of malfunction on either bird. The data from both birds is identical. I confirm the NUDET report."

Reeves didn't hesitate. One of the reasons he was a general was that he had no difficulty making decisions. He was on the hot line in seconds. Messages began to flow out of Colorado, notifying the President, the National Command Authorities, and the commanders of the principal combat commands and the heads of key civilian agencies. Within minutes a coded message flashed up from Washington to a communications satellite and was relayed to the United States Embassy in Cairo. The message was short and cryptic even when decoded. It said "Activate Task Force Sphinx."

**2**

Colonel Nazir Sadiq sat at his desk, staring intently at a map of Egypt and the Sudan. The desk was old and battered, a relic of the days when the sun never set on the British empire and the Sudan had been a British colony. He liked that idea. A hundred years ago the British empire had been the strongest power in the world, seemingly invincible. Now it was gone, swept out of Africa by determined men who wouldn't submit to British rule. That was a comforting thought. Sadiq was fighting against the Americans and their allies. They had seemed invincible since the Gulf War, but he was determined to break their power, destroy their allies and drive the Americans once and for all from the Middle East. He lived for the day when the Arabs would be a single, powerful, unified nation. He would make that happen or die trying.

There was a knock on the door. Instantly, without thinking, Sadiq's hand moved to grip the 9 mm Browning automatic pistol that lay on the desk. He was not being paranoid. There were a great many people who would rejoice to see him dead. Somebody whose mortal enemies include the CIA, the Iraqi secret police and the Israeli Mossad must be ready to defend his life at a second's notice. He put his thumb on the Browning's safety and pointed its muzzle at the door. There were thirteen rounds in the Browning's magazine, and a fourteenth in the chamber. If there were assassins outside, he would take one or two of them with him.

"Who is it?" he asked quietly, and pushed the Browning's safety off.

"Saada Almori, Colonel. May I come in?"

Sadiq relaxed. He knew the voice. Saada Almori was one of his most trusted agents. She must just have arrived from Egypt, probably with vital information. He had to speak to her immediately.

"You are always welcome, Saada. Please join me," he said politely.

Saada came in. She was a tall, dark, pretty woman. Instead of her usual fashionable Western clothes, she wore a loose, flowing Sudanese robe. She carried in a heavy brass tray laden with a pot of steaming tea and some small sweet cakes. Saada was the picture of a simple Arab country girl, bringing her hardworking father some tea and cakes. But Sadiq knew that appearances were at times deceiving. She was highly intelligent and totally dedicated to the cause, and in her way, as deadly as any of Sadiq's commandos.

Sadiq was genuinely glad to see her, but he knew this wasn't a social call. There was a thick envelope on the tray. He stared at it as Saada poured the tea. She looked at him warmly. "Do not be concerned, Colonel. I have brought the information, but drink your tea and have a cake before you examine it. Major Tawfiq is concerned about you. He says you do not eat enough or rest enough. You must take better care of yourself. The movement would be lost without you."

Sadiq smiled. The Americans had incredible power and technology on their side, but he had dedicated followers, loyal men and women who believed and were willing to fight and die for the Arab Nation. With them, and the help of God, he would win. He sipped his tea and nibbled a cake politely.

"You see, Saada," he said, "I follow your advice in all things. Now, what news from our friends in Egypt?"

It was Saada's turn to smile. It is always pleasant to report success. "We have succeeded in penetrating the headquarters of Egyptian Special Operations Command, their famous Lightning Force. Their best units are conducting joint training exercises west of Cairo with Americans from the United States Special Operations Command, SOCOM."

Sadiq nodded. This was interesting. If the Egyptians learned his plans and came after him in Sudan, their Lightning Force would be the unit they sent. But there was more to it than that. He could tell by Saada's expression that there was something else, something important.

Saada opened the envelope and spread a stack of eight-by-ten glossy color prints across the desktop. "These photographs were taken at the start of the joint training exercise. These are pictures of the American commanding officers. There can be no doubt. I know these men. It is Omega Force."

Sadiq felt the thrill of a hunter who sees a man-eating tiger. He had fought Omega Force in Libya and in Lebanon, but he had never seen their leaders. Now he was looking at the face of the enemy. Sadiq was a superb planner. He had once been the operations officer of one of the crack divisions of Iraq's elite Republican Guards and had fought against Americans in Kuwait and Iraq. He regarded war as a game of chess, with carefully planned moves and countermoves. These were the men he was going to play against. He did not underestimate them. They had won in Libya and Lebanon, not by much, perhaps, but they had defeated him. Now it was time for a rematch. This time he would win.

He must not be overconfident, however. Omega Force was the key piece on the board, the unit the Americans would be certain to use against him if they learned his plans. He must learn everything he could about their leaders, how they thought and how they would react. "You saw these men and talked to them in Lebanon, Saada. What can you tell me about them and their famous Omega Force?"

Saada smiled. She was pleased that the colonel valued her opinion. She glanced at the first photograph. It showed a stocky, powerful-looking man with a battered face. The kindest thing that could be said for him was that he had rugged good looks. "This man is Major John Cray. He is the commanding officer of Omega Force. He is not given to talking a great deal, but he is a strong leader. His men believe in him. One of his sergeants said he would charge Hell with a bucket of water if Cray led the attack."

Saada pointed to the second photograph. It showed a tall, blond man wearing BDUs and a green beret. "This is Captain David Tower. He is the executive officer, the second in command. He looks like a handsome young man without a thought in his head. Do not be deceived. He is highly intelligent. He speaks our language fluently and understands our customs. That makes him very dangerous."

Saada pointed to another picture. "This man is their commander. He makes the key decisions which Omega Force carries out. He is General James Sykes. I did not have much contact with him, but I saw enough to know that he is a clever and ruthless man. Cray and Tower trust him. They carry out his orders without question, and where they lead, their men will follow."

Sadiq stared at the picture of Sykes, memorizing every detail. A big man, well over six feet tall, he was staring at the camera with cold gray eyes. Even without seeing the silver star on each shoulder, Sadiq knew that he was a leader. He radiated authority and command presence. Sadiq's face grew grim. Sykes was obviously a worthy opponent. They would see who would win the match.

"Who is the tall red-haired woman standing behind the general? His aide?"

"No, that is Captain Amanda Stuart. They say that she is an outstanding helicopter pilot. General Sykes was there for the start of the exercise. She flew him here in his special helicopter. She was waiting to fly the general back to Cairo."

Sadiq laughed. "The general is a fortunate man! Would that I had such a helicopter and such an attractive pilot to fly me around!"

Saada's tone grew noticeably cooler. "Yes, most men think her very attractive. She is good-looking in a crude sort of way. If she knew how to dress and use makeup properly, she would not be ugly, but she likes to dress like a man in that uniform and pretend to be a soldier."

Sadiq smiled to himself and noted that Saada Almori wasn't particularly fond of Amanda Stuart. He would remember that. One never knew when something like that might be extremely useful. "What can you tell me about their Omega Force?"

Saada thought for a moment, as if weighing her words. "I am not a military expert, as you know, but in my opinion, these men are very dangerous. Omega Force is a group of specially selected U.S. Army Rangers and Green Berets. Each is a volunteer, and they have special training and equipment. As you would expect, the officers chosen to command such a unit are highly capable. When I was with them in Lebanon, I was using my cover as a free-lance journalist. I asked them many questions. They are not fools. They would not tell me their plans or show me their secret equipment, but they talked freely about their unit. The name Omega Force comes from the last letter of the Greek alphabet. It means that they are the Americans' last option before they go to all-out war."

"You are the only one of us who has seen these men. What do you think of them?"

Again Saada paused to consider her answer, and then spoke slowly and carefully. "They are extremely dangerous, more dangerous to us than the Americans' long-range missiles and atomic bombs. We do not offer an easy target for those weapons, and using them is very difficult, politically, for the Americans. Omega Force is different. It is a secret organization. The Americans will not admit it exists, and they do not have to explain what it does. If they learn our plans and find out where we are, they will not hesitate. They will send them after us. They call it a surgical strike. That means they will kill us all very precisely, if they can, with minimum damage to the surrounding area."

Colonel Sadiq shook his head. "Surgical strike." He thought he spoke English rather well, but some things the Americans said were very difficult to understand. "Very well, Saada, I understand. Now, what should we do about them?"

She didn't hesitate. "Kill them all! We must destroy their entire force at once, if we can. If that is not possible, we must kill their leaders. Without their key officers, Omega Force will be crippled."

Sadiq smiled again. Whatever you might think of Saada, she wasn't a shy, delicate creature who would faint at the sight of blood. If she had a weapon pointed at Omega Force, she wouldn't hesitate to pull the trigger.

"Your advice is good, as always, Saada," he said smoothly. "We will carry out your recommendations if we can. I need someone in Egypt to be my eyes and ears and to coordinate the operations of our people and our Egyptian friends. Are you willing to go back to Egypt and do this task for me?"

Saada hesitated for a moment. It would be very dangerous for her to go back to Egypt. It could be very unpleasant for her if she were discovered; the Egyptian secret police weren't known for treating suspected terrorists in a kindly manner. The fact that she was a woman would make no difference, but it was her duty. She considered herself to be a soldier of the Arab Nation. She would die for what she believed in if she had to.

"I will go, Colonel," she said proudly. "God willing, I will carry out the mission. I will kill them all!"

Colonel Sadiq was proud of Saada, but he couldn't help feeling sad. He hated to send a young woman into danger, but he, too, believed in the Arab Nation, and he would do anything he had to for the cause. "Go with God, Saada," he said softly, "go with God."

THE FOUR MIRAGES flew across the desert fast and low, engines howling as they flashed toward their target at five hundred miles per hour. Captain Dave Tower was painfully aware that he was standing only two hundred yards away from the target point. The Egyptian commandos around him were hugging the ground like sensible men, and Tower would have loved to join them. However, Colonel Khier was standing, lecturing calmly as if he were in a classroom, and Tower would be damned if he would duck before the Egyptian commando group's commander did.

He kept his binoculars trained on the Egyptian planes. This was going to be hairy. The Egyptian pilots were determined to show their American visitors what they could do. They would impress them or die trying. Tower was willing to be impressed, but he disliked intensely the idea of being hit by friendly fire. Fortunately he did not have any more time to worry about it. The wings of the Mirages were suddenly haloed in orange fire as their rocket launchers ripple-fired lethal showers of 68 mm air-to-ground rockets. The rockets shot overhead, trailing orange flame and gray-white smoke. Tower watched, fascinated, as the rockets began to strike and detonate. The target was a low, sandy hill. It seemed to vanish in fountains of sand and the gray smoke of burning high explosives. Each Mirage had launched seventy-six rockets in a few seconds. Tower could not deny that the results were very impressive.

Colonel Khier smiled. The tall, dark Egyptian commander seemed to be enjoying himself immensely. "The first attack is for defense suppression, Captain. It confuses and demoralizes the enemy. Now, the—" Khier's words were lost in an ear shattering shriek as the four Mirages flashed by less than a hundred feet overhead.

Khier's smile broadened. "As I was saying, the next flight will deliver the main attack. Here they come."

Tower swung his binoculars. Four more Mirages were coming, flying even lower than the first four. He could see the noses of their bombs, ominous, hanging in olive drab clusters under their wings and fuselages. "Each of them carries eighteen 250-kilogram, or as you would say, 550-pound bombs," Colonel Khier remarked happily, "and 30 mm cannons, also. They will—"

Whatever else Khier was going to say was lost in the piercing howl of jet engines and the sudden sustained roar of 30 mm automatic cannon firing. Tower saw the bombs drop away as the Mirages shrieked overhead. Retarding fins snapped open to delay the bombs' fall and give the fighter planes time to clear the area before their bombs struck and exploded. The target area disappeared in smoke and dust, and the ground shook and shuddered as the bombs struck and detonated. The Mirages shrieked away and were gone. Tower was glad they were on his side. He was totally convinced that the Egyptian air force knew how to fly close-support missions.

"Time for the helicopter assault, Captain. Tell your Major Cray he is cleared to go in. We are eager to see how your Omega Force does this kind of operation."

Tower nodded. It was time to look good and impress their Egyptian friends and allies. He was about to contact Cray when a sergeant appeared at Colonel Khier's side. He saluted smartly and handed Khier a piece of paper. "Urgent message from army general headquarters, Colonel. It is the war-alert order."

Tower could speak fluent Arabic and understood every word the sergeant said, but he wasn't sure what was going on. Was this part of the exercise? He kept his mouth shut and waited.

When Khier's smile vanished as he read the message, Tower's doubts vanished. He could tell by the look on Khier's face that this was no drill.

"I am sorry, Captain, but the rest of our joint exercise is canceled. There has been a serious accident, perhaps an attack on Egypt. We may be at war. The 127th Commando Group is on full combat alert. This message also contains instructions for you from an American general named Sykes. You and Major Cray are to report to the American Embassy in Cairo as soon as possible. Omega Force is to prepare for immediate combat operations. You have been assigned to something called Task Force Sphinx."

CRAY AND TOWER slipped into the darkened briefing room. The tall, dark, intense woman at the speaker's stand glared at them as they slid into vacant chairs. She obviously didn't approve of people who were late to briefings. Cray looked at Tower and shrugged. It was not their fault. The Marine Corps guards had been suspicious of two men in civilian clothes who claimed that they were there to attend a top secret meeting. It had taken several phone calls and repeated ID checks before the Marines reluctantly let them through the door.

"As I was saying, the evidence points to a deliberate attempt to destabilize and overthrow the Egyptian government and replace it with a fundamentalist Muslim government that would be hostile to the United States. There have been a number of assassinations of pro-Western politicians, newspaper editors and government officials. Credit for these killings has been claimed by the Islamic Jihad, a fanatic fundamentalist terrorist group. Arms have been smuggled into southern Egypt, as well as a large quantity of extremely high-quality counterfeit Egyptian hundred-pound notes.

"This money is being used to finance a major propaganda effort against the government. Rumors are sweeping the country. Their theme is that God is angry with Egypt and will punish it with hellfire for its sins, which include turning away from God, making peace with Israel and fighting on our side against Iraq in the Gulf War. The Egyptian people will be spared only if they overthrow their sinful government and return to God's holy ways."

Someone chuckled. "Really, Dr. Rossi, are we supposed to take this seriously? I don't doubt your information, but are we really supposed to believe that the Egyptian government is going to be overthrown by a few religious fanatics spreading rumors in dark corners? Do you have any serious evidence of a real plot?"

Dr. Rossi glared at the speaker. It was obvious that she didn't like being interrupted. "Perhaps this will be serious enough for you, Mr. Givens!"

She paused for a moment and stared at her audience.

"What I am about to say is classified top secret—special access required—code word Sphinx. If you do not have this clearance, you should leave the room immediately. If you disclose the information I am about to give you to any unauthorized person, you will be subject to the full penalties of the espionage act."

No one left the room, but no one was laughing. The situation sounded serious. Cray sighed as he waited for Dr. Rossi to continue. He had been briefed on so many classified missions it would probably be a security violation if he talked to himself.

"Very well. Approximately thirty hours ago, a nuclear weapon was detonated in Egypt on the southwestern coast near the border with the Sudan. The weapons yield was equivalent to approximately sixteen thousand tons of TNT."

This was something Cray could understand far better than Middle Eastern politics. "What was the target? How was the weapon delivered? Were there casualties?" he asked quickly.

Dr. Rossi smiled. Apparently she felt those were intelligent questions. "The detonation took place at an Egyptian air force emergency airfield. Normally the airfield is unmanned. However, an Egyptian army commando company was there when the bomb exploded. They were all killed, approximately one hundred fifty officers and men. We do not believe the airfield or the commandos were the target in the conventional military sense. The weapon was apparently on board an airplane which was forced to land by Egyptian air force fighters. Either there was an accident or the plane's crew deliberately fired the weapon to prevent it from being captured. The Egyptians think it was deliberate. They believe the weapon was being smuggled into the Sudan to be used against Egypt."

"Jesus Christ!" someone exclaimed. Cray agreed with the sentiment. If there was going to be a nuclear attack on Egypt, Cairo was a logical target, and they were sitting in the center of the city.

Dr. Rossi smiled bleakly. "I agree, but it's worse than that! Those of you who are familiar with nuclear weapons know that they have a distinctive signature when they explode. That results from the different materials used in the bomb and the design of its firing system. Given the data, an expert can distinguish an American design from a Russian, or a French weapon from an Israeli weapon. Our experts have been analyzing the data from this explosion. It does not match the signature of any known nuclear weapon. It appears to have been designed and manufactured by a new and unknown source."

She paused for a moment and then went on quietly. "So, gentlemen, you see the problem. We are facing fanatic terrorists, and they are armed with nuclear weapons. They do not regard nuclear weapons as political power symbols or a means of deterring hostile attacks. All indications are that they intend to use them, which is an extremely serious threat! Our experts estimate that, if this weapon were detonated in downtown Cairo, there would be over one hundred thousand casualties from weapons effects alone. God only knows how many more people would die in the ensuing panic. That is serious enough even for Mr. Givens!"

Cray wasn't interested in Mr. Givens's feelings, one way or the other. He knew now why he and Tower were there, rubbing elbows with the State Department and the CIA. Omega Force had been created to solve problems like this, but he needed more information. "Where are the weapons, who controls them, and how are they guarded?" he asked quickly.

Dr. Rossi smiled again. Cray was happy that she still thought he was asking intelligent questions. He only hoped that he was going to get intelligent answers. The CIA wasn't always eager to share its secrets with the military.

"Well, gentlemen, those are the critical questions. The answer is, 'I wish to God we knew.' At the moment we simply don't have the information. All I can say is that we and Egyptian Intelligence are working on it twenty-four hours a day."

Givens saw his opening and exploited it smoothly. "Really, Dr. Rossi? Those of us in the State Department stand in awe of the capabilities of our colleagues in the CIA. Are you seriously telling us that all the resources of the CIA have been unable to locate a stockpile of nuclear weapons?"

Cray didn't like Givens's tone and felt a twinge of annoyance. It was not that Cray loved the CIA—far from it—but the situation sounded serious enough without wasting time on bureaucratic infighting.

Dr. Rossi tossed her dark hair and glared at Givens. If looks could kill, there would have been an opening in the staff of the Cairo embassy. "Any problem seems simple if you don't understand it," she remarked acidly. "For the benefit of those of you who do not understand the situation—" she paused for a second and stared pointedly at Givens "—the Sudan is physically the largest country in Africa. It is larger in area than all the nations in Western Europe combined. Nuclear weapons are not large, and they don't require special storage facilities. Several of them could be carried on a truck. They could be kept in an ordinary house or building. When they are inert, in a storage mode, they do not radiate anything that can be detected remotely. You would have to be within a few feet of one to detect it with scientific instruments. To put it in perspective, if there was a nuclear weapon concealed here in the embassy, we could only find it by conducting a room-by-room search."

There was a buzz of concern in the darkened briefing room. No one liked Dr. Rossi's example. Most Middle Eastern terrorist groups hate the United States with a pure and burning passion, and if one of them were going to set off a nuclear weapon in downtown Cairo, what better place for ground zero than the American Embassy!

"If we do locate these weapons, Dr. Rossi, what are our capabilities?" someone asked.

"General Sykes is the senior American military officer in Egypt. He will brief us on our military options."

Sykes moved to the speaker's stand. He looked like a general in his desert camouflage battle dress uniform. He was well over six feet tall and radiated command presence. He ran his hand through his closely cropped gray hair and went straight to the point. "Ladies and gentlemen, I am Brigadier General James Sykes, United States Army. At the moment there is almost no American military capability in Egypt. We have no bases in Egypt, and we normally have no forces stationed here. That will change. I have been talking to Washington via satellite, and the President and the National Security Council have decided we will support Egypt in this crisis and defend it if it is attacked. The Department of Defense has ordered that U.S. forces begin to deploy. They are moving now."

Sykes pushed a button, the lights dimmed, and a map of Egypt and the eastern Mediterranean appeared on the screen. He used a laser pointer to indicate spots on the map. "The Navy is deploying three carrier battle groups, each with an aircraft carrier and ten to twelve escort ships, cruisers, destroyers and frigates. The *George Washington* is here. She is moving from the gulf into the Red Sea. She will be on station and ready for combat operations in twenty-four hours. The *Saratoga* and her battle group are here. They left Naples two hours ago. They will be off the coast of Egypt in forty-eight hours. The *Theodore Roosevelt* will leave the East Coast in a few hours. A Marine Expeditionary Brigade is sailing with the *Roosevelt* group. That's sixteen thousand Marines. Unfortunately it will be at least ten days before they get here. Each of these carriers operates approximately ninety aircraft, F-14 Tomcats, F/A-18 Hornets and A-6E Intruders. When they are in position, they will guarantee us air superiority against any air force in the Middle East.

"The Army is preparing to deploy the 101st Airborne Division, the Screaming Eagles. The 101st is an air-assault division. It has approximately fifteen thousand officers and men. More important, it has several hundred modern helicopters and is completely transportable by air. As soon as the Egyptian government agrees to have U.S. troops in country, the 101st will be on the way."

Sykes smiled grimly. "I don't think the Egyptian government is going to say no. I expect the leading elements of the 101st is to be here in seventy-two hours. More troops will be sent if necessary. The Eighty-second Airborne and the Seventh Infantry Division are on alert. Any questions?"

"General, Dr. Rossi says we must keep this whole affair quiet to prevent panic in Egypt. The carriers I understand. They will be operating in international waters. There is nothing unusual in that. But how will we explain fifteen thousand U.S. troops suddenly arriving in Egypt?"

Sykes did not appear to be flustered by the question. International politics weren't his strong point, but he had thought of that. "We have conducted a series of Bright Star exercises with the Egyptian army over the last few years. They have involved significant numbers of American troops, and they were flown in from the United States. As far as the public and the media are concerned, this will be just another Bright Star exercise, one that just happens to be carried out at short notice."

"What about the Air Force?" Dr. Rossi asked.

"They will provide the airlift for the troops we send in, of course. Combat aircraft is a bit more complicated. The Egyptian air bases can only accommodate a limited number of additional combat aircraft. The Air Force is recommending that we deploy special-capability aircraft such as F-15E Strike Eagles. The Fourth Combat Wing has been alerted. It will deploy if we can work out the basing and logistic support with the Egyptians. They don't seem to be too concerned. They believe their own air force can handle anybody else in the Middle East except Israel, and, thank God, they are not involved."

There was a subdued chuckle at that. The Israelis were remarkably effective in combat, but they weren't the easiest allies in the world to deal with. Sykes looked around the room and concluded that his briefing was finished. He was about to leave the speaker's stand when Givens spoke again. "General, you have told us quite a bit about all the things the military will be ready to do in a few days, assuming your plan is approved in Washington, but that leaves one question. What if the weapons are located in the next forty-eight hours? What capabilities do you have before reinforcements arrive from the United States?''

Sykes stared frostily at Givens. He did not like the man's attitude. He struck Sykes as one of those know-it-all civilians who loved to criticize the military without the slightest knowledge of what was involved in moving thousands of men and their equipment five thousand miles. Still, he supposed it was a legitimate question.

''I said there is almost no American military capability in Egypt. That is correct, but we are lucky. We have SOCOM's best emergency special-operations unit, Omega Force, here in Egypt. This is a specially selected and trained company-size force. Every man is a Ranger or a Green Beret. They have the most advanced weapons and equipment, and they know how to use them. They can't stop a full-scale invasion, but if you can find the nuclear weapons, Omega Force can go in and take them out.''

''Really, General,'' Givens said sarcastically, ''two hundred men are going to do all that? Are your supersoldiers really that good?''

''They are.'' A cold, precise voice came from the back of the darkened briefing room. ''I have worked with them before, in Libya and Lebanon. They are not lovable, perhaps, but they are precisely as good as General Sykes says they are.''

Sykes was looking toward the slide-projector beam. He couldn't see the speaker, but he didn't have to. He resisted the impulse to take cover and draw his pistol. He knew that voice and he recognized the superior, slightly sarcastic tone instantly.

Givens did not. ''I don't recognize you,'' he said coldly. ''Who are you? Who do you represent, and why are you attending this meeting?''

Someone killed the slide projector and turned up the lights. A tall, thin man in an expensive dark gray suit moved to the front of the room. He looked coldly at Givens. No one spoke for a long moment, and Sykes noticed that Givens suddenly didn't seem happy with life.

At last the thin man spoke in a tone that seemed to chill the air. ''I will assume your questions are prompted by your concern for security, and not by an adolescent desire to show off. I am Dr. Peter Kaye of the Central Intelligence Agency. I represent the President of the United States and the National Security Council. They have assigned me to be the director of Task Force Sphinx, effective immediately. If you wish to verify this, you may communicate with the National Security Council, or perhaps you would prefer to check my credentials with the ambassador.''

A subdued murmur ran through the group. Peter Kaye! Most of them had never seen Dr. Kaye before, but everyone had heard of him. His reputation was fearsome. Kaye was the CIA's senior troubleshooter in the Middle East, and rumor had it that he was the CIA director's hatchet man. No one questioned Kaye's competence, but he was totally ruthless.

There was a saying in American government circles in the Middle East: "It doesn't pay to cross Dr. Kaye." Perhaps Givens was remembering that. He showed no signs of wanting to continue the conversation.

Kaye smiled bleakly. "Now that we have settled that, this meeting is adjourned. I would like Dr. Rossi and General Sykes and his officers to stay for a brief discussion. The rest of you please remain on call."

The task force members filed quickly out of the room. Perhaps some of them had hurt feelings at being excluded from the meeting, but none of them seemed inclined to discuss the matter with Dr. Kaye.

Kaye looked after them with withering contempt. "Task Force Sphinx! I wonder what idiot in Washington thinks a thirty-man committee can run a covert operation of this magnitude. God deliver me from gifted amateurs!"

He turned to Sykes and smiled again. "Well, at least I have you and your people with me, General. I know I can count on you and Omega Force. You are real professionals."

Sykes smiled thinly. "Thank you, Doctor. We're glad to see you again." That was a lie, of course. Sykes was not normally insincere, but he hated to work with Kaye. Kaye was a brilliant man, but he was consumed with ambition and was totally ruthless. He was determined to get the job done, and he did not care whom he sacrificed to do it. To him, Sykes and Omega

Force were just tools to be used to accomplish the mission. If they were all killed, Kaye wouldn't be concerned, as long as it did not make him look like a failure. Sykes didn't appreciate men who thought like that.

Kaye turned to Dr. Rossi. "You did a good job keeping this fire drill under control until I got here, Rossi. Now, get on secure communications to the CIA Khartoum station. Tell them I will be in Khartoum to contact the Sudanese and get their assistance as soon as clearance for the trip can be arranged. But they are not to wait for that. I want an all-out, maximum effort starting now. All agents and assets in the Sudan are to concentrate on locating the weapons. And Rossi, tell them I want results!"

Dr. Rossi nodded and was gone. Sykes was impressed. Though he didn't like Kaye, he had to admit he could make things happen.

There was a knock on the door, and Kaye looked up as a tall man in a desert camouflage uniform entered the room. "Ah, Colonel," he said, "there you are. Gentlemen, I believe you all know Colonel Khier. He is the Egyptian military officer assigned to Task Force Sphinx. I would like for you to move Omega Force to Colonel Khier's base. Be ready for combat operations in the Sudan within twenty-four hours, with or without the consent of the Sudanese government."

Kaye paused for a moment and smiled broadly. Sykes was sure he meant well, but when Kaye smiled, it reminded him of a shark about to bite.

"I know you will justify my confidence in you, gentlemen. I am sure you will take those weapons out."

Sykes nodded grimly. Kaye was right, of course. It was a critical mission. Omega Force would do the job or die trying.

**3**

The big black Mercedes limousine moved smoothly through the night. It was a new car in perfect condition, and Sergeant Blake was an excellent driver. Tower could see the taillights of the other car ahead of them. It, too, was a big new Mercedes. Tower smiled to himself. Task Force Sphinx certainly was not short of money, and Tower didn't have to justify Dr. Kaye's expense account.

Their tour of the pyramids had been interesting but sobering. Tower liked history, but the weight of seven thousand years of Egyptian history was almost oppressive. Still, he was glad he had seen them. The pyramids in the moonlight were a sight he would remember forever. Colonel Khier was certainly making an all-out effort to be hospitable. Tower was just thinking that they would have to do something to show their appreciation, maybe tap into Kaye's expense account, when Blake spoke up from behind the wheel.

"Captain," Blake said softly but urgently, "someone's following us. Two or three vehicles. They've been behind us for the last several miles. Now they're starting to move up."

Tower was instantly alert. He had served with Blake for several years. The small wiry master sergeant was Omega Force's weapons and demolition expert. Few things frightened Blake, and he did not imagine dangers that weren't there. If Blake thought they were being followed, they were being followed, and Tower knew it was not the Cairo Chamber of Commerce welcoming committee. Still, he had better check with Khier before he did anything drastic. It just might be the Egyptian secret police, and a firefight with them might sour American-Egyptian relations.

"Colonel, Sergeant Blake thinks we are being followed. Any chance it could be some of your people?"

Khier was alert. "I know. I heard your sergeant," he replied. He reached under his white linen coat and drew a big 9 mm Beretta automatic from a shoulder holster. "It is not any of our people. We had best be ready. Are any of your people armed?"

In answer Tower pulled a .45 Colt automatic from under his coat. He knew he was bending Egyptian law, but ten years in the Green Berets had made Tower unwilling to go anywhere unarmed if he could help it, and he didn't think Colonel Khier was going to complain. "I am," he said, "and Sergeant Blake and Sergeant Hall have pistols. I'm not sure about Captain Stuart."

Amanda Stuart had been dozing, but the sounds of weapons being drawn and checked had jolted her wide awake. She opened her purse and pulled out a flat, black 9 mm automatic. "I've got my 9 mm SIG-Sauer," she announced.

Five pistols were a lot better than nothing, but Tower wished they had rifles or submachine guns. He had a dismal feeling that the people behind them would be heavily armed. Well, pistols would have to do.

Tower hesitated for a second. Colonel Khier was the senior officer, but everyone else in the car was an American, and Khier didn't know their capabilities. Tower decided he had better give the orders. He could always apologize to the Egyptian colonel later, provided they both lived through the next few minutes.

"Signal the lead car, Blake," he ordered, "and let's get all the windows down now." That was absolutely essential. Tower knew that civilian cars were hard to shoot out of, but, unfortunately, easy to shoot into, and only targets right alongside could be engaged well. To fire at a car ahead or behind, the passengers have to stick their heads and arms out the window. Trying to shoot accurately that way from a car going sixty miles per hour would not be easy.

"Signaling now!" Blake announced, and flicked the big Mercedes's lights on and off several times. It was not a standard signal, but if Cray were alert, he would know that something was going on behind him. Tower watched tensely, and he saw the taillights in front of them suddenly blink on and off rapidly. Good. But Cray wasn't the only one who had seen the blinking lights. It was impossible for Blake to blink their Mercedes's headlights without blinking the taillights at the same time. The people behind them knew that something was going on, and they reacted.

"Heads up!" Blake shouted. "Here they come!"

The inside of the Mercedes was suddenly illuminated by the glare of headlights on high beam. A red-and-white Volkswagen van seemed to appear from nowhere and roar alongside them. Blake stepped on the gas, and the Mercedes's engine roared as he accelerated rapidly. The van was trying to pull ahead, and Tower saw the van's side windows fly open. His last doubts vanished. He held his big .45 in a firm two-handed grip and fired two shots in half a second in the deadly technique that experienced combat pistol shooters call the double hammer. The big Colt bucked in his hands. He saw the yellow flashes of metal striking metal at high velocities as the two .45-caliber full-metal-jacketed bullets tore through the van's side. Instantly he fired twice again.

A pulsing, bright yellow flash suddenly appeared in one of the van's side windows. Tower saw the distinctive yellow muzzle-flash of an AK-47M assault rifle firing full automatic. The muzzle seemed to be pointed straight at him, but there was no place to hide. He fired back as fast as he could, aiming at the muzzle-flash. Only one thing saved Tower then. The AK-47 gunner stayed on the trigger too long, firing a sustained burst of fifteen or twenty rounds. The strongest man couldn't hold an automatic rifle on target through a long burst, and the gunman's rifle muzzle climbed rapidly as the force of the rapidly repeated recoil drove it upward.

There was the shriek of tearing metal as several steel-jacketed .30-caliber rifle bullets smashed through the Mercedes's roof and howled off into the darkness. Tower squeezed the trigger again and the AK-47 stopped firing. Perhaps the gunner was hit, or perhaps he had emptied his magazine and was reloading. Tower tried to fire again but nothing happened. The slide of his .45 automatic was locked back. He had fired the big Colt empty. The basic directive to count the shots and reload while there was still a round in the chamber was much easier to follow on a training range than in the middle of a furious firefight in the dark. He reached for his belt to draw a spare magazine, but his position in the car seat made the usually lightning-fast reloading motion slow and awkward.

Time seemed to slow down as Tower desperately tried to reach his magazine holder. The van was beginning to pull ahead a little, and in the bright moonlight he could see another black barrel slide through the van's other window and point like an accusing finger at the speeding Mercedes. Something had to be done. He glanced at Amanda Stuart, who was sitting tensely in the middle of the passenger seat. She looked pale in the moonlight and the glare of the headlights, but her 9 mm SIG-Sauer was steady in her hands. She was ready to fire, but she had not dared to try to shoot past Tower's head. It would have been dangerous even if the car had been standing still, but it could be fatal in the bouncing, lurching Mercedes as it roared through the night.

She was their only chance. "Stuart!" Tower yelled at the top of his lungs. His parade-ground bellow cut through the sounds of the roaring engines. "Take the window! Shoot! Shoot! Shoot!"

Amanda did not hesitate. She lunged forward and thrust the muzzle of her SIG-Sauer through the window and began shooting as fast as she could pull the trigger. Her pistol was loaded with high-velocity M882 9 mm military ammunition. It was not elegant shooting. Amanda had never been trained to fire from a moving car, but the van was only a few feet away, and every shot hit it. The 9 mm bullets from her pistol were only half the weight of the big bullets from Tower's .45 Colt, but they were hard-jacketed, military bullets designed for deep penetration, and they were moving more than fifty percent faster. Against human targets, they would have been less effective. Against the van, they were superior. She couldn't be sure if she was hitting any of the men in the van, but she was sure she was making them unhappy.

Tower was not very happy himself. Amanda was doing exactly what he had told her to do and doing it very well, but he found himself looking at a 9 mm automatic in rapid fire less than two feet from his face. The muzzle-flash was dazzling, and the blast was deafening. He could feel a hot puff of burning powder gas and the sting of partly burned grains of powder from every shot. Fired cartridge cases bounced around the passenger compartment, and one of them struck Tower on the chin and rolled down the front of his shirt. He started to swear fluently. The damned thing was hot. He stared, almost hypnotized, as the SIG-Sauer spit bullets, hot gas and ejected cartridge cases. It seemed to go on forever. Actually Amanda fired thirteen shots in less than four seconds.

The SIG-Sauer's slide suddenly locked open. Amanda's pistol was empty now, and she searched frantically through her purse for a spare magazine. In the meantime Tower had located his magazine holder, and now he snapped a fresh magazine into his .45 and pushed the slide release, chambering a round. He aimed out the window, but the scene was changing rapidly. The van was accelerating. The driver was trying to get past the Mercedes and pull ahead of them. That could be fatal, as 'he men in the van could easily fire to the rear. The steel-jacketed .30-caliber bullets from their AK-47s could tear through the Mercedes from end to end, but it would be extremely difficult for anyone in the Mercedes to fire directly forward. The van had nearly passed them. Something had to be done immediately.

"Blake!" Tower yelled. "Don't let them get ahead!"

Blake had no time for conversation. All his attention was concentrated on his driving, but he could understand the situation as well as Tower. "Brace yourselves!" he shouted and slammed the gas pedal to the floor. The engine roared as the Mercedes shot forward and smashed into the rear of the speeding van. Tower heard the screech of bending metal and the crash of breaking glass. The impact threw him forward against the back of the driver's seat and spoiled his aim. He could see a flickering yellow flash as someone fired an AK-47 from one of the van's back windows. The impact seemed to have spoiled the gunner's aim. The long burst went high, but the Mercedes was straight behind the van now. What the hell was Blake doing? If the man with the AK-47 kept his head, he was not likely to miss again.

The black Mercedes shuddered, and the tires shrieked as Blake suddenly stood on the brakes. The van seemed to shoot ahead as the Mercedes slowed. Blake swung the wheel to the left and floorboarded the accelerator again. The engine roared into redline, and the transmission howled as the big black car swerved to the left and accelerated forward again. Now the van was to the Mercedes's right. Momentarily, the men in the van were confused. The rifleman had to shift to the van's left-hand windows to fire to the left.

Colonel Khier was already in position. Tower heard the spiteful crack of his 9 mm Beretta as Khier opened fire. For a second the Americans had the advantage as the car and the van roared through the night side by side, but it wouldn't last long. In a few seconds it would be AK-47s against pistols. Blake had bought them a little time, but they were still outgunned. But Tower had forgotten Sergeant Hall. Hall was never outgunned. He could make up in skill what he lacked in firepower. He had been unable to fire past Blake when the van was on the Mercedes's left side. Nothing stopped him now. He had a clear field of fire. Tower saw Hall raise a big snub-nosed stainless steel revolver in a firm two-handed hold and aim at the van alongside.

It was the largest short-barreled revolver Tower had ever seen, a huge Smith & Wesson. Tower had heard wild rumors about Sergeant Hall's pocket pistol, but nothing had prepared him for what happened next. Hall took a fast sight picture and squeezed the trigger smoothly. There was a roar like a cannon firing, and Tower's ears rang. Even with the car windows open, the muzzle blast was appalling. The big Smith & Wesson seemed to explode in balls of orange fire as Hall fired shot after shot as fast as he could align his sights and squeeze the trigger.

Hall's revolver was a .44 Magnum. With every shot, it drove a heavy, blunt, nearly cylindrical bullet into the van at more than thirteen hundred feet per second. The .44 Magnum cartridge was designed to be used in a long-barreled revolver. It lost a little power when fired in Hall's short-barreled weapon, but no one on the receiving end would ever notice the difference. A superb shot, the best in Omega Force, Hall seldom missed, and he didn't miss now. The big blunt-nosed .44-caliber bullets were twice as heavy as those from an AK-47 rifle, and each delivered more than half a ton of kinetic energy. Metal tore and glass shattered as six rounds smashed into the van's front seat.

Hall's hammer clicked on a fired chamber. He had shot all six rounds in the big Smith & Wesson's cylinder, and he was out of action until he could reload. But it was no longer that crucial. One of the heavy Magnum bullets had struck the driver in the left side. He immediately lost interest in driving or anything else, since the human body lacks enough resistance to stop a .44 Magnum bullet. The huge bullet expanded to more than .60 caliber and struck the man in the passenger seat. He died instantly. The van roared on down the road at sixty-five miles per hour with two dead men in the front seat. It drifted to the right and suddenly cartwheeled off the road, turning over and over in the sand until it crashed to a stop in a cloud of dust.

Blake stood on the brakes, and the Mercedes screeched to a halt, tires screaming. Tower was half-dazed from muzzle blast and flash, but he reacted with the combat instincts honed by eight years in special operations. It would have been most unwise for him to assume that all the men in the van were dead, and God only knew what weapons they might have inside. They must close in and hit them now, before they recovered from the crash. "Come on!" he shouted as he threw the door open and leapt out of the car, but Hall and Colonel Khier had reacted instinctively, already getting out the other side.

Tower ran toward the van as fast as he could. He felt half-blind without his night-vision goggles, but he could see the van lying on one side in the bright moonlight. Its side and rear doors flew open as the men in the passenger compartment leapt out. They may have been shaken up, but Tower could see they still held weapons in their hands. He could not shoot accurately while running in the dark, so he skidded to a halt and swung up his .45 Colt automatic. The first man out was swinging a rifle in Tower's direction, not taking the time to bring his rifle to his shoulder, but preparing to fire from the hip.

Time seemed to slow down. It took forever for Tower to bring his .45 to bear. He was grateful he had fitted it with night sights. The glowing green dot of the front sight was pointing at the man's chest, and Tower was pressing the trigger as the man fired. A pulsing, bright yellow flash suddenly appeared in one of the van's side windows. Tower saw the flickering yellow muzzle-flash of an AK-47M on full automatic. Its muzzle seemed to be pointed straight at him. A burst of .30-caliber bullets flashed past Tower, and a few feet behind him the ground suddenly exploded in a dozen gouts of dust as steel-jacketed rifle bullets struck and ricocheted away. The urge to duck and take cover was almost overpowering; but there was no cover, and the man with the AK-47 was only ten yards away. Only fast and accurate shooting could save Tower now.

He kept all his attention on his front sight and squeezed the Colt's trigger as fast as he could without throwing off his aim. The big .45 automatic bucked and roared as he fired two shots as fast as he could. Two heavy .45-caliber full-metal-jacketed bullets smashed into the man's chest. Tower saw him stagger, but he was still on his feet. Instantly Tower fired again, another double hammer. The man fell limply, like a puppet whose strings have been cut. Tower had seen men fall like that before and knew he wouldn't need shooting again.

Tower caught a blur of movement out of the corner of his eye. Another man was coming quickly around the other side of the van with an AK-47 rifle held low and ready for action. Tower tried desperately to turn, but he was too late. The muzzle of the AK-47 was pointing straight at him. Then a blinding flash lit up the area, and Tower heard a deafening roar as Hall triggered several fast shots from his short-barreled cannon. The heavy .44 Magnum bullets struck the man with the AK-47 like a sledgehammer and bounced his limp body back against the van.

Another man was kneeling at one corner of the van. He held a long slender tube over one shoulder, and was pointing it straight at Tower. Tower was good at weapons identification. Even in the moonlight he recognized an RPG-7 rocket-propelled grenade launcher. The Russian-made RPG-7 was a deadly weapon, firing 85 mm rockets with five-pound, high-explosive fragmentation warheads. Effective against almost anything but a main battle tank, it was a favorite weapon with

Arab soldiers who had access to Russian weapons. It was overkill to use an RPG-7 against one man, but Tower would be very dead indeed if the rocket struck him.

Instantly Tower swung his .45 automatic, pivoting smoothly from the waist, and snapped two quick shots as fast as he could at the RPG gunner. If he didn't hit him, perhaps he could spoil his aim. Tower saw two yellow flashes as the heavy .45 bullets struck the metal of the van and ricocheted away. He swore under his breath. He had not missed by much, but he had missed.

The RPG-7 gunner was a combat veteran. He didn't like near misses from large-caliber weapons, but he kept his eye on the cross hairs of his optical sight and pulled the RPG-7's trigger. The rocket whooshed from the launcher and shot toward Tower. He felt a puff of hot gas and smelled the acrid odor of burning rocket propellant as the rocket hissed past his head at four hundred feet per second. Tower would have sworn it missed him by inches; actually, it was at least two feet. The rocket shot past him and streaked toward the Mercedes, trailing gray-white smoke. It struck the trunk, and its five-pound warhead detonated in a blast of yellow fire. The Mercedes exploded in a huge ball of orange fire, and the shattered wreck began to smoke and burn. Tower hoped to God Blake and Amanda Stuart had gotten clear of the car. If not, he was going to have to write letters of condolence to their next of kin.

Although he realized that the RPG-7 gunner had been firing at the Mercedes, not at him, that did not make Tower like him any better. He could see the gunner's arm moving up toward the spare rocket pack on his back, reaching for another rocket to reload. Tower didn't want to be within kissing distance of another RPG-7 rocket. He concentrated all his attention on his .45 Colt's front sight and sent another double hammer blasting into the RPG man. The man shuddered and fell heavily, the RPG launcher slipping from his hands as he went down.

Things were suddenly quiet. The action seemed to have stopped. Tower's ears were ringing from muzzle blast, and he was shaking with after-action nerves, but he forced himself to concentrate. He couldn't afford to relax until he was sure all the attackers were dead or disabled.

Then he heard Amanda Stuart's voice, clear and carrying through the suddenly silent night. "Look out! There's somebody coming up the road behind us!"

He whirled and stared down the road. Amanda was right; he could see the lights of a truck approaching rapidly down the road from the west. Anyone coming up behind them was almost certainly hostile. The truck was three or four hundred yards away and it would arrive in less than twenty seconds. Amanda had already swung around and was pointing her 9 mm SIG-Sauer at the oncoming vehicle. She was not shooting yet, but coolly waiting until the truck was in effective range. That was the right reaction. Amanda could be counted on to keep her head in a fight, but she wasn't likely to stop a speeding truck with a pistol. Tower had reloaded his .45 without thinking, but two pistols were not much better than one.

He was getting awfully tired of being outgunned. Khier was firing at someone near the van. Tower could hear the repeated crack of his big 9 mm Beretta automatic. That would give Tower some cover, at least for a few seconds. Tower dashed toward the van and crouched quickly beside the body of the RPG gunner. He seized the long cylindrical launcher in one hand and reached for the gunner's spare rocket pack with the other. He slipped the long, thin, cylindrical rocket motor body down the muzzle of the launcher tube and checked to see that it was properly seated.

A burst of green tracers shot over Tower's head. Someone in the back of the truck was firing. There was no time to waste. He swung the RPG-7 launcher over his shoulder and peered through the optical sight. Two or three weapons were firing from the truck, and they all seemed to be firing straight at him. He put the illuminated cross hairs of the sight between the truck's headlights, grasped the pistol grip and pulled the trigger. The ejection cartridge shot the rocket grenade from the launcher. Its fins snapped out, the rocket motor ignited, and it hissed toward the truck, trailing orange flames and gray-white smoke.

The rocket struck, and its high explosive fragmentation warhead detonated. Tower heard a loud explosion and saw steel fragments tearing into the sand around the truck. Flames and smoke began to pour out from under its hood. Tower slipped in another round and fired again. The second rocket flashed at the truck. It smashed through the shattered windshield and detonated in a blast of yellow fire. The firing stopped and the truck began to burn spectacularly.

Tower heard the booming roar of Hall's big .44 Magnum and the spiteful crack of smaller-caliber weapons behind him as Hall, Blake and Colonel Khier fired shot after shot into the wrecked van. Suddenly everything was quiet. The silence was deafening after the sustained roar of many weapons firing. Tower found himself shaking with post-combat reaction. He felt as if he was having a nervous breakdown. He was sure that he had earned it, but he had no time to waste. The winners had better be damned sure they had won before relaxing and starting the celebration. One determined soul with an automatic weapon could turn things around in a hurry. It was better to check to be sure it was over.

Tower advanced carefully toward the van, keeping his pistol ready. All their attackers were crumpled on the ground, seemingly dead. Tower did not intend to take any chances. One of them might still be alive, determined to take an American with him when he died. But no one moved. There was nothing remarkable about them. They all appeared to be Arabs between the ages of twenty and thirty, dressed in rough work clothes or old military fatigues. Nor was anything unusual about their weapons; AK-47s and RPG-7s, the standard Russian infantry arms that saturated the Middle East.

Blake also moved forward and began to search the bodies. He shook his head. The dead men carried no identification. They could be from anywhere in the Arab world. Except for their weapons, they were no different than hundreds of thousands of men on the streets of Cairo. It gave Tower a queasy feeling. It could happen again and again. There could be dozens more waiting to attack, and there would be no warning, no way to identify them until they started their assault.

Tower heard sirens in the distance. The Egyptian police must be on their way from the pyramids, and no wonder. The fireworks they had just staged were certainly not part of the usual tourist attractions. Tower was glad Colonel Khier was with them, since he wouldn't have wanted to try to explain things to the Egyptian police without him.

Khier appeared out of the darkness. With a small tactical radio in one hand. "I have called for helicopters and a reaction team to secure the site. We must return to base at once. There is a message from Cairo. Your embassy has arranged a meeting with the Sudanese government. You are to leave with General Sykes and Dr. Kaye for Khartoum at 0800 hours."

Tower looked at his watch. That was less than seven hours away. He grinned weakly. There was no rest for the wicked! Khier turned away. The other car was approaching, accompanied by several Egyptian police cars with flashing lights.

Blake who had been standing quietly a few feet away, moved to Tower's side and held out his left hand. There was something in it, a piece of cloth, but Tower couldn't see what it was. Blake took a miniflashlight out of his pocket and shone it on the cloth. Tower saw a faded red triangle sewn on a piece of cloth cut from a military fatigue uniform. Blake pointed at one of the dead men.

Tower's stomach turned over. He knew what it was instantly. He had seen that simple insignia a hundred times before in Iraq and Kuwait. The Guards, the damned Iraqi Republican Guards. And he knew what it meant. The attack had not been an accident. Their security had been penetrated; their assailants had known who they were and where to find them. but that was not the worst of it. They were not up against ordinary terrorists, but men sent by the most dangerous man in the Middle East, Colonel Sadiq. If Sadiq was involved, all hell was going to break loose. He would strike again. It was only a question of when and where.

**4**

Dave Tower sat in the back seat of the old Mercedes as it moved slowly through the streets of Khartoum. The sun was blazing in the bright blue sky like a huge ball of molten yellow fire. The heat was brutal, with the temperature well over a hundred degrees, and Tower could feel every degree. The hot air coming in the open windows seemed to beat at him and provided no relief at all. The Sudanese army captain in the front seat had insisted on keeping the windows down since they left the American Embassy. It was a wise precaution. If they were attacked, having the windows down might save a critical second.

Captain Jabir obviously knew his business. His red beret showed he was an officer in the Sudanese army's elite 144th Parachute Brigade, which the Sudanese called the "Coup Stoppers." Tower noticed that he kept his .30-caliber German Heckler & Koch assault rifle ready across his knees. Tower knew soldiers. The captain and his men were obviously alert, ready for trouble. The paratroopers had the look of men who had been in combat. They were heavily loaded with spare magazines and hand grenades and kept their weapons ready for action.

They were not the only ones. Most of the soldiers Tower saw on the streets were heavily armed with weapons of varying types and vintages. The exotic panorama of constantly moving people grabbed his attention, and Tower found it hard to tear his eyes away from the striking mixture of ancient and modern. Colorful flowing robes and camels alternated with cars, trucks and Western clothes. And more than once they passed small groups of Saladin and Ferret armored cars parked at intersections, fully manned and ready for action. The capital was tense, a tension that could be felt in the air. Tower glanced at General Sykes and pointed at a Saladin. The general appeared to be almost asleep, dozing in the heat, but he had not survived twenty-five years in the Rangers by ignoring what was going on around him. It was obvious that the Sudanese army was expecting trouble.

They were on the outskirts of the city now, on El Geish Road, which rings the old city, moving faster as the traffic thinned. They turned onto a side road, and the driver suddenly stopped and pulled over to the side. A column of tanks was moving slowly toward them. Tower recognized Russian built T-55s. They were not the latest models, but their 100 mm high-velocity cannons and thick armor were still formidable. It was not a parade. The T-55s looked ready for action, with belts of cartridges dangling from the 12.7 mm antiaircraft machine guns mounted on the tops of their turrets. He counted over thirty tanks, a full battalion. He didn't want to appear to be staring, but he took in every detail. The more he knew, the better. He had no way of knowing whether he would be fighting with the Sudanese or against them, but either way, the quality of their troops would be very important.

The Sudanese captain looked at Tower and smiled. "They are from the Seventh Armored Division. They are going north to reinforce the Ninth Infantry Division at Shendi. You see, we have no secrets from our American friends."

"Their tanks seem well maintained," Tower said politely. "I have heard that Sudanese are good fighters and excellent soldiers. I can see for myself that this is true."

Captain Jabir's smile broadened. He knew he was being flattered, but he was proud of his unit and his army. He knew very little about Tower or why he was in Khartoum, but he recognized Tower's green beret and knew what it meant. Even in the Sudan, they had heard of the American Army's Special Forces. Tower's opinion was worth hearing.

They were slowing down now. There was a gate ahead, and signs on either side proclaimed in Arabic and English that they were approaching the headquarters of the Sudanese People's Armed Forces. Unauthorized persons were definitely not allowed. The sentries on the gate looked neat and efficient, their rifles in their hands ready for action. They saluted and checked

Captain Jabir's identity carefully before saluting again and waving the Mercedes through. Tower would not have liked to try to crash the gate. Two six-wheeled Saladin armored cars were carefully parked to cover the gate, their 76 mm cannons pointing threateningly toward the entrance. They were not there for show. One fifteen-pound high-explosive round would be more than enough to blast a car to pieces.

The Mercedes came to a stop in front of a large, dingy white building. The red-and-black-and-white-and-green flag of the Sudan hung from a flagpole outside the entrance, dangling limply in the heat. Tower and Sykes followed the Sudanese captain into the building and down a long corridor. He led them into a large room sparsely furnished with a table, some chairs and a big map of the Sudan on one wall.

Two men sat behind the table, waiting quietly. One of them was a large dark-skinned man in a military uniform. The other was a short, stocky civilian wearing a white suit and sunglasses. They looked at the Americans coolly. Tower noticed that there were no refreshments on the table. That was a bad sign. If the Sudanese considered this a friendly visit, their visitors should be offered tea or coffee.

The Sudanese captain saluted and reported formally. "Sir, these are the American visitors, General Sykes and Captain Tower. Gentlemen, this is Major General Rashid, and this is Dr. Minyar, the assistant director of military Intelligence."

General Rashid returned the captain's salute and spoke quietly in excellent English with a faintly British accent. "Gentlemen, we have been told that you have information, extremely important military information, vital to the security of the Sudan. Our government has appointed us to receive this information and discuss it with you. If you have no objection, Captain Jabir will remain. He commands the counterterrorist force in the 144th Parachute Brigade. If your information involves terrorist activity, he and his men will probably be involved. Please proceed. We await your information with great interest."

General Sykes didn't miss the tone of skepticism in General Rashid's voice, but it made no difference to him. He was here to do a job, and he would give them the facts, whether they liked it or not. He moved to the map. "I am Brigadier General James Sykes, United States Army. I am the executive officer of the United States Special Operations Command, SOCOM. At the moment I am the senior United States military officer in Egypt."

Dr. Minyar smiled bleakly. "We know who you are, General Sykes, and we have heard of your famous organization. We know that you have been conducting joint combat exercises with the Egyptians' Lightning Force. Units of that force and other major Egyptian military units are moving south toward our borders. This appears to be a threat. We know what is happening, but not why. Perhaps you would like to tell us?"

"That's what I'm here for, Gentlemen. Events in the last forty-eight hours have convinced the Egyptian government that there is a high probability that Egypt will be attacked by Sudanese forces or forces acting from Sudanese territory. They are moving their forces to your border to be prepared for combat. The United States government is a friend of Egypt and the Sudan. We wish to do anything possible to prevent war between the two countries."

"What?" General Rashid leapt to his feet. He was no longer calm. His dark face was livid. "This is preposterous! With all due respect, General, you have been listening to Egyptian propaganda. We are a poor country. There are twenty million Sudanese and seventy million Egyptians. Their armed forces outnumber ours five to one. We have rebels in the south. The Libyans are trying to overthrow our government. There is evidence that the fundamentalist groups may try to stage a coup. This is absurd! Surely you must know these things are true. How can you believe we threaten the Egyptians?"

Sykes was not there to argue. "I agree that the military situation is as you say it is, General, but it neglects one fact. Someone in the Sudan has nuclear weapons. One has already been used against Egypt. Nearly two hundred Egyptian soldiers were killed. Nuclear weapons completely change the military balance, and the Egyptians are right to be concerned. If they cannot be assured that these weapons have been destroyed, they will take military action against the Sudan. Those are the facts."

Dr. Minyar's face was ashen. "Nuclear weapons, General? As God is my witness, we have no nuclear weapons. I would know if we did. They must be planning to attack us! These lies about Sudanese nuclear weapons are a provocation! If the United States is truly our friend, you must stop them."

General Rashid stared at Sykes grimly. "Your Egyptian friends have tried to conquer and rule the Sudan before. They failed many times. We soaked the sands with their blood. It took the British army to defeat us. If they attack us, we will fight them to the end! Tell them that."

This was not going well. Sykes had stumbled into the midst of one of the old hatreds that plagues the Middle East. He took a deep breath and continued carefully. "I'm sure that the Egyptians know you will defend your country, just as you know they will defend theirs. I am not here to threaten you or to take sides. We want to prevent a war, not fight one."

"So you say, General," Dr. Minyar said suspiciously, "but there are some facts that seem to indicate otherwise. You have troops in Egypt, some of your elite special-operations units. You are, in your own words, the senior United States military officer in Egypt. That is not all. We may seem primitive to you, but our Intelligence service is efficient. We know that one of your U.S. Navy carrier battle groups is moving into the Red Sea, and there are reports that American troops and aircraft are on their way to Egypt. Tell us again that you are not taking sides."

Sykes paused for a moment. He was a soldier, not a diplomat. He was not skilled in evasive answers. He would simply tell the truth. "What you say is true, Doctor. Egypt is a friend of the United States. It is threatened with attack. The Egyptian government has asked for U.S. support. We will give it. If Egypt is attacked, we will help defend it, but that does not mean that we are your enemies. We will not support an unprovoked Egyptian attack on the Sudan or an Egyptian attempt to conquer your country. The nuclear weapons are the problem. We need your cooperation to locate and destroy them. The United States and Egypt are ready to assist you in doing this."

Dr. Minyar thought for a long moment. When he spoke, it was obvious that he was choosing his words very carefully. "Let us assume for the moment that everything you say is true, General. Suppose some group or organization has nuclear weapons in the Sudan. What do you propose we do about it?"

"First, we need your help in locating the weapons and identifying the group that controls them. You said that your Intelligence services are efficient. I am sure that is true. These weapons are very difficult to detect with remote sensors, and human Intelligence is vital. People are going to have to locate them, people who know the country and its inhabitants. Obviously no one can match Sudanese Intelligence when it comes to that. Your people can make a vital contribution."

Dr. Minyar smiled. It was obvious that this was true, but it was flattering and reassuring to see that this strange American general understood it. "Certainly Sudanese Intelligence will make every effort to find them, General. My government is not amused at the thought that unknown terrorists control nuclear weapons inside our borders. After all, they may be intended for use against our government. There are fanatic groups inside the Sudan who would not hesitate to do so."

Sykes frowned. He could have gone all day without hearing that. It complicated the situation, and it was already far too complicated to suit him.

"However, General, there is one very important point you have not mentioned. Suppose we find these weapons. What will you do then? Do you intend to destroy them with an air strike or with guided missiles? Remember, they are on Sudanese soil. What will happen if one or more of the weapons is detonated or if radioactive materials are released during your attack? We must know exactly what you propose to do."

It was a reasonable question. No government in the world can be expected to be indifferent to possible nuclear explosions within its territory. Fortunately Sykes was prepared to answer. "We have no intention of bombing the weapons site," he responded quickly. "That would be very dangerous. And there would be no way for us to be sure that we got them all, no matter how heavy our bombing was. Men have to go in, search the area and seize the weapons. We recommend that this be done by a joint Sudanese-American-Egyptian strike force. That way your government and the Egyptian government will be absolutely certain that the problem has been solved. Once we have control of the weapons, the United States will assume custody and remove them from—"

"Impossible!" Dr. Minyar interrupted. He was no longer smiling. "Absolutely impossible! We will never allow Egyptian troops to operate in the Sudan. If their soldiers cross our borders, it means war."

Sykes started to say something conciliatory, but Minyar held up his hand and stopped him. "Hear me out before you protest, General. It is obvious that you do not understand the political situation in the Sudan, or you would never suggest such a thing. Listen for a moment, and I will explain it to you."

Sykes sighed. Politicians seemed to be the same the whole world over. They needed to settle on a plan and get ready for action. Instead, he was about to get a lecture on the damned political situation in the Sudan. Perhaps he sighed a little louder than he intended because Dr. Minyar smiled bleakly.

"Oh, I know, General. Like all military men, you are a man of action. You are impatient with politicians, but if you do not understand our situation, none of your recommendations will make sense to us. You must understand what we can and cannot do without tearing our country apart." He paused for a second and stared straight at Sykes. "And remember one thing, General. As poor and backward as we may be, it is our country."

Sykes could not argue with that. Besides, much as he hated to admit it, he knew Minyar was right. The political situation was always a factor in military operations, just as important as the power of weapons or the range of aircraft. Perhaps more so. The United States had learned that the hard way in Vietnam. "Sorry, Doctor," Sykes said apologetically. "You're right. We're not familiar with the situation in the Sudan, and we need to be. Fill us in."

Dr. Minyar's smile returned. Perhaps the big American general was not as unreasonable as he had assumed. It remained to be seen how clever he was. It was Minyar's job to persuade Sykes to accept the views of the Sudanese government and recommend them to his government. That should not be too difficult. In Minyar's experience, Americans were a simple people, rich and powerful, with wonderful machines, but unsophisticated and possessing little knowledge of how the world outside their borders really worked. Still, it would not be wise to be overconfident. He chose his words carefully.

"The recent history of the Sudan is not a happy one. The Egyptians conquered the north in 1821. They used it to exploit the south. The Sudan has no gold or other natural riches. What the Egyptians wanted was slaves. The northern Sudan is basically Arab and Muslim. The people in the south are mostly black. They are not true believers. They are Christians or pagans. Khartoum itself was founded by the Egyptians in 1821 as a base for the slave trade. Vast numbers of blacks were taken in the south and sold as slaves. Whole areas were depopulated. The slave trade was carried out by Muslims, who were Arabs. People in the Sudan have long memories. You can understand, General, why Muslims are not popular in the south."

Sykes nodded. That seemed reasonable to him. If he were a southern Sudanese, the sight of some Muslims from the north would make him reach for his rifle.

"But that was not all," Minyar continued quickly. "At first the Arabs in the north profited from the slave trade. Then the Egyptian government imposed heavier and heavier taxes on them until most were reduced to poverty. They hired British officers as mercenaries to command their troops and act as their governors in the Sudan. The British conquered Egypt in 1882 and made the Egyptian government their puppet. But things did not change for us. The British did not want to use their soldiers in the Sudan. They continued the Egyptian rule. We protested, but they would not hear our words. They laughed at our suffering and called us ignorant savages. One British lord said that the Sudan should be left to stew in its own juices. Everyone in the Sudan, black and white, Muslim or Christian, was oppressed by the Egyptians and their British masters. There seemed to be no hope.

"Then God sent us a leader to rally all true believers and drive the foreigners out of the Sudan. He was Muhammad Ahmad ibn as-Sayyid Abdullah, the Mahdi. At first he preached repentance and called for justice for our people. The government laughed at him and called him a religious fanatic.

But when he preached against their unjust taxes and told true believers to resist their tax collectors, they stopped laughing. They sent soldiers to arrest him. He escaped and he preached jihad, the holy war, and called on all true believers to fight against the foreigners and those who served them."

Sykes was puzzled. This was interesting history, perhaps, but how did it relate to what was happening now? Sykes was not a great historian, but he was an excellent judge of men. He could see a change in Minyar as he spoke. He was no longer a dry, unemotional bureaucrat. His face was flushed, and his eyes were shining. It was obvious that what he was saying meant a great deal to him.

"The Mahdi called the true believers who rallied to the jihad Ansars, which means faithful followers. It is a title of honor in the Sudan to this day. My people were among the first to follow the Mahdi. I am a Hadendowa Beja. The British laughed at our quaint customs and the way our warriors wore their hair in battle. They called us fuzzy-wuzzies. They did not laugh at our swords when they felt their edges! The government sent two armies against us, Egyptian soldiers with British commanders. We fought them with our spears and swords against their rifles. But God is great and protects the faithful! We shed their blood and destroyed both their armies utterly."

"God is great!" General Rashid and Captain Jabir said together. It was obvious from the looks on their faces that this was not dry, ancient history to them. Sykes had the feeling he was witnessing a religious ritual.

"The Mahdi and the Ansars won victory after victory. The people rallied to the Mahdi's cause. The British sent their famous general, Chinese Gordon, to be governor-general of the Sudan. Gordon called for reinforcements and said he would 'smash the Mahdists and restore order to the Sudan.' He was a brave man and a good soldier, but he could not stop the Mahdi. Soon he was besieged in Khartoum. Gordon himself could have escaped to Egypt, but he was an honorable man. He would not desert his men.

"Gordon held Khartoum for three hundred days. The Mahdi called on him to surrender. Gordon was an infidel, but he was a brave man. He would not surrender. Finally the Mahdi gave the order, and the Ansars stormed Khartoum. Gordon and his garrison were destroyed to the last man.''

"It was my people, the Baggara, who stormed the governor's palace,'' General Rashid said proudly. "Gordon was there alone. The rest had fled, but not he. Four of our men rushed forward with their spears. He met the Ansars with his sword in his hand and died fighting. The Ansars cut off his head and took it to the Mahdi. God had granted victory to the faithful! Khartoum was ours. The Sudan was free from foreign rule.''

Minyar paused for a moment. He had made the story real. Sykes had been in many battles. He could almost hear the war cries and smell the powder smoke. Sykes didn't know much about Chinese Gordon, but a general who died with his troops rather than run away and leave them was Sykes's kind of soldier.

"We were free for thirteen years,'' Minyar continued quietly, "but the Mahdi died the year after he took Khartoum. He was succeeded by the Khalifa, Abdallahi. He was a brave man and a good leader, but he was not the Mahdi. The British never forgave us for their defeat and Gordon's death. They could not endure being defeated by poor and ignorant savages. In 1898 they sent an army against us. This time we faced British regulars. The Khalifa summoned the faithful to battle. We met them at Omdurman, a few miles north of here. Our people fought well. Even the British said no one ever fought them as fiercely as we Sudanese. But times had changed. The British had new weapons, long range cannon, repeating rifles, and machine guns. We lost. When the battle was over, eleven thousand of our people were dead. The British lost forty-eight officers and men. They blasted the Mahdi's tomb and took his skull to show their general. They made the Sudan a British colony.''

Minyar smiled bleakly. "Perhaps we should learn from that. Faith may not be enough if you lack modern weapons. I will not bore you with further details. The British ruled us until 1956. Then we regained our independence. We are proud of our past, as you can see, but we are a poor country. We have been crippled by civil war. The people in the south want to break up our nation and establish their own country. Even now there is steady fighting in the southern provinces, and the situation is precarious. There is evidence that foreign governments are supplying arms to the rebels.''

Foreign governments? Sykes wondered if that included the CIA. If so, no one had told him. Perhaps he was happier not knowing. ''This is very interesting, Dr. Minyar,'' he said politely. ''It certainly helps us understand the Sudan. But I don't see how it affects the question of the nuclear weapons and what to do about them. Perhaps you could explain that in simple terms so that we can understand.''

Minyar looked at Sykes narrowly. Was the big American general being sarcastic? He decided to be careful. Perhaps the Americans were more clever than they appeared.

''Certainly, General Sykes. I will be glad to do so. Our government came to power in 1989. The most important faction is the National Islamic Front. We are dedicated to making the Sudan a true Islamic state. We are fundamentalists, but we are not fanatics. Forty percent of our people are not believers— they are Christians or pagans. We do not want to persecute them or convert them by force. When the *sharia,* the fundamental Muslim code based on the principles of the Koran, was proclaimed the law of the land, we exempted the southern provinces. This has caused great unrest among true believers. The government is criticized for being weak and tolerant of foreigners and unbelievers.

''A new religious leader has arisen. He preaches a return to the true faith and the principles of the Mahdi. He says that our problems are caused by the corruption of the true faith by lip-serving rulers and foreigners. God is going to punish the Egyptians with hellfire, and He will punish us if we do not return to the true faith. He calls for jihad against the south and casting out the foreigners. His followers call themselves Ansars, and many are ready to become holy martyrs and die for the faith. He calls himself the Khalifa, meaning he is a successor of the Mahdi, but his followers whisper that he is a new Mahdi, or the old Mahdi come again.''

Minyar stared at Sykes and Tower intently. ''Can you see how powerful these words are in the Sudan? This man and his followers are everywhere, and they are gaining power every day.

At any moment they may try to overthrow the government. Now, do you understand? What you ask cannot be done. A joint Sudanese-American-Egyptian military strike force is impossible. If people learn that Egyptian soldiers have entered the Sudan at the invitation of our government, there would be rioting and bloodshed in the streets. The Ansars would move to overthrow the government, and they probably would succeed. Nor can we use government forces to search for these weapons, which may or may not exist. It would be said that we were persecuting true believers because foreigners have said we must do so. No, such things are impossible, utterly impossible!''

Sykes's face flushed. He understood that the Sudanese government had problems; but he had problems, too, and Dr. Minyar seemed determined to ignore them. Sykes had no tolerance for people who told him nothing could be done. The temptation to swear and pound the table was strong, but he was representing the United States government. He took a deep breath and spoke as diplomatically as possible. "Thank you for the briefing, Doctor," he said quietly. "I'm sure Captain Tower and I understand the situation in the Sudan much better now, but there's a problem. You seem to be saying that there's nothing that can be done, nothing at all. Believe me, I sympathize with your government's problems, but that answer is completely unacceptable! Remember why we are here. We are trying to prevent a war between Egypt and the Sudan, a war in which nuclear weapons may be used in attacks launched from the Sudan. If that happens, God only knows what will happen then to Egypt, to the Sudan, to all of us. We can't just sit here and wait. Something must be done to stop it!''

Dr. Minyar smiled faintly. The big American general was taking the bait. "I did not say that nothing can be done, General, only that what you have suggested is impossible. The Sudanese government has the utmost trust in the United States of America. Your good deeds are well-known throughout the Middle East and Africa. And we have the greatest respect for you and your Omega Force.''

Minyar looked at Sykes closely. Was he laying on the flattery too thick? Sykes was staring at him intently. It was obvious he was extremely interested. Minyar put his best political smile on his face and continued quickly. "What we propose is this. We will give you all possible help in locating the weapons. Once they are found, you will neutralize them. It must be an American operation, completely American, and no larger than absolutely necessary. When you have the weapons, you may remove them from our territory. General Rashid will arrange it so that our armed forces will not interfere with Omega Force, but our troops will not participate in the operation. Officially my government will know nothing about the operation, nothing whatsoever. Is this acceptable to you?"

Sykes kept his poker face, and he was a very good poker player indeed. You clever bastard, he thought. You think you're conning me! You want to have your cake and eat it, too. We take all the risks and do all the work. If anything goes wrong, you'll say you didn't know anything about it. We'll take all the blame. Still, in a way, it was what Sykes wanted. He knew what Omega Force could do. There was no telling what would happen if they tried a joint American- Egyptian-Sudanese operation. It could be the goddamnedest mess imaginable. All right, he decided, let them think they are conning the simpleminded Americans.

"I believe your proposal is acceptable. However,—" General Sykes paused meaningfully, and Dr. Minyar frowned. He did not like that *however.* "However," Sykes repeated, "I believe an Egyptian officer should accompany Omega Force. The Egyptians will want eyewitness confirmation from one of their own people. I also want a Sudanese army liaison officer to accompany our team. He can provide on-the-spot advice, and be an eyewitness for your government."

Dr. Minyar smiled. "I am sure that will be acceptable, General, provided the Egyptian officer wears an American uniform and carries no identification. If he is killed and his body is found, there must be no way of proving he was an Egyptian."

Minyar turned to General Rashid. "Is there any objection to one of our officers accompanying the Americans?"

"None at all. It seems an excellent plan. Captain Jabir will act as our liaison officer."

"Excellent. The general and I will contact our senior officials. They are meeting with your Dr. Kaye at the American Embassy. You will have an answer in a few hours. In the meantime Captain Jabir will escort you to your hotel. I am pleased to have met you, gentlemen. Allow me to wish you good luck."

Sykes smiled bleakly. He was afraid they were going to need all the luck they could get.

**5**

Dave Tower walked slowly down the dimly lit second-floor hall of the Safa Hotel. The hall seemed to be deserted, but he took no chances. He moved carefully, checking every spot where someone might be waiting in ambush. Some people would have smiled and said that Tower was too careful, but he had survived eight years of special operations because he never took unnecessary chances. He had carefully inspected the three adjacent rooms that Dr. Kaye had rented. The rooms were simple and clean, with fans and air coolers in the windows. The CIA was paying thirty-two Sudanese pounds for each double room, which was approximately eight U.S. dollars. Even the most eagle-eyed auditor from the government accounting office would find it hard to complain about that.

Tower had carefully swept each room with one of Sergeant Blake's magic black boxes. This marvel of electronic technology swore that there were no bugs in the rooms, at least none of the electronic variety. It had no opinion concerning the kind that bite tourists. They would have to take their chances there, but Tower was far more concerned about listening devices than the local insects. If someone learned their plans, it could be fatal.

He knocked on the door of General Sykes's room and identified himself carefully. That was just as well, since he noticed that Sykes was casually holstering a big .45 Colt automatic as Tower came in. Sykes wasn't trigger-happy, but he was very high on the list of people whom Tower did not want to startle.

The general was sitting quietly, sipping a large glass of orange juice. That was not his usual evening beverage, but the Sudanese government was placating the fundamentalists by enforcing strict prohibition. The porter who had showed them to their rooms had offered to get them a bottle of Scotch for a hundred Sudanese pounds, but Captain Jabir had pointed out that the penalty for being caught with illegal alcohol was a public flogging. That made orange juice seem much tastier, somehow.

"All secure, General," Tower reported. Sykes nodded and motioned for Tower to be seated.

"Where's Captain Jabir?" Sykes asked quietly.

"He's gone to his quarters to get ready to go with us. He should be back shortly."

Sykes nodded. That seemed reasonable. They could not expect Jabir to go to a foreign country with nothing but the uniform on his back, but there was still a nagging question in his mind. "What do you think, Tower? You've spent more time in the Middle East than I have. Do you think we can trust Jabir?"

Tower thought carefully for a minute. It wasn't an easy question to answer, and he wanted to be fair to Jabir. "Probably as much as we can trust anyone here," he said at last. "The Sudanese government obviously trusts him. He wouldn't be an officer in their elite 144th Parachute Brigade if they didn't, but he is a Muslim and an Arab. That means his religion is one of the most important things in his life. Maybe the most important. If he becomes convinced that this new Mahdi really is a divinely inspired leader, sent by God to save the Sudan, that would override all his other loyalties."

Sykes frowned. "All right, we'll play it straight. But keep an eye on him, and don't tell him anything he doesn't really need to know."

Tower nodded, although he did not like it. Jabir had appeared to be straightforward and cooperative. In a way, it did not seem fair, but special operations missions were seldom fair. "All right, General. I understand. Where's the rest of the party?"

"Dr. Kaye is at the embassy, talking to the powers that be in Washington on the SATCOM. Captain Stuart is with him. They should be here shortly. Blake and Hall are with them in case there's any trouble on the way."

Tower smiled. The American Embassy was less than half a mile from the hotel, but it was a wise precaution. Blake and Hall could handle a lot of trouble quite competently if it came to that.

There was a knock on the door, and Sykes's .45 automatic was instantly in his hand. He was careful not to stand in line with the door.

"It's Peter Kaye."

Sykes nodded. It certainly sounded like the CIA's rising star. "Speak of the devil," Sykes said softly under his breath as he moved quietly to unlock the door. Tower smiled again. It would be a cold day in hell when Sykes and Kaye were friends.

Kaye entered the room, mopping his face with a handkerchief. His elegant white linen suit was soaked with perspiration. Tower could sympathize. It was still brutally hot outside. There was someone with Kaye, a tall, elegant young black woman in a flowing multicolored robe.

"Gentlemen," Kaye said formally, "this is Miriam Mboro. We met at the embassy. She is a Sudanese journalist. Miss Mboro, these gentlemen are—"

"I know what they are, Dr. Kaye." She glared fiercely at Sykes and Tower. "All I have to do is look at them. It's obvious what they are, hired killers, trained assassins! Some of your famous Green Berets, brought here to kill, torture and terrorize the peace-loving citizens of the Sudan!"

Oh, God! Tower thought. One of those! Why the hell had Kaye brought her here? "I'm pleased to meet you, Miss Mboro," he said politely, extending his hand.

Miriam Mboro stared at Tower's hand as if it were dirty. "Well, I'm not pleased to meet you," she said in her husky contralto voice. "I hate mercenaries! How many women and children have you killed today, Tower?"

Tower flushed to the roots of his dark blond hair. He was a soldier in the United States Army and proud of it. He was tempted to deck Miss Mboro on the spot, but there was probably something in the regulations against punching Third World female journalists, no matter how much they deserved it. Then an alarm bell began to ring in the back of his mind.

Tower! She had called him Tower! Dr. Kaye had not finished his introduction, so how did she know his name was Tower?

Tower did not hesitate. He would have been dead a long time ago if he took the time to think deep thoughts when his instincts told him he was in danger. Instantly he drew his pistol, pushing off the safety as he swung into the firing position. "Freeze!" he shouted. "Move, and I'll blow your head off!"

Miriam Mboro found herself looking into the cavernous muzzle of a Colt .45 automatic. It was an utterly convincing argument. She froze.

Kaye stared at Tower. It was obvious he was astounded. "Why are you doing that, Tower?" he asked.

Tower was concentrating totally on his front sight, his finger on the trigger. "My name! How the hell does she know my name?"

Tower heard a harsh, rasping sound. Dr. Kaye was laughing. That in itself was alarming. He had never heard Kaye laugh and hadn't been sure that Kaye was capable of laughter. However, whatever Kaye thought, Tower did not find the situation funny.

Kaye clapped his hands in sarcastic applause. "Bravo! As you can see, Miriam is a splendid actress. She loves to deceive people, but I think she picked the wrong man this time. It's all right, Tower. You can put your weapon away. I vouch for her. She knows your name because I told her. Miss Mboro is one of us, the crusading-journalist act is part of her cover. She is the CIA agent in the Sudan who coordinates our support for the Sudanese rebels, the SPLM. She has the proper clearances, and she is briefed on our mission. Her contacts with the rebels are excellent. She is using them to try to locate the nuclear weapons."

Tower glared at Kaye and Miriam Mboro. He didn't like their little joke. He hated being made to look like a fool by a pretty woman. He felt utterly stupid menacing her with a .45 automatic, but it had been the right thing to do. "Very funny!" he said sourly, and slipped his big Colt back in its holster.

Miriam Mboro laughed and held out her hand. "I think we're even, Captain. You scared the hell out of me with your damned pistol! No hard feelings?"

Tower smiled. Personality conflicts could not be allowed on a mission. He might have to work closely with Miriam Mboro, but that would not be too hard to take. She was a very attractive woman. "I'm still pleased to meet you, Miss Mboro."

"Good," Kaye said in his usual superior tone of voice. "Now that we are all good friends, it's time to settle down and get some rest. There is nothing more to do until I hear from the embassy. Unless there are any questions, we can relax until then."

Sykes had been sitting quietly, enjoying the show, but his curiosity was aroused.

"Tell me something, Doctor," he said. "I realize that it's probably highly classified, but I'm cleared for top secret, and as the local U.S. military commander, I think I need to know. You say Miss Mboro is coordinating U.S. support for the rebels. I thought we were supporting the Sudanese government. Is the United States really supporting them, or are we supporting the rebels in the south?"

Kaye looked totally astounded. Sykes had never seen him look so surprised since he had first met the man during the Libyan operation a year ago. "You want to know if we are supporting the Sudanese government or the SPLM?" Kaye asked carefully.

Sykes nodded. "Yes, Doctor. I'm not just asking because I'm curious. I really need to know."

Kaye shook his head in disbelief, as if considering whether the question was for real. "Well, General, I think the answer is obvious. The CIA is supporting both of them, of course."

It was Sykes's turn to look astounded. "We're supporting both of them? But the SPLM is trying to overthrow the government. How the hell can we possibly be supporting both of them?"

"Really, General," Kaye said with his usual superior air, "I should think the answer is obvious. We support the government because, as Muslim governments go, it is really quite moderate. We don't want it overthrown and replaced by a radical fundamentalist government which would be completely hostile to the United States and its allies in the Middle East. Therefore, we are supporting the current government and have given it limited amounts of economic and military aid. On the other hand, if the radicals do become the government, they will persecute the Christians and the pagans in the south. We will then help them to resist, and overthrow the radical government if that is possible. To effect that, we support the SPLM, who are opposed to both the present government and the radicals. As you can see, General, it's completely logical for us to support the SPLM and give them limited military aid now."

Sykes shook his head. It might seem perfectly logical and straightforward to Dr. Kaye, but not to him. Sykes was a soldier and had fought for the United States in a dozen campaigns. He had killed many people, but he thought of himself as a straightforward and honorable man. To support both sides in a civil war and help them kill each other seemed like the height of hypocrisy. It was obvious that he did not live in the same world as Dr. Kaye. "All right," he said quietly, "I understand what you say, but I don't like it."

"It doesn't matter if you like it, General," Kaye said coldly. "You don't make national policy, and neither do I. We just see that it is carried out, whether we like it or not."

Sykes shrugged. Perhaps he was getting old-fashioned.

Miriam Mboro sighed softly. Kaye and Sykes glanced at her. Sykes did not know her well, but it seemed to him that she was very unhappy. Kaye stared at her and smiled his cold, bleak little smile. "That makes Miriam unhappy, too. She is probably the best agent the CIA has in this country, but she is a Christian and her family came from the southern Sudan. She thinks we should support the people in the south because they are right, and the government is oppressing them. She wants us to fight for freedom and the right." He shook his head. "God deliver me from idealists!"

Miriam Mboro kept her mouth shut, but if looks could have killed, Dr. Kaye's promising career with the CIA would have ended abruptly. But Kaye didn't seem to care.

"Miss Mboro will be spending the night with us," he said. "Will you escort her to Captain Stuart's room, Tower? I must wait for a call from the embassy."

Tower glanced at General Sykes. He would much rather spend time with pretty women than with Dr. Kaye, but he took his orders from Sykes, not from Kaye. When Sykes nodded, Tower opened the door and carefully scanned the dimly lit hall. It still seemed to be deserted, but he wasn't taking any chances. It would be impolite to move down the hall with a pistol in his hand, but his .45 automatic was ready in its holster, and he could draw and fire very rapidly if he had to.

All clear. He motioned to Miriam to follow him. She stalked into the hall, slamming the door behind her. It was a good thing that the Safa Hotel was well built, or it might have suffered structural damage. She followed Tower down the hall, seething.

"Damn that man!" she said in a tone of voice that could peel paint off the walls. "Why did the Agency have to send him here? He's a brilliant man, but he's a pretty sorry excuse for a human being!"

Tower said nothing. He was busy scanning the hall, but he felt that Miriam Mboro was an excellent judge of character. They traveled the short distance to Amanda Stuart's room without incident, and he knocked loudly and identified himself. Amanda unlocked the door and told him to come in. She was fetchingly attired in a large, thick towel, but Tower noticed she had her pistol in her hand. He smiled approvingly. Amanda had been around Omega Force long enough to pick up the attitudes that kept them alive in dangerous situations.

Amanda raised an eyebrow when she saw Miriam Mboro. "Would you like to introduce me to your girlfriend?" she inquired sweetly. Tower winced, not sure Miriam would like being referred to as his girlfriend. He quickly did the honors. Amanda was gracious. "You're welcome to stay with me, Miriam," she offered. "Can I do anything for you?"

Miriam looked at Amanda's towel and wet hair. "Do you have a shower? This damned robe is colorful, but it's like wearing a tent in this heat. I'd kill someone for a shower!"

Amanda laughed. "You don't have to go that far. Be my guest."

Miriam set her leather carryall down by the sofa and began to undress. Tower noticed that her carryall made a distinct metallic clunking noise when she set it down. He said nothing, but decided to check it out while she was in the shower. When

Miriam pulled off her robe, Tower found the view entrancing. She was decently dressed in a sensible white bra and panties. He could have seen more at a beach, but she did have an excellent figure. He was trying to think of something clever to say when someone knocked softly on the door.

When Amanda Stuart looked inquiringly at Tower, he motioned to her to wait. Whoever was outside knocked again. He did not like that. Sykes, Blake or Hall would have identified themselves immediately. Of course, it might be Dr. Kaye. His Ivy League education and CIA training might not have included the art and science of room defense. And if it wasn't Kaye, it might be some innocent tourist who was simply at the wrong door. Tower slipped his .45 automatic from his holster and moved to the wall of the room next to the door.

He shot a glance at Amanda Stuart and Miriam Mboro. Amanda had been through close-quarters battle training with Omega Force. She was moving toward the left wall of the room, her compact 9 mm SIG-Sauer P228 automatic pointing at the door, ready for action. Tower smiled grimly. He had been in combat with her before, in Libya and Lebanon. If you had to be in a tight spot, Amanda Stuart was a damned good person to have on your side. But where the hell was Miriam Mboro? She seemed to have vanished. Had she panicked and slipped into the bathroom to hide?

He heard the hiss of a large zipper being opened. Miriam was lying prone on the floor just to the right of the large sofa. She opened her leather carryall and pulled out something flat, black and deadly. Tower was good at recognizing weapons. He identified it as a 9 mm Swedish Carl Gustav submachine gun. It was not a standard U.S. military weapon, but the CIA had used and loved them since Vietnam. Tower heard a metallic click as she unfolded the metal stock and snapped in a 36-round magazine. Tower smiled again. He did not have to worry about Miriam Mboro.

The knocking came again, louder and more insistently this time. Tower thought for a second. The lights were on and they had been talking freely, so no one was going to believe the room was empty. He gestured to Amanda with his left hand.

She put her back against the left wall of the room, carefully avoiding the corner. "Who's there?" she called.

"It is I, Hassan, the porter, madam. I have brought you refreshments, bread and cheese, and a fine bottle of whiskey."

"There must be some mistake," Amanda said quickly. "I didn't order any refreshments."

Hassan chuckled. "Ah, there is no mistake, madam. They are a gift from Dr. Kaye. He wishes everything done to see that you are comfortable."

Instantly Tower's fingers tightened on his .45 Colt automatic. That was wrong, dead wrong! If Kaye had any friends, they weren't in Omega Force. He didn't care whether Tower and Amanda Stuart lived or died, or were comfortable or not, as long as his mission was accomplished. They were merely tools to him.

Amanda thought quickly. "Ah... I'm not dressed. Could you leave the refreshments outside? I will put your tip on the bill."

"I am so sorry, madam, but someone must sign the chit. Whiskey is very expensive here, a hundred pounds a bottle, and I am a poor man. If no one signs for it, I will be suspected of stealing, and I will lose my job."

Amanda looked at Tower. Hassan, if that was really who it was, was not going to go away. Tower signaled to Amanda not to move toward the door, and then nodded.

"All right, Hassan, we can't have that," she said casually. "Just a minute while I slip on a robe."

Good thinking! That would buy them a few seconds. Tower stayed against the wall and stretched forward until the fingertips of his left hand touched the doorknob. He pushed quickly and the knob started to turn. He jerked his hand back and flicked off the light switch. The world seemed to explode. The hall was filled with the ripping roar of automatic weapons firing rapidly. The center of the door seemed to disintegrate in showers of splinters as dozens of metal-jacketed bullets tore through the wood and sprayed the room beyond. The mirror on the back wall shattered into a hundred pieces, plaster flew from the wall, and the sofa jerked and shuddered as bullet after bullet smashed into it. A bullet struck something hard and shrieked like a lost soul as it ricocheted away. The firing seemed to go on endlessly. If Tower or Amanda Stuart had been standing in line with the door, they would have been cut to pieces. Tower resisted the temptation to shoot back through the door. He didn't think the opposition was stupid enough to stand directly in front of it, and he had no ammunition to waste.

There was a momentary pause in the firing, and Tower dropped to the floor and rolled away from the wall, still staying well clear of the door. He brought his pistol up in a hard, two-handed grip and covered the door. He had a damned good idea what was coming next. He heard a muffled bang, and metal shrieked and tore. Someone was shooting out the lock. The door smashed open and slammed against the wall. A man dived into the room and lay prone, but he did not fire. Tower knew that trick. He was waiting for a defender to fire. Tower aimed at the man, the soft green glow of his night sights centered on the man's body.

Perhaps two seconds had gone by. The automatic weapons snarled into life again. Two men were firing; Tower could see them illuminated by the flickering yellow light of their muzzle-flashes. One man was at each side of the door, and they raked the back wall and blasted both corners with long sustained bursts. They weren't foolishly wasting ammunition, since the corners of a room were the positions a defender would take almost automatically if he had not had close-quarters battle training. The room vibrated with the continuous muzzle blast. The firing seemed to go on forever. What the hell were they firing, belt-fed machine guns?

Tower was not the only person who could see them. Miriam Mboro didn't know who the men were, but she didn't have the slightest doubt that they were hostile. She pulled the trigger of her Carl Gustav and fired a long burst at the man to the left of the door. It was not elegant shooting. She stayed on the trigger too long and fired too many shots, but half a dozen 9 mm bullets tore into the attacker, and he fell heavily.

But the man waiting on the floor now knew where Miriam was. The muzzle-flash of her submachine gun had given her position away. He swung his weapon toward her, but Tower was ready. Instantly he pulled the trigger of his big Colt automatic twice in a deadly double hammer. Two heavy .45 bullets smashed into the man's side. He twitched and lay still.

Amanda's pistol cracked as she fired three or four quick shots through the open door. Someone outside raked the room with a long burst. If the CIA had to pay for damages, the bill was going up. Amanda Stuart gasped. Tower hoped she was not hit, but he had no time to look. He was tired of being outgunned. He rolled to the side of the man he had shot and ripped his weapon from his hands.

It was a heavy, short-barreled submachine gun with a thick, old-fashioned wooden stock and a large, round drum magazine protruding from the bottom. A Thompson? No such luck! For a second Tower was baffled, but he was good with foreign weapons. In a second he knew. It was a Russian PPSh 41, the famous Russian burp gun. He'd heard that some retired Russian generals swore that the PPSh 41 was the weapon that won World War II. Tower's war was not that big, but the solid weight of the weapon in his hands and the knowledge that its fat, round drum magazine held seventy-one cartridges ready to fire was extremely comforting.

That was just as well. There were more men outside, and they were still determined to kill the people in the room. The threat of Miriam Mboro's submachine gun was stopping them from rushing in. One of them began to fire around the right side of the door into the room, one 8- or 10-round burst after another. They were trying to get Miriam to return fire so that they could pinpoint her position and cut her to pieces. Miriam took the bait and fired back, one burst, two as she traded shots with the attacker, but she had started with thirty-six rounds in her magazine. Tower heard a hollow clunk as the bolt of Miriam's Carl Gustav slammed home on an empty chamber.

Tower wasn't the only one who heard. A second man had been waiting just to the left of the door. With a snarl of triumph, he took a step forward and swung the lethal muzzle of his PPSh 41 toward Miriam Mboro. Tower could see the big round drum magazine of the PPSh 41 in his hands. He took a flash sight picture, his sights silhouetted against the dim light in the hall, aiming just below the edge of the magazine and pulled the trigger. The burp gun snarled and vibrated in his hands. A dozen 7.62 mm bullets ripped into the center of the man's body. His snarl of triumph changed abruptly into a shriek of agony. He staggered forward, his hands convulsing on his weapon. His PPSh 41 erupted into one long, continuous burst. Tower could see the flickering yellow of the blazing muzzle-flashes as the weapon's lethal muzzle swung toward him.

Puffs of dust and shreds of carpet flew as the striking bullets moved toward Tower. To his left, he heard the flat crack of Amanda's pistol as she snapped a fast double hammer into the man's side, but he still didn't go down. His weapon was still spitting flame and bullets. He must be dying on his feet, but that would be cold comfort if he took Tower with him. Tower pulled the trigger of his own PPSh. He had no time for precise shooting. The PPSh's small, fast, 7.62 mm bullets were lethal, but they lacked the instantaneous stopping power of a .45. Tower had to depend on the cumulative effects of multiple hits, and he had to get those hits fast! He held his trigger back and fired one long, sustained burst into his attacker.

The heavy PPSh quivered and its steel butt plate slammed repeatedly into Tower's shoulder. The deafening roar and dazzling light of the muzzle-flash seemed to go on forever as he fired thirty rounds in less than two seconds. The blasts of bullets struck like an angry swarm of hornets. Flesh and blood could only endure so much. The attacker's weapon slipped from his nerveless fingers and he fell limply to the floor. Tower had seen men fall like that before. He was not going to need shooting again.

There was at least one man still outside, probably more, but they had lost enthusiasm for coming through the door. Miriam Mboro was reloaded now, and Tower was ready to fire again. The crossfire from two automatic weapons made the door a death trap for anyone who tried to come through. But that worked both ways. They were still trapped inside the room. If the attackers had grenades, they were doomed.

Tower thought furiously, but he could think of nothing he and the two women could do but stay in the room and shoot it out. Stalemate. For a long moment there was silence, each side waiting for the other to make a move. Then shouting came from the hall, and then the echoing roar of sustained firing. Someone was blasting away with far more powerful weapons than submachine guns or pistols. Tower heard the dull boom of a hand grenade detonating. The walls shook and shuddered. Someone screamed in pain, then everything was quiet. Tower listened intently. He was still a little deaf from the concentrated blasts of automatic weapons fired in a small, closed room. At first he could not be certain, but then he was sure. People were moving slowly and carefully down the hall in his direction. He kept his sights on the door, ready to fire, and waited tensely.

"Captain Tower? Captain Stuart?" someone called softly. They were speaking English, but with a slight Arabic accent. Tower didn't know the voice, and did not answer. Someone outside had hand grenades. If he called out and gave his position away, the reply might be fatal.

Someone else spoke. "Captain Tower? Captain Stuart? It's Sergeant Hall. Hold your fire. There are friendlies coming down the hall." Tower felt a great surge of relief. He knew that voice. He would have bet a month's pay that there was no one in the Sudan who could counterfeit Hall's soft southwestern twang.

"Roger, Hall, understood. We will hold our fire. Come ahead." Tower flicked on the room lights. This was no time for confusion. Accidental friendly fire could kill them just as dead as shots from their worst enemy.

Hall came cautiously in the door, his big .44 Magnum in one hand. He was followed by several men in camouflage uniforms and red berets. The Coup Stoppers had arrived. Hall looked around the room. The walls were pockmarked with bullet holes and the floor was littered with pieces of plaster, broken glass and fired cartridge cases. The smell of burnt powder drifted on the air.

Miriam Mboro stood up. Her submachine gun was still in her hands, and she was still fetchingly attired in her bra and panties. Amanda Stuart was still wearing her towel and was examining her left leg. A large splinter from the door was embedded in her thigh, and a small trickle of blood was oozing down her leg. Amanda spoke fluently about splinters and people who shot at her. She had learned some interesting words in her Army career. Even Tower was impressed.

Sergeant Hall stared at the scene. He lifted one eyebrow. "Well, Captain," he said softly, "it looks like you've been having quite a party." It was an unusual situation. Tower had been in a good many firefights, but he had never led a combat team of two scantily clad women before. He considered trying to explain the situation. That was no good. Anything he said would just get him in deeper. It was time to change the subject.

"What's the situation, Sam?" he asked quickly. "How are General Sykes and Dr. Kaye?"

"They're all right," Hall said with a grin. "Three of these people tried to take them out, but the general got two of them with his .45 and Kaye got the other with his little .38 Special revolver. Kaye really ought to carry a serious gun, but he managed to get the job done. Blake and Captain Jabir's men are with them." Hall's grin widened. "I think the doctor is a little shook up. He's not used to shooting it out with people face-to-face."

Captain Jabir appeared in the door and stared at the scene. Miriam Mboro had produced a first-aid kit and was bandaging Amanda Stuart's thigh. Jabir looked startled, but whatever he thought, he managed to keep his opinions to himself. "Captain Tower, we must leave the hotel immediately. I have checked with the hotel management, There are several other groups of Americans staying here, but they were not attacked. This action was aimed directly at your group. The terrorists knew who you were and where you were staying. Our security has been penetrated. You must leave for the airport immediately. I have two platoons of my men here. They will escort us."

Jabir paused for a moment and cleared his throat politely. "If the ladies would put some clothes on, we will be on our way. I fear they will attract a great deal of attention dressed as they are."

Ten minutes later they were on their way to the military airport, escorted by stony-faced paratroopers. No one had much to say as they drove along. Tower kept alert, but no one on the streets seemed to want to annoy the Coup Stoppers. Amanda's

Blackhawk was surrounded by a platoon of heavily armed Sudanese paratroopers. Jabir spoke quickly to the lieutenant in charge, and waved them into the troop compartment. Amanda completed her preflight checks in record time, and the Blackhawk's twin turbine engines whined into life. Kaye spoke urgently to Miriam Mboro. Tower could not hear what he said, but Miriam nodded and stepped back out the door. Tower was puzzled, but there was no time to ask questions. Hall closed the door when the whine of the turbines rose to a shriek, as Amanda Stuart went to full power, and the Blackhawk lifted off.

Tower looked out a window as Amanda went to full pitch and headed north. He would have liked to have had more time to see Khartoum and the rest of the Sudan, but perhaps it was just as well they were leaving. It seemed like a hard place to stay alive in.

Kaye was sitting next to Tower, staring out a window as the Blackhawk began to follow the Nile northward. He seemed preoccupied with his thoughts, but Tower didn't like being in the dark. He would ask a few questions, and if that upset Kaye, that was too damned bad.

"Where's Miriam Mboro, why isn't she coming with us?" he inquired.

"What? Yes, I had better fill you in. I didn't want to say anything until we were airborne. The hotel and the vehicles could have been bugged. Miriam is on her way to the north in a Sudanese army helicopter. Our agents there think they have located the weapons. Miriam will check it out. If she confirms their location, she will meet you when you go in."

Tower smiled bleakly. It sounded as if he had not seen the last of the Sudan, after all. "How soon will that be, Doctor?" he asked quietly.

"Twenty-four to forty-eight hours. It will take Miriam that long to get ready," Kaye said absently. His mind did not seem to be on the conversation.

Tower was puzzled. "That sounds like good news, Doctor, but you don't seem very happy about it. Is something wrong?"

Kaye looked at him scornfully. "For God's sake, Tower, I always thought you were one of the few intelligent soldiers I have ever met. How can you ask a stupid question like that? Of course something is wrong! They tried to kill us in Egypt and they almost succeeded. They tried again just now in Khartoum, and we were lucky to get out alive. It should be obvious that our security has been compromised. Operation Sphinx is leaking like a sieve. They know who we are, where we are and what we're doing. We have got to start outsmarting them for a change if we want to stay alive.''

It was hot in the Blackhawk's troop transport compartment, but Tower still felt a chill. He did not like Kaye's tone of voice, but it was hard to argue with his cold logic. They had managed to stay alive so far, but the enemy was winning.

**6**

The big Air Force Lockheed C-130 flew steadily on through the night. Captain Dave Tower sat in one of the cramped nylon web seats in the troop compartment and worried. There was really nothing else for him to do until they got to the target. He was strapped snugly but uncomfortably into his web equipment and his parachute harness. He had strapped on his gear four hours before and had been sitting in the big plane for half of that time. His legs and buttocks were numb, and his back was aching and throbbing from the constriction of his harness and that damned seat. Tower liked C-130s. They were strong, reliable aircraft that always got him to his destination, but if he ever met the man who had designed their troop seats, he would kill him on the spot.

The C-130 was no ordinary Lockheed Hercules. It was one of the new MC-130H Combat Talon II models, designed and equipped for special-operations and missions. The plane and its crew were from the Air Force's Eighth Special Operations Squadron, and that made Tower happy. The Eighth SOS had flown him into Iraq and Kuwait. If anyone could get Tower and Omega Force to the right place at the right time, they could. Tower hoped his faith was justified. The attack order had been received forty minutes ago. They had turned in from the Red Sea and crossed the Sudanese coast half an hour ago. He was just considering that they should be already approaching the target when the Air Force loadmaster suddenly appeared, moving quietly through the dimly lit crew compartment. He looked at Tower for a second to be sure he had the right man. In the dark all the Omega Force team looked the same in their dull black, nonreflective uniforms, Kevlar helmets and combat gear. Tower was not wearing his silver captain's bars; he wasn't going to make life easier for enemy snipers.

"Captain Tower?" the Air Force sergeant asked, and Tower nodded. "Captain Lynch says to tell you we are on final approach for the drop zone. Course and location confirmed by the inertial navigation system and satellite global position system." Tower smiled. He was happy that the MC-130H's marvelous technology insisted that everything was going perfectly, but he could not help remembering the old joke that ends, "Nothing can go wrong…go wrong…go wrong…go wrong." It would be extremely embarrassing if he and his elite assault team came floating down in the wrong place.

He told himself to settle down and relax. A high-altitude, low-opening parachute jump was not the safest thing in the world, but everyone in Omega Force had done it many times. Tower was not quite so sure about Colonel Khier and Captain Jabir. He would have been happier if there had been more time to check them out. Although they were both experienced paratroopers, they were not used to American equipment and procedures. That worried Tower. He knew there were no unimportant details in a HALO jump. Small mistakes could kill you.

Tower was in command. As usual, Major Cray had wanted to lead the HALO jump in person, but General Sykes had vetoed that and assigned Cray to lead the main attack if the rest of Omega Force had to be sent in. Cray had argued with Sykes, but he had lost. That was not surprising: majors seldom won arguments with generals. Tower had been selected to lead the assault team. He was a veteran of more than two thousand jumps, and he was their only officer who could speak fluent Arabic. Tower sighed. There were times he thought that learning to speak Arabic had been a serious error. This was one of them. He smiled to himself. He always felt scared just before he jumped, but he had never frozen in the door yet, and he was not going to start now.

The steady whine of the four turboprop engines changed as the pilot throttled back and leveled off. Sergeant Hall came slowly down the aisle, breathing from the oxygen bottle on his chest. Hall would act as the jump master. He was a good choice. Hall had made as many HALO jumps as anyone else in Omega Force, and he kept cool when things got bad.

"Get ready!" Hall's voice rang through the troop compartment, loud and clear over the whine of the engines. All eyes were on Hall now. Tower felt a cold knot in his stomach. He did not really like parachute jumping. He did it because it was part of his job, but at times like this, he had trouble remembering just why he had wanted to be a Green Beret.

Hall gestured upward with both hands. "Jump party! Stand...up!"

Grunts and wordless groans filled the troop compartment as the fourteen-man assault team heaved themselves to their feet, each man fighting the drag of one hundred forty pounds of parachutes, weapons and combat equipment. Tower could feel the shoulder straps of his parachute harness cutting deeper into his aching shoulders, but he had no time to brood over his troubles.

"Check equipment, prepare for depressurization!" Hall shouted.

Quickly Tower checked his equipment and the equipment of the man to his left and right. Now for the critical step. Everyone in the troop compartment had to go on oxygen. The transport plane had been climbing steadily since it left the Egyptian air base, and it was flying at thirty-three thousand feet. The MC-130H's aft compartment must be depressurized now. The HALO jump would require opening the tail door, and if the pressure inside did not match that of the thin outside air, a hurricane of air would blast through the compartment the instant the door was opened. That meant Tower and the assault party had to start breathing oxygen from the two individual bailout bottles strapped to their harnesses before the door was opened. Each bottle could supply thirty minutes of oxygen. Their bailout bottles would keep them alive until they were below ten thousand feet.

The four-minute-warning light was on. Tower and the assault team were breathing from their bailout bottles now. Hall gave each man a final equipment check. He looked to see that each man's head and face was covered by his jump helmet and oxygen mask. Boots, gloves and insulated jumpsuits protected the rest of their bodies. It was sixty-five degrees below zero outside, and the air would be howling past the MC-130H's fuselage at one hundred thirty knots when they jumped. It would be like stepping into an ice-cold hurricane. Any unprotected skin meant instant frostbite. When each man gave the thumbs-up ready signal, Hall nodded and pointed at the tail door.

Slowly, careful not to tangle their equipment, the team moved toward the tail door. They would jump at five-second intervals. Tower would go first. He would be the jump leader, the low man. Sergeant Hall would be the last man out. If anything happened to Tower during the jump, Hall would take command of the assault team.

Two-minute warning. They were standing at the end of the cargo compartment now, facing the C-130's tail door. When the door opened, there would be nothing below them but air. The pilot was waiting until the last moment to open the door. Hall signaled for the final oxygen check. Red warning lights came on, and with the high-pitched whine of hydraulic motors the tail door was lowered and locked open in the horizontal ready position. Icy air filled the cargo compartment. Tower stared into the blackness outside.

One-minute warning. Tower looked back and made a thumbs-up gesture to his team. Each man returned the gesture with his own thumbs-up signal. They were all ready to go. No one was having breathing problems or trouble with his equipment.

The thirty-second-warning light came on! There was a sudden change in the roar of the engines as the Air Force pilot throttled back. He was holding the MC-130H as close to its stalling speed as he dared in order to reduce the strength of the airflow around the big plane's fuselage. When he was satisfied, he would push the ten-second-warning light. Unless Tower or Hal called an abort, the team would go.

The big plane began to shake and vibrate as its speed dropped to within a few knots of stalling. Satisfied, the Air Force pilot pushed the button. The ten-second-warning light came on.

"Standby!" Hall shouted. The standby order was the last warning before the jump. Tower felt a quick surge of adrenaline. There was nothing left for him to do now but pray.

Suddenly the go light went on.

Tower heard Hall scream "Go! Go! Go!" He took two long strides along the ramp and dived through the open door out into the dark. Instantly he was in free-fall. The slipstream spun and buffeted his body like a rag doll. Looking back, he saw the bright moonlight reflected from the huge wings and fuselage of the MC-130H. The whine of its engines faded as it pulled away and vanished into the dark. Tower used his arms and legs to turn his body and assume a facedown position.

He was falling through the dark. The only sounds were the sighing of the air as it rushed past him and the harsh, rasping sounds of his own breathing inside his mask. He looked down. All his AN/PVS-7 night-vision goggles showed him were the tops of a thick layer of clouds below. The scene did not seem to change. Tower knew he was falling several hundred feet each second toward the ground below, but he seemed to be suspended in space. He hated free-fall from high altitudes, but the plan called for opening their chutes at two thousand feet. Until then, he would have to grit his teeth and bear it.

He had spent enough time brooding about his own troubles. Time to think like an assault-team commander! Hall should have jumped and cleared the aircraft now. He should be above everyone else. "High man, give me the count," Tower said. The sound of his voice activated the microphone on his throat, and the low-probability-of-intercept radio transmitted his message. In theory, his radio was almost impossible to intercept, and even if someone on the ground picked it up, the message was scrambled. Still, people on the ground would certainly be alerted if they detected mysterious, undecipherable messages coming from the sky overhead. He must keep radio transmissions to a minimum.

"I only see four, Lead," Hall reported in his soft southwestern drawl, "but everyone cleared the plane." Tower found that reassuring. All fourteen men were falling through space toward the target now. Even if someone had passed out from oxygen-mask failure, their chute would open automatically when they reached a thousand feet.

Tower looked down again. He no longer had the sensation of being suspended motionless in space. He was close to the cloud tops now. It looked as if he were falling toward the tops of snow-covered mountains. He checked his altimeter—sixteen thousand feet. The clouds seemed to be rushing at him at breakneck speed. Suddenly he was surrounded by thick gray mist. Moisture condensed on his goggles, obscuring his vision. Then he was through, bursting out into the air below the clouds.

His goggles cleared. Tower checked his altimeter again—twelve thousand feet. He began to scan the land below. The view did not offer much except flat, rolling, arid dirt and sand, broken here and there by a low-lying rocky hill. He could see why this part of the Sudan was called the Nubian Desert. In the distance he could see a cluster of dim lights. That must be the town, but that was not what he was looking for. Then he spotted it. There it was! From the edge of a wide, flat patch of ground, the beacon began to blink, sending out pulses of infrared. It would have been invisible to the naked eye, but Tower's night-vision goggles showed him a steady series of bright, flashing pulses. The beacon's light was shrouded by a funnel-shaped shield. Even with night-vision equipment, it would be invisible to anyone on the ground.

The beacon was putting out a steady, rhythmic series of infrared pulses. That was the go code. If the operator thought the landing zone was not secure, he would have pushed the warning button and the beacon's output would be a series of faster, flickering pulses. It was a standard U.S. special-operations clandestine beacon. Miriam Mboro or some of her people must be at the landing zone.

But it was time to concentrate on landing. They were a bit to the right of the landing zone, but their special, rectangular, MT1-XX ram-air canopy parachutes could be flown like hang gliders, allowing them to come down at angles as great as forty-five degrees. They should all come down close together near the blinking infrared beacon that marked the center of the landing zone.

He checked his altimeter—four thousand feet. Time passes fast when you're having fun! he thought wryly. He kept his eye on his altimeter dial and grasped the rip cord's D-ring. He was counting to himself without thinking as he glanced quickly to

the left and right. All clear. Three! Two! One! Tower pulled his
rip cord. His pilot chute deployed, pulling the special high-
performance ram-air canopy out of its pack and into the air.
The canopy blossomed, and Tower felt a bone-jarring jolt as it
filled with air and abruptly slowed his fall. Quickly he slipped
his hands into his steering loops, ready to maneuver if he had
to. A collision with one of his team could ruin the landing, or
if it collapsed Tower's canopy, it might ruin Tower.

"High man, give me the count," Tower said again.

There was a second or two of silence. Hall was a careful man.
"I see thirteen, Lead," Hall said in his soft drawl. "Approxi-
mate team dispersion is thirty yards, with one man one hundred yards to the left."

Tower felt a surge of relief. He looked around him quickly
and counted. Everyone's chute had opened. No one seemed to
be in trouble. Someone was a bit off course, probably Khier or
Jabir, but not enough to matter. Now it was time to concentrate on his landing.

He pulled on his steering loops and began to move to the
right, toward the steadily blinking beacon. He had to make a
good parachute landing fall, since no operational jump was
worth a damn without a good PLF. A broken knee or ankle
deep inside the Sudan was likely to be just as fatal as a burst
from a well-aimed AK-47. The ground was getting closer and
closer.

Knees and elbows were the most vulnerable points in a PLF,
so Tower tensed and slightly bent his knees, keeping his hands
in the steering loops with his elbows turned inward, close to his
chest. He was almost on top of the beacon. He released his
equipment rucksack. It dropped away and dangled fifteen feet
below him on the end of its heavy nylon line.

He pulled on the steering loops and went to full brake. His
forward motion stopped, and he went straight down. He felt a
jolt through the nylon line as his rucksack hit the ground. Now!
Feet together, damn it! Feet together and roll! Tower felt a jolt
through every bone as he struck the ground in the controlled
crash landing of a heavily loaded military parachutist. He did
a forward roll and came to a stop. Everything seemed to be in
one piece. He felt a surge of relief. He was down and safe.

No time to celebrate. First things first. He must be ready to defend himself before he worried about anything else. He reached for the nylon weapons case under his left arm, snapped it open and pulled out his dull black M-16A2 automatic rifle. There was a round in the chamber, and a full 30-round magazine was inserted in the receiver. Tower flicked the selector switch to automatic. Now he was ready to fight. He would worry about getting out of his parachute harness when he was sure the landing zone was secure.

He saw a flicker of motion in his night-vision goggles. A tall, slender woman was crouching in a cluster of scrubby bushes fifty feet away. She held a submachine gun ready in her hands. It certainly looked like Miriam Mboro, but he had better make sure. He dropped to a prone position and covered her with his M-16. He kept his finger in the trigger guard but did not touch his trigger. It would be a tragedy if he accidentally shot Miriam. The only thing worse would be if she shot him.

She didn't seem to have seen him. She was looking away from him and up, apparently amazed at what she saw. Tower heard a soft sighing noise as Sergeant Blake glided in to a perfect stand-up landing. Above and behind him, the rest of the assault team was flying in, appearing one by one like giant black bats out of the dark.

"Dagger!" Tower whispered loudly, issuing the challenge.

The woman was startled and whirled toward the sound of Tower's voice. It was a perfect response. The muzzle of her submachine gun swung to point at the sound, but she kept her head. "Arrow!" she responded. Tower relaxed. It was the correct response, and he recognized Miriam Mboro's husky voice. She stared at Tower and Blake in amazement as they slipped out of their parachute harnesses. In their Kevlar helmets and with their faces obscured by their night-vision goggles, they looked like warriors from another world.

Miriam Mboro laughed. "You guys sure know how to make an entrance! Welcome to the Sudan!"

**7**

Dave Tower crawled slowly toward the top of the low, sandy ridge. He kept down, flattened to the ground, his rifle cradled across his arms. It was a tiring, uncomfortable way to move, but it made him extremely difficult to see in the dark, even for someone scanning the area with night-vision equipment. The little ridge was the last real cover between the assault team and their objective four hundred yards ahead. If Tower had been planning the defense, he would have posted sentries on top of the ridge. That thought made him careful. He would have been dead a long time ago if he was stupid enough to believe that his enemies were not very smart and highly capable.

He stopped twenty yards from the crest and scanned it carefully through his AN/PVS-7 night-vision goggles. All he saw was sand, broken here and there by clumps of rock and clusters of scraggly bushes. Nothing moved. Everything was quiet. If anyone was on the ridge line, he was perfectly camouflaged and staying absolutely still, waiting to blow the head off any intruder who offered him a target. Tower did not like that thought, but that made no difference. All the miracles of modern science had not developed a substitute for the infantryman. There was only one way to be sure. Tower put his hand on the pistol grip of his rifle and pushed the selector switch to full automatic. The weight of the M-16A2 in his hands was comforting. For the next sixty seconds, it would be the only friend he had.

His nerves crawled as he inched forward, ten yards, then five. Now he was at the top. Tower discovered he had been holding his breath for the last few yards. He took a deep breath and looked around himself carefully. The top of the low-lying ridge was deserted. He inched toward a clump of rocks ahead. He was careful not to stand up and look over the top of the rocks. That would silhouette him against the sky behind him. Instead, he stayed low and peered around the right edge of the rocks. That way, his body would blend into the shape of the rocks if anyone were looking. It was true that the enemy would have to have night-vision equipment to see him, but Tower was not about to bet his life that they did not.

He scanned the area ahead carefully. There it was! Tower had memorized the satellite photographs of the objective. He instantly recognized the group of shabby buildings and rusty machinery at the end of a dirt road that ran past the ridge. He felt a pardonable sense of pride. Omega Force had come several hundred miles through the dark and had found their target perfectly. The mission was certainly not over yet, but they were off to a damned good start. He scanned the buildings carefully through his night-vision goggles. He saw no sign of life. The oil-exploration station had been abandoned years ago, and it still seemed to be deserted.

Tower unclipped a mini-infrared flashlight from his web equipment and signaled Blake to bring up the command group. The coded pulses from the tiny flashlight were invisible to the human eye, but Blake would see them through his night-vision goggles. Tower waited patiently as Blake came crawling through the darkness, followed by Colonel Khier and Captain Jabir. Tower was glad to see that Khier and Jabir stayed low, keeping close to the ground. He didn't doubt that both of them were brave men, but he was pleased that they knew when to be careful. Bravery and professional competence are related, but they aren't always the same thing.

Sergeant Blake and Colonel Khier slipped quietly forward and joined Tower. Jabir stayed back a few yards, keeping his rifle ready, scanning the area around them steadily. He would provide security while the rest of the group studied the target. Blake opened his pack and took out something that looked like an amateur astronomer's telescope. Next he opened the tripod and pointed the cylindrical body at the target and began to check it carefully. It was a AN/TAS-6, a thermal acquisition sight. Tower sometimes liked to tease Blake about his unlimited enthusiasm for SOCOM's high-technology devices and weapons. Tower felt that some of them were too complicated to be worth their cost and weight, but he had no doubts about the AN/TAS-6. It was complicated and bulky, it weighed nearly seventy pounds and required liquid-nitrogen cooling bottles and regular replacement of its batteries. But Tower had used them in Iraq during Desert Storm, and he was convinced there were times when they were worth their weight in gold. This was one of those times.

Blake finished his tests and began to activate the AN/TAS-6. There was a soft hiss as liquid nitrogen was released from the cooling bottle, instantly evaporating into an immensely cold gas and cooling the array of tiny metal detectors inside the device to nearly three hundred degrees below zero. As the detectors cooled, they became extremely sensitive to infrared light and began to emit electrical signals that were converted to a clear television image in the AN/TAS-6's optics. Blake had set it for 12X, maximum magnification. He could now see the buildings as well as if he were standing only thirty-five yards away in broad daylight.

He began to scan the target area while Tower waited impatiently. Only one man could use the AN/TAS-6 at a time, and Blake was by far the best operator in Omega Force. If there was anything to see, he would find it and report. Tower knew this, and there was no point in trying to hurry Blake. That might make him careless, with highly unpleasant results. Still, Tower couldn't help feeling tense. If the buildings were actually deserted, he and his team had come a long and dangerous way for nothing.

"Jackpot!" Blake said softly. "There are people down there, Captain. I see at least five or six. They all have rifles. I think we had better get organized and pay them a visit."

"Let us not be too hasty, Captain," Colonel Khier interjected. "They may be local people using this place as a campsite. There are many bands of nomads in the northern Sudan."

"Well, Colonel, if they're friendly local nomads, they're awfully damned well armed," Blake said casually. "All the rifles I see are AK-47s, and there is a belt-fed heavy machine gun near the corner of the big building sited to cover the road. It looks like a Russian 12.7 mm or a 14.5. There are three men near the gun, and you can see that it has a belt in it, ready to fire."

Tower did not like the sound of that! A Russian 12.7 mm was the equivalent of an American .50-caliber machine gun. The 14.5 mm was even more powerful, but either one could hit and kill men at a thousand yards or tear a jeep apart in a few seconds. This was not going to be a walkover, and he wondered just how many men they were up against. There was no way to be certain. Blake had reported eight or nine, but there could be a lot more men inside the buildings. Marvelous as modern infrared sensors are, they cannot see through walls.

Blake completed his scan. Without waiting to be asked, he moved to one side and let Tower use the AN/TAS-6. Tower searched the area carefully. He was not doing anything that Blake had not done, but two sets of eyes were better than one, and he needed to see things for himself before he made his attack plan. He confirmed what Blake had reported and studied the men around the buildings. The clear, sharp, black-and-white images let him pick up small details. The men he was looking at were not casually armed bedouins. He could see that they were all carrying several spare magazines for their automatic rifles, and most of them had hand grenades attached to their ammunition belts.

Tower had seen enough. He motioned to Colonel Khier to take a look. It was the courteous thing to do. Tower was in command, but Khier was a senior officer and an experienced commando.

Khier looked through the eyepiece. "God is great! Your equipment is marvelous," Khier exclaimed. "I can count every hair in their beards! I would give everything I possess if my battalion could have such equipment."

Tower grinned. He understood how Khier felt. But he had better remember that this was a multinational mission. If he neglected Jabir, it might cause an international incident. Besides, Jabir was Sudanese and he might pick up something foreigners would miss. He motioned to Jabir to come forward and take the scope. Jabir, too, was impressed by the AN/TAS-6. He scanned their objective carefully.

"It is indeed a wonderful thing," he said as he finished. "Did you see that some of those men are followers of the Mahdi?"

It was Tower's turn to be surprised. The AN/TAS-6 was a marvelous device, but he didn't see how it could tell a man's political affiliation. "No," he said quickly, "how can you tell that?"

Jabir smiled politely. It pleased him that, even with their advanced technology, the Americans did not know everything. "Look again," he directed, "at the three men on the big machine gun and the two men sitting by the door of the large building."

Tower stared through the AN/TAS-6. He looked at the men carefully, but he could see nothing unusual. Except for their weapons, they looked like ordinary Arabs. He would have passed them on the streets of an Arab town without a second glance.

"They all have several patches on their clothing," Jabir pointed out. "Notice that the patches are large squares. Do you know what that means?"

Tower shook his head. He was not sure it meant anything. Perhaps the opposition believed in spending their money on weapons instead of new clothes.

"It means they are dervishes. That is a word that is hard to translate into English, but it means poor in all things except faith. The Mahdi's followers wore patches like those a hundred years ago to show that they had given up everything in this world to follow him. The followers of the new Mahdi have taken up the old custom. The patches are both a symbol of their faith and their uniform."

Tower thought that was interesting, yet why was Jabir taking the time to tell him this now? But it was obviously important to Jabir. Tower had known the Sudanese captain long enough to know that he was a very intelligent man. He had better find out why Jabir thought Tower must know this. "I understand what you say. Why is it important?"

Jabir sighed. In many ways, Americans were wonderful people. But for all their wealth and machines, they were ignorant when it came to the really important things in men's lives. "They are dedicated men," he said patiently. "It means they have already sacrificed their lives for the faith. They are willing to die for it. You would call them fanatics. We would say that they are holy martyrs. You do not know what such men are like. If we attack them, they will not run away. They will not surrender. They will fight you until they are all dead. If you wound one of them, he will try to kill you as he is dying, and he will die happy if he can take you with him. This may be hard for you to believe, but it is true. Be warned.''

Tower shivered slightly. Jabir was wrong; Tower believed him completely. He had served two tours in Lebanon and he remembered the holy martyrs in Beirut, who would willingly drive a truck loaded with high explosives into an American position and blow themselves up. One of them had killed two hundred forty U.S. Marines in a single attack. It was not pleasant to think that he was about to fight many men like that, but that didn't matter. The Army paid him to do unpleasant things. They would attack.

Tower turned over the AN/TAS-6 to Sergeant Blake. Tower had to concentrate on making a plan, and Blake would alert him if there were any sudden changes in the situation. Khier and Jabir looked at Tower expectantly. Tower didn't waste any time on polite conversation. ''Gentlemen, I'm convinced that this place is our objective. We are in the right place, and this many armed men are not here to guard empty buildings. Do you agree?''

Khier and Jabir nodded. They had no doubts.

''All right, with nine or ten on guard, there are probably thirty or forty men altogether. There are more of them than I like, but we came here to do a job. I say we attack. Do you agree?''

''You are in command, Captain,'' Khier said quickly, and Jabir nodded in agreement. ''It is your decision.''

Perhaps they were just as happy they did not have to call the shots. That did not bother Tower; he wasn't afraid of responsibility. ''I agree. It is my decision, but I value your advice.''

It was the right thing to say. Both Khier and Jabir seemed pleased. ''We have one big problem. We are outnumbered three to one. To win we have to take them by surprise, hit them with everything we have and knock them out before they can get organized. To do that, we're going to need our crew-served weapons. Our vehicles are twelve hundred yards back. Noise carries a long way out here in the desert. I don't see how we can bring them much closer without being detected. Fifty-caliber machine guns and automatic grenade launchers are big, heavy weapons. It will take hours to carry them up and emplace them by hand, and we haven't got hours. I want to get the job done and get to the airstrip before dawn. It could be very unhealthy around here once the sun comes up.''

"There is no alternative but to use the vehicles," Khier said quietly, "but you are right. They will hear us coming. What will you do about that?"

"There is a way of attacking using heavily armed light vehicles. The Israelis developed it. It's been refined in the U.S. Army by the Second Ranger Battalion. We call it 'gun jeep tactics.' We get as close as we can without firing. If we go in bold as brass with our lights on, they will probably take us for a Sudanese army patrol. They'll hesitate to fire on us, at least for a minute or two. If they fire, we go in fast with all guns blazing. We depend on firepower and surprise to dazzle and overwhelm them. With any luck, we'll get it over with quick and fast and get the hell out of here."

Colonel Khier thought for a moment. "It is a daring plan, but as the British say, 'Who dares, wins!' Let us dare, then, and if God is willing, we will win."

One down and one to go. Tower looked at Jabir. The Sudanese captain was thinking hard. "It is an excellent plan," he said at last. "However, I have a suggestion for you to consider."

Tower didn't like that. They did not have time for a long debate on tactics, but he had listened to Colonel Khier and he must show Jabir the same courtesy. "Certainly, Captain," he said politely. "What's your idea?"

"Your idea is to drive toward the buildings appearing to be a Sudanese patrol and get as close as possible before you must open fire?"

"That's the idea," Tower agreed.

"Would it not be better to deceive them completely, be on the objective, and have the guards and the doors to the buildings covered before opening fire? I think that would make your plan much more effective, don't you?''

"Hell, yes," Tower said. "That would be great. The trouble is, I'm fresh out of miracles. I don't see how we can do that."

"There is a way," Jabir said quietly. "It is not without risk, but there is a good chance it can be made to work. Your plan is to make the terrorists think we are a Sudanese army patrol and get close to them, ready to attack, before they can be sure that we are not. Let us carry it one step further and show them a Sudanese army patrol. I will ride in the lead jeep. They will see my Sudanese uniform and my red beret. I will tell them we are a counterterrorist patrol from the 144th Parachute Brigade. I speak Arabic with a Sudanese accent, so there is no reason why they should not believe me. I think it is a good plan, but you are in command. It is your decision. What do you think?"

Tower thought hard. It was a daring plan, but it could work, and there would be a big payoff if it did. Still, he thought he saw a flaw in Jabir's plan. "That's a good plan, Captain, but I think there's a problem. These people are terrorists. They don't want attention. They're not likely to fire on a Sudanese army unit that seems to just be passing by. But if they're the Mahdi's men, the Sudanese government is no friend of theirs. Your 144th Parachute Brigade is an elite counterterrorist unit, the coup stoppers. If you drive up and tell them who you are, they'll think you may be after them. They're likely to shoot first and ask questions later. How will you get around that?"

Jabir smiled to himself. The American was clever, but Jabir had thought of that. "I will sew patches on my uniform to show that I, too, am a follower of the Mahdi. Many people in our army are, so they should believe that. I will say I have just smashed a plot by Christian terrorists to strike at them because they are followers of the Mahdi. The Mboro woman was one of them. She is my prisoner. My radio was damaged during the firefight with the terrorists. I need to use their radio to communicate with Khartoum, and I need fuel for my vehicles. They should be overjoyed to help such a loyal follower of the Mahdi. They will welcome us with open arms."

Yes, and with loaded weapons! Tower thought, but he still liked Jabir's plan. It was dangerous, but it offered the chance to achieve complete, devastating surprise, and surprise has won a hell of a lot of battles. Tower was not afraid to take chances when he had to. If he were, he would not have been in Omega Force. Besides, he could think of nothing better.

"All right," he said, "let's do it!" Tower felt a surge of relief. He always felt better when the worrying was over and a decision was reached. Going into action was easier for him than the burdens of command. He activated his low-probability-of-intercept radio and told Sergeant Hall to bring up the rest of the team and the vehicles. The next twenty minutes were full of highly organized confusion as weapons and equipment were checked out and everyone briefed on his role in the plan. It took much longer than Tower liked, but there was no help for it. Rushing off before everything was checked and ready could be committing suicide.

It seemed to take forever, but at last everyone was in the jeeps and they were driving through the night toward the base. Tower was taking every man he had except for Sergeant Hall, who was waiting patiently on the ridge with his big .50-caliber M82A1 sniper's rifle. Hall was incredibly accurate with that rifle, and for him, four hundred yards was point-blank range. It was a comforting thought to know that Hall would be covering the assault team. Hall also had the LT-5C SATCOM radio. If the assault party did not come back, Hall would report what had happened to General Sykes in Egypt. That was not such a comforting thought, but a good commander must plan for failure as well as for success.

They were approaching the terrorist base now. Tower was driving the lead jeep. It was not the orthodox position for the raid commander, but the lead driver must speak Arabic, and Tower desperately needed to see what was going on. It was an odd sensation to be driving down the dirt road toward the enemy, headlights blazing, instead of slipping quietly through the dark.

They were almost there. Tower made one last, quick check. Jabir was sitting beside him in the passenger seat. He looked tense but ready. Colonel Khier sat in the back, manning the pedestal-mounted .50-caliber Browning machine gun. The jeep's windshield was folded down over the hood and locked in place, giving him a perfect field of fire. Miriam Mboro sat beside him, her weapons concealed. Tower had tied her hands loosely behind her back with a piece of parachute line. She could free herself instantly, but unless someone made a close inspection, she would look like a prisoner.

Blake was in the second jeep, manning its Mark 19 40 mm automatic grenade launcher. He was definitely the right man for the job. Blake loved explosions, and the Mark 19 could produce a lot of explosions very rapidly. Corporal Chavez brought up the rear. His jeep was towing a high-mobility trailer loaded with Blake's demolition equipment. Tower hoped no one threw a grenade into the trailer. If all Blake's explosives went off at once, a nuclear weapon would not be needed to wipe out this part of the Sudan.

They came around a bend in the dirt road. The entrance to the abandoned oil-exploration station was about fifty yards ahead. Tower slowed to a crawl as he approached the entrance. The scene was deceptively peaceful. The lights were on, three men were standing by a ramshackle guard shack, and no one else was in sight. But Tower would have bet his last dollar that a dozen weapons were trained on his jeep. One of the guards held up his hand. Tower stopped the jeep and Captain Jabir stepped out. The three men stared at his red beret and camouflage uniform. One of them gasped and pointed at Jabir. Tower hoped to God they were favorably impressed by the black patches sewn on Jabir's uniform. Jabir didn't wait for them to ask questions.

"I am Captain Jabir of the 144th Parachute Brigade. You are in danger. I must speak to your commander immediately!"

The three men looked puzzled. "Commander?" one of them said. "We have no commander. We are only poor men, hired to guard these buildings so that the thieving nomads do not steal everything here."

Jabir smiled. "It is well to be cautious, but only a fool is too cautious. Call whoever is in charge, then."

The guard shrugged and shouted. Three men emerged from the large building and came toward the jeep. It all seemed very casual, but Tower could feel the tension in the air. He kept his hand close to his pistol holster, and he kept his eyes on the tall man in the center. He was dressed in military fatigues and wore a large brown leather holster on a military web belt. He wore no insignia of rank, but everything about him said soldier. He had an air of command. He stopped a few feet from Jabir and spoke politely. "I am the manager here, Captain. How may we serve you?"

The words were smooth enough, but Tower thought the man seemed suspicious. Jabir did not hesitate. "God is great! I am Captain Jabir of the 144th Parachute Brigade. I have come to warn you. You are in great danger. I am on antiterrorist patrol and I located and attacked a group of Christian rebels only a few miles from here. They had radios and signal lights. It is obvious that they were there to make contact with parachutists. Egyptian commandos may already have landed. I think you are their objective."

"I think you must be mistaken, Captain. Why would Christian rebels or Egyptian commandos attack an old oil station?"

Jabir smiled knowingly. "Because of the things you are guarding here. The enemies of the Mahdi will do anything to capture or destroy them."

"Your men carry strange weapons and wear strange uniforms, Captain," the leader said skeptically.

Jabir sighed. "I have told you, we are an antiterrorist patrol. Naturally we have special equipment. Let us not stand here and babble. If you do not believe me, use your radio. Contact your headquarters in Khartoum. You leaders will vouch for me."

"I have already done that. No one I can contact has heard of you. Our leaders are meeting with the Mahdi himself. They cannot be disturbed. Until I can speak to them, I must take precautions. If you know my mission, you will understand. I must ask you to dismount your men and give up your weapons. They will be returned to you as soon as I verify your story."

The feeling of tension increased. Two of the guards started to unsling their AK-47s. Jabir shrugged. "Very well, if you insist." His hand moved casually towards his pistol holster. The

guards relaxed. Jabir seemed to be giving in. "But this is fool-
ish, I am telling you—"

In midsentence, Jabir's hand closed on the checkered grip of
his 9 mm Browning Hi-Power. He drew and fired with blinding speed, putting four shots into the leader's chest before
anyone else could move. The startled guards reached for their
rifles. Tower drew his .45, but Colonel Khier's hands were already on his .50-caliber machine gun. He pressed the trigger,
and the big gun roared into life.

Tower's ears rang from the muzzle blast. He could feel the
hot powder gasses sting his cheek as Khier fired short bursts two
feet over his head. The Browning .50-caliber machine gun is
one of the most powerful weapons that can be fired and controlled by a single man. At point-blank range, its effects were
devastating. The heavy bullets blasted men from their feet like
rag dolls. The group of men around the jeep was cut down before they could fire.

For two seconds the assault team had the advantage of mind-
numbing surprise. Then the defenders reacted. The heavy machine gun at the corner of the large building opened fire, and a
swarm of green tracers flashed at the jeep. Tower heard the
tearing shriek of tortured metal as the heavy .60-caliber bullets
struck the jeep's hood. Khier instantly switched targets. Red
and green tracers crisscrossed as he dueled with the heavy machine gun's crew. Other, lighter weapons were opening
fire. Some of the lights had been shot out, but the jeep was still
illuminated. Stopped at the entrance, the jeep was a magnet for
bullets. Tower put it in gear and stepped on the gas. The jeep
jerked forward a few feet, emitting terrible grinding noises, and
lurched to a stop. The engine must be torn to pieces.

Another burst of bullets tore into the engine block. There was
nothing more that Tower could do. The jeep was becoming a
death trap. He grabbed his rifle and rolled out the door. Miriam Mboro was already gone. She dropped to a prone position
and began to fire back at the flickering muzzle-flashes around
them. Khier stayed on his gun, blasting bursts of .50-caliber
bullets at the enemy. Tower tried desperately to get his sights on
the heavy machine gun. He heard repeated, rhythmic thuds as
Blake opened fire with his Mark 19. A cluster of bright orange

flashes suddenly bloomed around the hostile heavy machine gun. Tower heard the repeated dull booms of 40 mm high-explosive grenades detonating. The heavy machine gun abruptly stopped firing. Blake swung his weapon and blasted away at a new target.

Tower felt a surge of relief. The plan was working! They had caught the enemy by surprise. Their leader was dead, and their heavy weapons had been knocked out. There was no organized counterattack. Resistance was wilting under the concentrated fire of the American heavy machine guns and grenade launchers. In another minute it should be over.

Then Tower heard a sound that froze his blood. Someone shouted a battle cry that has echoed across the world's battlefields for twelve hundred years. "God is great! God is great! Kill the enemies of God!" The sound swelled until men were shouting it on all sides. Then the Mahdi's followers came rushing out of the dark to kill and be killed. One of them fired an RPG-7. The rocket hissed at Tower's jeep, struck the radiator and exploded. Steel fragments shrieked over Tower's head. Khier's gun stopped firing. Tower had no time to check to see if Khier were dead or alive. He was too busy fighting for his life. The dervishes were not making a coordinated military attack, but instead hurled themselves at the Omega Force team like a pack of man-eating tigers, all the while shouting their battle cry.

Four or five men came running toward Tower and Miriam Mboro. Tower fired a quick burst into the chest of the leader. The big man staggered. Tower knew he must have hit him, but the small, light bullets from the M-16A2 didn't put the man down. He snarled and swung his AK-47 toward Tower. He might be dying on his feet, but he was determined to kill Tower. Tower fired a second burst and a third. Still, the man came on, and the muzzle of his AK-47 was almost lined up with Tower's chest.

Tower felt a surge of fear. It was like a scene from a horror movie. He seemed to be fighting enemies that bullets could not stop or kill. Tower fired again, and again, emptying the last rounds in his rifle's magazine. He could see the dust fly from the man's patched shirt as the .223-caliber bullets slammed home. The AK-47 snarled into life. Its bullets tore into the ground as the man fell. But more men were rushing straight toward him. Tower knew how Chinese Gordon must have felt when the dervishes stormed Khartoum.

There was no time to reload his rifle. Tower reached desperately for his pistol as another man came straight at him. Miriam Mboro fired a long burst from her submachine gun. The 9 mm bullets struck home, but still the man came on. Miriam snarled and swore in a language Tower did not know. She fired another long, ripping burst. The man staggered, but he did not go down. Tower had his .45 Colt out now. He pressed the trigger twice, as fast as he could, and sent a deadly double hammer smashing into the man's chest. Only Tower's choice of pistols saved him then. John Browning had designed the .45 Colt automatic to stop religious fanatics in the Philippines. Half a world and eighty years away, it still did the job. The two large, heavy bullets struck like a sledgehammer, and the man went down.

Two more terrorists were rushing at him. One of them had an AK-47 in his hands, but the other seemed to be unarmed. Tower swung his sights smoothly onto the man with the AK-47 and fired a double hammer. The big .45-caliber bullets struck the man in the right side just as he was squeezing the trigger of his rifle. It was just in time. The tremendous impact twisted the man around just as he pulled the trigger. A burst of .30-caliber bullets missed Tower by inches. The man was still on his feet. Instantly Tower fired again, another double hammer, as fast as he could press his trigger and keep his sights on. It was not pretty shooting, but it did the job. The man fell heavily, his AK-47 dropping from his nerveless hands.

The last man was rushing straight at Tower. He still seemed to have no weapons. His fists were clenched as if he meant to beat Tower to death. Miriam Mboro fired at him, a short 2- or 3-round burst. Tower could hear her swear. Her magazine was empty, but it would all be over before she could reload. Tower could not understand why an unarmed man was charging straight into the gaping muzzle of his .45. Perhaps he was momentarily crazed by the emotional stress of close-quarters combat. It did not matter. Tower was not going to take any chances.

He centered his sights on the man's chest and squeezed the Colt's trigger. There were two rounds left in the big automatic, so he had better make them good. He saw something drop away from one of the man's clenched hands, a curved piece of metal. Then Tower knew, and the knowledge flashed through his mind like a bolt of lightning—grenades! And the fuzes were burning. Only perfect shooting could save him now. Tower squeezed the trigger, once, twice. His slide locked open. His .45 Colt was empty. But the big, heavy bullets had smashed home. The man fell forward heavily. Tower flattened himself against the ground frantically. The fuzes were still burning.

He heard a muffled blast, and then another as the grenades exploded. He felt the shock of the blast, then something smashed against his Kevlar helmet. Tower was dazed. By sheer reflex, he reached for a spare magazine and reloaded his .45. Someone was crouching over him. It was Miriam Mboro, shaking like a leaf. Tower did not blame her. It had been a damned near thing, and Miriam had done her share. If she needed to shake, she was certainly entitled to do it.

Tower struggled to his feet. Things were suddenly calm and quiet, and it was an eerie feeling. No one was firing. All he could hear was someone groaning in pain and the crackling flames from a burning jeep. The fight was over, but the mission was not. He had to get things organized.

Tower found himself trembling with reaction. His body was still filled with adrenaline, and his heartbeat would have raised his doctor's eyebrows. It did not matter. He was a team leader on a special-operations mission and had no time for a nervous breakdown. Quickly he organized a defensive perimeter and had the outside lights turned off. He didn't have enough men to really defend the base against an attack, but their night-vision equipment would give them an edge as long as it was dark.

Blake was already at the door of the large building. He checked it carefully with one of his marvelous black boxes, then nodded cheerfully. Nothing electronic. He took out a pencil flashlight and examined the door frame carefully. A simple mechanical trip wire couldn't be detected electronically, but it could fire a booby trap and kill them just as dead as the latest high-tech models. Inwardly Tower seethed with impatience. It seemed to take Blake forever, but Tower knew better than to hurry him when he was working.

At last Blake nodded and gave the thumbs-up signal. The door was safe, so it was time to go in without knocking. Tower would have loved to throw in a few grenades, but starting explosions inside a building that might contain nuclear weapons was not a good idea. He nodded to Blake and dived through the door, his M-16A2 ready for action. No one fired. The room seemed empty except for a canvas-shrouded object on a dolly standing against the far wall.

Blake moved toward it carefully, took another black box from his pack and slowly scanned the object. Tower heard a steady buzzing, clicking sound.

"Jackpot, Captain," Blake said softly. "I'm detecting radioactivity."

Tower did not like the sound of that. "How much radioactivity?"

Blake smiled. "Not enough to do us any real damage unless we stayed here a long time, but there's definitely a significant source here." He flipped the canvas cover back to reveal a dull gray cylinder about four feet long and two feet in diameter. It did not look dangerous. In fact, it reminded Tower of a hot-water heater lying on its side. An access panel on the side was open where two black electric cables snaked inside. Blake brought his black box close to the opening, and the buzzing, clicking sound immediately became faster and more insistent.

"That's it, Captain, mission successful. One live nuclear weapon."

Tower was not quite as happy as Blake. He didn't like being within ten feet of a live nuclear weapon. "What's it doing, Blake? Why's it making that noise?" he asked suspiciously.

Blake lifted one eyebrow. It was hard for him to accept that the leadership of the U.S. Army was sometimes technically illiterate. "It's not doing anything, Captain. My scanner is making the noise. It's detecting ionizing radiation from the bomb's fissionable materials, Uranium 235 or Plutonium 239. The weapon is not armed or fuzed. It is not counting down to detonate. In fact, I think they were having trouble with it. It looks like they opened it up to check it out."

Tower sighed in relief. He did not care if he seemed a little dense to Blake or not. At least the damned thing was not about to go off, but that still left one critical question. "Is it safe to try and move it? If it is, get it ready to go and we'll take it back. Otherwise, get set up to destroy it."

Blake thought for a moment. "I think we can move it, Captain, but I'd better check it out first. I don't think they had time to booby-trap it, but I'd like to be sure."

Tower agreed wholeheartedly with that. A nuclear explosion would ruin his whole day. Blake busied himself with his checks, and Tower looked around the room. There were some papers on a table, but there was no time to read them now. He stuffed them in his pack. Nothing else in the room looked interesting.

Tower held his breath while Blake disconnected the cables and closed the access panel. Nothing happened. The buzzing, clicking noise from Blake's scanner faded to a slow click. Blake nodded and smiled. "Okay. We can load it now. It's—"

He stopped and pointed at Tower's chest. The low-probability-of-intercept tactical radio attached to his web equipment harness was blinking steadily. Hall wanted to talk to Tower immediately, and he would call only if his message were urgent. Tower pushed the receive button and acknowledged.

"Omega Blue, Omega Four, urgent-priority message from Eagle," Hall said in his soft southwestern drawl. Tower did not like the sound of that. General Sykes would not call him during a mission unless something important had happened. Tower had a dismal feeling he was not going to like what he was about to hear.

"Eagle says, 'Intelligence indicates heavy fighting in Khartoum and other Sudanese cities. Mahdi's followers are attempting to overthrow the Sudanese government and appear to be succeeding. Many Sudanese military units have gone over to the Mahdi's side. We cannot communicate with Sudanese defense headquarters. Our arrangement with the Sudanese government no longer effective. Assume all Sudanese military units encountered are hostile. Complete your mission and leave Sudanese territory as soon as possible.' Eagle's message ends, I have acknowledged."

Tower had heard worse news, but he could not remember where or when. "Roger, Omega Four, message understood. Reply to Eagle via SATCOM, urgent priority. Mission successful. Objective secured. Objects located. All Sudanese military forces are hostile. Request immediate preparations for air evacuation. Will depart objective for primary recovery zone as soon as possible. Estimate time of arrival, two to three hours."

"Roger, Omega Blue, will comply immediately. Captain, there's one more thing you've got to know. There is a column of vehicles moving toward your location from the south. Estimate eight to ten. They are driving fast with their lights on. They look like military vehicles to me. We'd better assume they're hostile. Do you want me to continue to observe them?"

"Negative, Omega Four. Get your gear together and get down here fast."

Blake was looking intently at Tower. He had heard his captain's side of the conversation and was no longer smiling.

"Get that damned thing loaded on a trailer," Tower snapped. "Company's on the way. Let's get the hell out of here!"

**8**

Tower was making his stand on a small, low-lying ridge about three thousand yards away from the recovery zone. But it might as well have been three thousand miles. It had been a wild chase through the dark. The Sudanese armored vehicles had not caught him, but they had cut him off. They were between his team and the airstrip. The assault team was outnumbered and outgunned. Dug in on the ridge, they might stand a chance, but if they tried to move across open ground, the armored cars would blast them to pieces.

It was starting to get light in the east. The sun would be up in another few minutes, which was not good. The Sudanese force didn't seem to have night-vision equipment. That was probably why they had not attacked already, but once the sun was up, that would no longer matter. Blake and Captain Jabir were studying the Sudanese force through the AN/TAS-6. When Blake motioned for Tower to take a look, he peered through the eyepiece and found himself staring at a six-wheeled armored car. He had seen that model in Khartoum. "Saladin armored car," he said confidently.

Blake was pleased. "That's right," he said cheerfully, "thirteen tons, one 76 mm cannon, two .30-caliber machine guns, one and a quarter inches of armor, crew of three."

Jabir was impressed. This American sergeant seemed to know everything.

Tower scanned the area. There were at least four Saladins, and something else. Something different. At least four vehicles—and all of the same model. They were like the Saladins but had larger, boxy hulls and no cannon. He pointed them out to Jabir. "What are those?"

"Saracens. They are the armored-personnel-carrier version of the Saladin. They mount no cannon, as you can see, but they carry ten infantrymen protected by armor."

Tower made a quick calculation. It did not make him happy; he didn't like the odds. "Who do you think they are?"

"I do not think. I know! I recognize the markings. That is a unit of our Border Brigade. They are picked men, well trained, elite troops. They are responsible for internal security in this area. They will almost certainly attack as soon as it is light. Unless you have antiarmor weapons, they will wipe you out."

It did not sound good. By modern standards the Saladins and Saracens were obsolete, 1960's technology. An American armored unit would defeat them in a heartbeat. But the Omega Force team was a light infantry force. They would fight, of course, but it would certainly not be easy. Their .50-caliber machine guns could not penetrate the Saladins' armor. The Mark 19 40 mm grenade launcher was marginal, and it would take a lucky hit to accomplish anything. They would have to depend on the AT-4s, the only real antiarmor weapons the team had.

Blake had passed out the AT-4s, and Tower had four laid carefully against one side of his foxhole. They did look impressive. Their fiberglass-reinforced plastic launchers looked like three-foot-long sections of ugly, olive drab pipe. Tower had never seen one used in combat. His instructors had sworn they were wonderful, and he hoped to hell they were right.

He was about to find out the hard way. The early-morning quiet was suddenly broken by the whine and rumble of engines starting. Jabir had been right—the Sudanese were coming. The rumble of the engines deepened as the attacking force moved out, the Saladins leading, the Saracens following them about fifty yards behind. Tower saw a bright yellow flash from the turret of the leading Saladin as its gunner sent a fifteen-pound 76 mm high-explosive shell shrieking into the American position. Tower braced himself, but there was no barrage. The Sudanese commander was conserving his ammunition, firing occasionally as they came to cover their advance, but clearly the serious shooting would commence when they got in close.

Tower picked up an AT-4 and swung the thirteen-pound weapon to his shoulder. It did not seem like much to stop a thirteen-ton armored fighting vehicle, but it was all he had. He pulled back the cocking lever on the top of the AT-4, readying himself to fire. The Saladins were advancing in a loose line, about fifty yards apart. One of them was coming straight toward Tower, which didn't make him happy, but it would give him a good shot. The AT-4 was not a guided weapon. It had to be aimed like a rifle. It was up to Tower to get a hit. Things would get very bad very rapidly if he missed.

Tower placed his sights on the front of the Saladin. It was camouflaged in a mottled tan-and-brown pattern. It looked ugly to him, but not half as ugly as the cannon and machine gun protruding menacingly from the front of its turret. The machine gun suddenly emitted a series of rapid yellow flashes, and Tower ducked as a burst of .30-caliber bullets raked the sand a few feet in front of his position. He did not think the gunner had actually seen him. He was just firing on general principle to discourage evil-minded people with antiarmor weapons.

Tower aimed again. The armored vehicles were coming on steadily, their six-wheel drive allowing them to move easily across the rough ground. The Saladin's machine gun fired again. This time the bullets were off to his left, and Tower kept his sights on the target. Few things are harder than to be shot at without shooting back, and the temptation to fire was almost overwhelming. Every nerve in Tower's body shrieked for him to pull the trigger, but the Saladins were at least five hundred yards away. In theory, the AT-4s could score at that range, but a hit was much more likely if he held his fire until the target was closer.

Four hundred yards, three hundred, two hundred—the Saladin was coming straight at him now. He would not have to lead the target. Now! Tower squeezed the trigger and felt the launcher quiver as the AT-4 fired. There was no recoil. The 6.6-pound 84 mm HEAT, or high-explosive antitank, projectile hurtled through the air at 985 feet per second. Tower saw a bright yellow flash as it struck the Saladin just under the turret and detonated. Had it been an ordinary high-explosive projectile, it would have failed completely, but the AT-4's HEAT round was designed to penetrate armor. The exploding warhead vaporized its metal liner and drove forward the jet of superheated metal. The blast penetrated the steel and sprayed the interior of the Saladin with white-hot gas and molten metal. The ready rounds for the 76 mm gun detonated in a shattering series of explosions, and the armored car shuddered to a halt, spewing flames and greasy black smoke.

Tower grabbed another AT-4 and looked for a new target. Another Saladin was burning brightly to his left, and a Saracen was stopped a hundred yards away. Bursts of bullets from one of the .50-caliber machine guns were beating on its armor. Tower placed the sights of the AT-4 on their side and pulled back the cocking lever. Before he could fire, a number of objects arced from the Saracen and struck the ground around it, and gray-white smoke began to billow up around the Saracen. Smoke grenades—the Saracen was firing its smoke-grenade launchers, laying down a smoke screen to cover its withdrawal. The Sudanese were pulling out. Tower no longer had a target, but he did not care. He had seen enough Saladins and Saracens to last him a lifetime. He had nothing against the Sudanese Border Brigade. If they would leave his team alone, he was willing to live and let live.

Blake was shouting something and pointing south. Tower brought up his field glasses and scanned the road to the south. No wonder Blake sounded grim; a column of armored vehicles was coming rapidly up the road. Tower could see the lead vehicles clearly. They were six-wheeled armored cars, camouflaged in a mottled tan-and-brown pattern. Saladins! The Sudanese were not giving up—they were reinforcing!

IT WAS two hours later. The Sudanese were probably plotting their next move, but at the moment nothing was happening. Tower was almost dozing. The sun was well up now, and the heat was paralyzing. He was thinking wistfully of oceans of ice-cold beer when he heard the beep of an electronic warning device. That was more effective than a bucket of cold water in the face. Tower was instantly awake, wondering what was happening. He looked at Blake. Blake had his usual cheerful grin on his face, but that was not a fail-safe guarantee that things were going well. Blake usually smiled no matter how bad things were.

Blake was pointing at the LT-5C SATCOM. The incoming-message alert light was blinking steadily, indicating that someone wanted to talk to them urgently. Tower took the headset and acknowledged. He heard General Sykes's voice loud and clear.

"Omega Blue, this is Eagle. Fast movers headed in your direction from the southeast. Shadow has been diverted. Make air defense preparations immediately."

Even in the brutal heat of the northern Sudan, Tower felt a chill. Fast movers! Jet aircraft were headed toward his position, and Tower knew he had no friends coming from the south. "Roger, Eagle. This is Omega Blue. Message understood. Preparing for air attack immediately. We are pinned down by Sudanese forces in company strength. They have light armor. We have held them off so far, but the situation is extremely serious. Can you get us air support and get us out of here?"

There was a moment of silence. To Tower, the few seconds seemed to drag on forever. Sykes was not the sort of commander who told his men fairy tales. Tower knew Sykes would tell him the truth, but he had a dismal feeling that he was not going to like it when he heard it.

"Sorry, Omega Blue. I still have orders that no U.S. combat aircraft are to cross the border and enter Sudanese airspace. I will contact Washington immediately and try to get that changed. In the meantime, hold your position."

Tower resisted the temptation to swear. What the hell else was he going to do, withdraw in broad daylight in the face of Sudanese armored cars and jets? There are simpler ways of committing suicide. But Tower was a soldier, and training overcame emotion. "Roger, Eagle, understood. I hold my position as long as possible. I do not withdraw. Question. I am heavily outnumbered and outgunned. I may be overrun. In that case, what shall I do with the device?"

There was a long silence while Sykes thought that over. "The device must not fall into enemy hands. If you cannot hold out, have Blake destroy it completely." Sykes paused for a moment. He was no longer a general speaking formally to a captain, but a man talking to a friend he may just have condemned to death. "Good luck, Dave. Eagle out."

Tower appreciated the thought. He was going to need all the luck he could get. He turned to Blake, who was already scanning the sky to the south through his binoculars.

"There they are, Captain, four fast movers at azimuth 2460. I estimate their altitude at thirty thousand feet."

Tower snapped his own binoculars up. Blake was right. He could not see planes at this distance, but four white contrails showed clearly against the bright blue sky. It was almost a pretty sight, but not to Tower. Death was coming at him at six hundred miles per hour. He did not know what kind of planes the Sudanese air force flew, but it didn't matter. Four jet fighters could blow the hell out of a small ground force. But they were not defenseless. Blake was looking at Tower expectantly, and Tower nodded. They had only one chance, but it was a good one. They just might give the Sudanese pilots a nasty surprise.

"Break out the Stingers, Sergeant."

Blake smiled. He loved high-tech weapons. He moved quickly to his jeep, staying low. Tower grinned as he watched him go. He could always count on Blake in a tight spot!

Colonel Khier was twenty feet away in the next foxhole. He had to be told what was happening, and Tower called and beckoned. Khier came over, using the flat-to-the-ground crawl of an experienced infantryman who knows he may be fired on at any moment. Tower explained the situation. Khier was not happy.

"In God's name, I do not know what your government is thinking. To send us here and then refuse to send combat aircraft to support us when we need them is insane!"

Tower understood perfectly, but he did not make national policy. "General Sykes is doing all he can, and at least we have the Stingers."

Khier was still angry. "Thank God for that. I hope they are as good as I have heard. In the meantime, I wish to use your

SATCOM to speak to my commanders. I must be sure they understand the situation."

Tower agreed absently, his attention focused on the Sudanese jets. They were getting closer and closer. Then he saw that Blake had made it back from his jeep to place two long dark cylinders on the ground and take off for more. Just as the four jets were passing overhead, he was back with two more. Tower studied the jets through his binoculars. There was something familiar about their shape—single seat, swept-wing fighters with a single large-engine air inlet in the nose. He had seen planes like that before. Tower had been in Afghanistan, training the freedom fighters to use Stingers. The jets looked like MiG-19s.

He passed the glasses to Blake. "MiG-19s," Tower said casually, smiling to himself. He seldom got a chance to tell Blake anything about foreign weapons.

Blake stared intently through the binoculars. "That's close," he said cheerfully. "They're Chinese Shenyang F-6s. They're a close copy of the MiG-19."

Tower sighed. Someday he was going to tell Blake something he did not know, but today was not the day.

He got his glasses and watched as the four planes whined overhead. They seemed to be maintaining their speed and altitude, and for a fleeting second he had the wild thought that maybe they were on a routine mission that had nothing to do with the Omega Force team. But it was not Tower's lucky day. Even as he looked, the picture changed. The contrails suddenly stopped, indicating that the planes were losing altitude and were heading down rapidly. He could see bombs and rocket launchers under their wings. They were armed for ground attack. Tower didn't kid himself; they were getting ready to attack, and his team was the only target in the area.

The F-6s were vanishing below the horizon. When they came back, they would come low and fast, and they would probably come shooting. Tower picked up a Stinger and began to prepare for firing. A team leader didn't ordinarily shoot missiles, but Tower was the best man with a Stinger in the team. Blake was almost as good. Tower smiled grimly. Four jets against his few men was long odds, but he didn't think the Sudanese pilots were going to enjoy the next few minutes.

Khier had finished his conversation with Egypt. It had not made him happy. He spit in the sand. He was so angry he forgot and spoke in Arabic, but Tower understood. He cursed Egyptian politicians bitterly and fluently, and while Tower was willing to believe that Egyptian politicians were no better than American, it was hard to believe that they had actually done all those things with their female relatives.

"The sons of diseased whores are leaving us here to die! God grant they burn in the hottest fires of hell!"

"I'll drink to that, Colonel, but we'd better get organized. Blake and I will handle the Stingers. Will you act as team chief and spot targets for us?"

Khier understood. Once Blake and Tower were looking through the sights of the Stingers at their initial targets, they would be vulnerable to other planes coming rapidly from unexpected directions. Tower picked up a Stinger and placed the launcher tube over his right shoulder. He checked to be sure a battery-coolant unit, or BCU, was screwed in place. Without a BCU, the Stinger system's tracker would not activate. He opened the IFF, identification friend or foe, antenna array and snapped the sight assembly with his left hand, making sure it locked in the open position. The familiar drill was reassuring. Tower was ready to fire now, and he was just in time. A distant, rumbling whine began to grow louder and louder. The F-6s were supersonic aircraft, but not at low altitude and carrying heavy weapons loads. They would be able to hear them coming.

The sound was coming from the north. Khier swung up his binoculars and scanned the horizon. "Standby! Here the sons of Satan come! Two aircraft at azimuth 040 and five hundred feet. Targets are hostile!"

Tower heard the roar of a 76 mm cannon firing, one blast and then another. The Sudanese armored cars were firing. Just as suddenly they stopped. Why only two rounds? The shells struck and exploded. A column of white smoke began to drift upward. Swell! The Saladins had marked the target for their jets. The rumbling whine grew louder. Tower swung his Stinger to the north and looked for a target. There they were! Two silver jets were coming low and fast, straight at him.

Tower aimed at the leader. He centered the image of the F-6 in the range ring and pressed the IFF interrogate button at the rear of the launcher's grip, but that was just force of habit. Tower knew there were no friendly jet fighters in the area. The IFF unit emitted a series of rapid, strident beeps. Hostile target! The image of the F-6 was swelling larger and larger in Tower's sight. He pressed the tracker activation switch and kept the F-6 centered in his sight's range ring. He heard a steady tone as the tracker activated.

Suddenly the F-6 seemed to burst into flame. Huge yellow muzzle-flashes erupted from under the nose and wing roots as the F-6 seemed to fire right at him. Each F-6 carried three NR-30 30 mm cannons. Bursts of fifteen-ounce high-explosive shells shrieked into the American position. Fountains of dirt and dust blasted skyward. It took a certain cold courage for a man to stand and face a ten-ton jet fighter armed with nothing but a small shoulder-fired missile; the urge to duck was immense, but Tower stayed in firing position and kept the F-6 centered in his sight ring.

The steady tone suddenly changed pitch. Lock on! The tracker had the target. Tower pressed the uncage switch. The Stinger was locked on the leading F-6 and ready to fire. The whine of the jet engines rose to an earsplitting shriek and orange balls of flame blossomed under the F-6's wings as its 57 mm rocket launchers sent a shower of lethal rockets at the American position. Tower raised the launcher on his shoulder so that he could see the three sight notches just below the range ring. There was no need to lead the target. The F-6 was coming straight at him. He centered the F-6 and the Stinger shot from its launcher. Its solid-propellant rocket motor ignited, and the Stinger flashed toward its target.

The Stinger raced at the F-6 at fifteen hundred miles per hour. Its guidance unit was locked on the heat radiating from the plane and would follow it and home in no matter what the pilot did. The pilot saw the slender, lethal shape flashing toward him and tried to turn aside, but the Stinger struck the nose of the F-6 and detonated in a flash of yellow fire. The stricken jet shuddered and began to belch flame and smoke as it staggered through the air. The five-hundred-fifty-pound bombs under its wings detonated like a string of giant firecrackers, and the F-6 vanished in a huge ball of orange flame. Pieces of blackened, twisted aluminum rained down.

Tower had no time to celebrate. The F-6's pilot was dead, but he and his wingman had already launched their rockets. The deadly swarm of 57 mm rockets shot toward the target area. No single rocket was precisely aimed, but the area was sprayed like the blast of a giant shotgun. Tower heard the hiss of the incoming-rocket motors and dropped to the bottom of his foxhole. There was nothing else he could do but pray. The rockets struck, and their four-pound warheads exploded. The ground shook. Clouds of dirt and sand filled the air, and Tower could smell the acrid scent of burning high explosives.

The explosions stopped. Tower popped up and grabbed another Stinger. The surviving F-6 shrieked overhead and began to fly away. Tower was not ready to fire again, but Blake had held his fire, waiting for a certain target. Now he pulled his trigger, and Tower saw the slender shape of the Stinger shoot from the launcher and race after the retreating plane, trailing orange flame from its rocket motor. The F-6 was moving away at five hundred miles per hour, but the Stinger was three times faster. The trail of hot gas pouring from the plane's two engines made it an ideal target for a heat-seeking missile. Frantically the pilot tried to twist from side to side, but that made no difference. The Stinger matched every maneuver with ease and struck the F-6's tail. As its warhead detonated, most of the vertical and horizontal tail surfaces disappeared in a yellow flash.

The pilot lost control, and the F-6 arched across the sky, trailing a banner of thick gray smoke. Tower saw a flash as the F-6's canopy blew off and the pilot ejected. Tower wished him luck. He had nothing against the Sudanese pilot now that he was no longer trying to kill him.

"God is great!" Khier yelled happily. "Got the sons of Satan! We got them both!"

Tower was quickly readying his second Stinger for firing, hurrying through the familiar drill as fast as he could. Although he shared Khier's exultation, he had not forgotten the other two F-6s, and their pilots had not forgotten him. The rumbling whine of jet engines began to rise to a howling shriek as the second pair of jets raced toward the Omega Force position. Fountains of dirt and dust shot skyward as their pilots opened fire with their 30 mm cannon.

Tower was ready now. He swung the Stinger launcher over his shoulder and stared through the sight. He was looking at another F-6 flying straight at him. He reached for the trigger, but the wingspan of the target's image was larger than the sight range ring diameter. The fighter was too close, inside the Stinger's dead zone. He would have to hold his fire and shoot as the F-6 pulled away. He pivoted smoothly to follow the F-6 as it shrieked overhead. The image grew smaller as the plane raced away. Now! Tower pulled the trigger. The Stinger shot from the launcher and accelerated smoothly toward its target, irresistibly attracted by the superheated gas from the jet's engine exhaust.

The Stinger struck, and its warhead detonated. For a second nothing seemed to happen. Then greasy gray smoke began to pour from the F-6's exhaust. The plane was still flying, but the pilot had had enough. He pushed the button and ejected. Tower had no time to cheer since there was still one plane left. He was reaching for his last Stinger when he heard Colonel Khier shout "Down! Down! For the love of God, down!"

Tower did not waste time asking Khier what he meant. He dived for the bottom of his foxhole. He heard a screaming whine and looked up. Blake had hit the last F-6 squarely on the nose. The canopy was riddled with holes. The pilot had to be dead, but ten tons of fighter were still shrieking toward the ground in a shallow dive, trailing flames and smoke. There was nothing Tower could do but stare in horror as the stricken F-6 seemed to come straight at him.

The screaming whine rose to an intolerable pitch. The F-6 flashed over Tower, just a few feet above his head. He could feel the heat from the flames and smell the acrid smoke. Smashing into the ground with tremendous force, the F-6 was engulfed in a huge ball of orange fire. The ground shook and shuddered. A giant, invisible hand seemed to slap Tower

against the side of his foxhole. The air was filled with dust and
smoke. The F-6's bomb load had exploded!

Tower was dazed by the blast for a few seconds. He seemed
to be in one piece. The air attack was over, and they had survived, but something was wrong. Khier was shouting something and pointing down the ridge.

They might have won the battle, but the war was not yet over.
The Sudanese Border Brigade commander was still determined to win. The distant rumble of engines grew louder and
deeper as the attacking force began to move forward. This time
they were doing it right. Tower counted nine Saladin armored
cars and eight Saracen armored personnel carriers. The com-
bination was deadly. The Saladins would blast the American
position with their 76 mm cannon, and the Saracens would
move the Sudanese infantrymen forward, protected by armor
until they dismounted for the final assault. Tower's team had
only a few AT-4s left, and they were unlikely to score hits on
moving targets until the range fell to two hundred yards or less.
The Sudanese infantry would be looking for antitank weapons, and they would concentrate rifle and machine-gun fire on
anyone who tried to fire one.

Tower was a brave man, but he was not a fool. This time they
were not going to stop them. They would be overrun and wiped
out. It was time to think about destroying the weapon. He was
turning to Blake to give the order when the tactical radio
clipped to his web equipment harness suddenly crackled into
life.

"Omega Blue, this is Gunfighter. I am inbound to your position. What is your situation? Acknowledge."

Gunfighter? Tower did not know the call sign but the message was on the correct channel, and the name certainly
sounded promising! A few F-15E Strike Eagles or A-10
Warthogs could take care of the attackers neatly. He pushed his
transmit button. "Gunfighter, this is Omega Blue. My situation is serious. I am under attack by approximately two-zero
light armored vehicles. My antiarmor weapons are nearly ex-
hausted. I require assistance immediately."

"Roger, Omega Blue. We'll give you all the help we can. I
understand you have been using Stingers. Verify Stingers tight."

That was only logical. No pilot likes the idea of accidentally being shot down by friendly missiles.

"Roger, Gunfighter, Stingers are tight. We will fire only on aircraft visually identified as hostile. What type of aircraft are you flying?"

"Four-engine transport aircraft, C-130 Hercules type. We—"

Whoom! The ground shook and dirt and dust rained down. Steel fragments whined menacingly overhead. A fifteen-pound 76 mm high-explosive shell had just missed Tower's foxhole by less than twenty feet. A second and a third shell shrieked in and exploded. The Saladins were firing steadily as they moved forward, but their rounds were not precisely aimed. The Sudanese were simply blasting the American position to provide cover for their advance. They were telling the defenders they had better keep their heads down. It was a very persuasive argument.

Tower's .50-caliber machine guns opened fire. Their gunners were shooting well. He could see yellow flashes as the heavy bullets smashed into two Saladins, but the bullets ricocheted away. The armored cars were protected by more than an inch of steel armor plate, and .50-caliber machine guns could not penetrate them. The Mark 19 opened fire, sending a burst of 40 mm grenades at an oncoming Saracen. Tower could see bright yellow flashes as the high-explosive, dual-purpose grenades detonated. He watched tensely. The 40 mm HEDP rounds were supposed to penetrate light armor.

For a moment nothing seemed to happen. Then smoke began to pour out of the Saracen, and it lurched to a halt. A jet of molten metal and superheated gas from one of the grenades had penetrated its armor and started a fire. The hatches flew open, and the crew began to bail out frantically. Tower did not blame them. The Saracen's Rolls-Royce engine burned gasoline! The Saracen suddenly blew up in a ball of orange fire. Score one for the good guys. But the Mark 19 had revealed its position when it fired, and armored-vehicle crews hated anti-tank weapons with a burning passion! The turrets of two of the Saladins rotated smoothly, and their 76 mm cannons opened rapid fire. Shell after shell howled into the American position, searching for the grenade launcher. It fired one return burst and fell silent as a 76 mm round scored a direct hit.

Tower felt a cold knot in the pit of his stomach. That was what was waiting for him when he fired his AT-4. They were four hundred yards away now, almost close enough, but he had only one shot. He had better make it a good one. He did not believe in surrendering. He would take a few of them with him when he died. He centered his optical sight on the nearest Saladin, which was three hundred yards away, then two hundred. His radio suddenly came to life.

"Omega Blue, Gunfighter. We have your position in sight. Targets are armored vehicles advancing. They're a little close to you. Keep your heads down. Firing now!"

That certainly sounded encouraging, but nothing seemed to happen. The Saladin was looming larger and larger in the AT-4's sights. The long barrel of its 76 mm gun appeared to be pointing straight at Tower like an accusing finger. Tower suddenly heard a noise, the unmistakable howl of incoming artillery. Something smashed into the Saladin and exploded. The Saladin erupted in a series of shattering explosions as the ready rounds for its 76 mm cannon detonated and tore it to pieces. Its turret was blown off and sailed into the air. There was nothing left but a blackened, shattered wreck. Another shell flashed in and tore a Saracen to pieces.

A firestorm beat on the Sudanese force. They were in the middle of a boiling cauldron of explosions. Tower turned and looked behind him. Olive drab C-130s were making a shallow turn behind his position, their sides seeming to explode in continuous blasts of flame. It took Tower a moment to realize what he was seeing. They were not ordinary C-130 cargo planes but AC-130U gunships armed with a 105 mm cannon and 25 mm Gatling guns, and those lethal weapons were aimed by the AC-130's computers and laser range finders. They did not miss!

The slope of the ridge was littered with burning and exploding vehicles. The surviving Sudanese vehicles were retreating, smashing through the scrubby brush as fast as they could move, frantically trying to escape the deadly killing zone swept by Gunfighter's lethal cannons. There was nothing else to do. They had no antiaircraft missiles. To stay and try to fight would be committing suicide.

Tower's radio spoke. "Omega Blue, this is Gunfighter. I think we've taken care of your problem. Move to the airstrip immediately. Shadow will be landing in five minutes. We will stay on station and take care of anyone who tries to bother you."

"Roger, Gunfighter. We will move out immediately. Thanks a lot. The beer's on us when we get back!"

Tower leapt to his feet. "Come on," he shouted to his team, "let's get the hell out of here!"

9

Sykes and Cray were finishing the debriefing. The Egyptian base commander had assigned them a room in his headquarters building. The room was adequate, but it was obvious that the Egyptian army did not waste its money on fancy facilities. The equipment was limited to some battered wooden furniture and a map of Egypt and the Sudan on the wall. At least the coffee was excellent, strong and hot. Colonel Khier was giving his version of what had happened on the mission when Dr. Kaye walked in.

"I am sorry to be late, gentlemen. I've been on SATCOM to Washington until a few minutes ago. Things certainly are in an uproar back there. They think the new government in the Sudan means nothing but trouble for us, and they are probably right."

"What do they think about the mission?" Sykes asked.

"They consider it a partial success, General, not what they would have liked, of course, but better than nothing."

Cray slammed his fist on the table. "Partial success? Goddamn it, Tower and the team did a hell of a job. They got to the objective, took it, captured the weapon, found themselves in a hell of a mess and managed to get out with it. What the hell do they want, miracles?"

Kaye raised an eyebrow and stared coldly at Cray. "I think that is obvious, Major. They wanted all the nuclear weapons captured or destroyed. Your team got one of them—the terrorists still have the others. It was a partial success. No one is blaming Tower and your men, if that is what concerns you. We had imperfect intelligence and bad luck. But results are what count, and we did not get all the weapons."

Kaye paused and looked around the room. "Speaking of Tower, where is he?"

"He's at the base hospital. The doctors are treating him for a mild concussion. He was a little too close to a 76 mm shell."

"That explains it then. He looked haggard and upset about something when I saw him earlier."

Cray wondered what Kaye would look like if he had been with the assault team in the Sudan instead of waiting in Egypt. Before he could say anything nasty, Sykes interrupted smoothly. "You're very perceptive, Doctor. Tower's upset, and Major Cray and I are upset. Do you realize that we suffered fifty percent casualties?"

Kaye looked puzzled. "Yes, I know that. Such losses are regrettable, certainly, but surely you expect them in your profession. You can't make an omelet without breaking eggs. I don't understand your emotional response."

Cray was tempted to kill Kaye on the spot. He did not think his men's lives counted for no more than eggs. He stood up and glared at Dr. Kaye. "I'm going to see about Tower," he said angrily, and stalked out of the room. He slammed the door behind him. Cray was a large, strong man. The door just barely remained on its hinges.

Kaye stared at the door. "Your officers seem to be very temperamental today, General. Is there something wrong, something you haven't told me?"

Sykes sighed, swearing would do no good. Kaye was undoubtedly a brilliant Intelligence officer, but he lacked something as a human being. "There is a problem, Doctor. Have you ever heard of the selection-destruction cycle?"

Kaye looked blank and shook his head. Sykes smiled to himself. You seldom got a chance to tell Kaye something he did not know.

"Elite special-operations units are controversial, Doctor. Many high-ranking officers oppose them. One of the main arguments against them is the selection-destruction cycle. The theory was developed by an English officer who studied Allied and German elite units that fought in World War II. He says the cycle is inevitable. I'm not absolutely sure I agree with that, but it certainly can happen, and I'm afraid it may be happening to Omega Force."

Kaye was still puzzled. "Just what is this cycle, General?" he asked. "Why is it important?"

"How do you create an elite unit and why is it effective? You call for volunteers. You screen and test them carefully and select only the best men. In the case of Omega Force, we had twelve hundred volunteers. We selected one hundred sixty men. The officers went through the same process. I personally handpicked Cray and Tower. After they were selected, we gave them the best possible training and equipment. For example, each man fires over twenty thousand rounds of practice ammunition a year. You should hear the bean counters in the Pentagon scream about that! It's no wonder they're good—they're the best we've got."

Kaye nodded. "I understand, General. Everything you have said seems completely logical, and from what I have seen, it works. Omega Force was extremely effective in Libya and Lebanon. It is a valuable tool for carrying out national policy. I don't see how it can be considered controversial."

"Yes, they are good," Sykes said somberly, "but now we come to the destruction side of the cycle. You have created an elite unit. For particular types of missions its the best unit you have. Then you go to war or you have a series of crises. There are really critical missions that must be accomplished, so you send them in. Since they are good, they get the job done. But these special missions are extremely dangerous. You suffer casualties, often heavy casualties. You ought to stop using the unit and give them a long rest and time to train replacements for the men they've lost. But there are more missions that are absolutely critical. You haven't any choice, so you send your elite unit in again and again. You suffer more casualties. Your key men begin to show the cumulative effects of stress. They start to make mistakes, and casualties go up. In the end the combat effectiveness of the unit is gone. That's the destruction cycle, and the men you've lost were the best you had. They may literally be irreplaceable."

Kaye stared at Sykes for a moment. He had never considered generals to be deep thinkers. He was surprised to hear that military men studied such things and were concerned about them. Although he did not like what Sykes had said, he understood it completely. "You are afraid this has happened to Omega Force, General?" he asked quietly.

"It hasn't happened yet, but it may have started. Omega Force has conducted three major missions in the last eight months. If you add up their losses in Libya, Lebanon and now here, they are over thirty percent. Cray and Tower are beginning to show the effects. If they are, so are the other officers and men. They aren't supermen, just some of the best soldiers we've got. They are afraid when people are trying to kill them, and they bleed when they're shot. I think we can still count on them, but there's a limit to what they can take."

"I understand, General. What can you do about it?"

Sykes shook his head. "Nothing, not a goddamned thing. This mission is absolutely critical. I have no alternative. I don't like it, but I have no choice. If your people can find the nuclear weapons, I'll have no choice. I'll have to send them in again.

MAJOR JAMAL TAWFIQ had never heard of the selection-destruction cycle. That did not prevent him from being an expert in destruction, and he was ready to destroy. His force was concealed in a group of dilapidated warehouses in a slum in western Cairo. He had infiltrated his men and equipment into Egypt with great skill and care. As far as he could tell, he hadn't been detected. He had contacted the Egyptian supporters of the Arab Nation. There was nothing to do now but wait. Like most soldiers, Tawfiq hated to wait, but he believed in his leader. Until Colonel Sadiq gave the word, Tawfiq would wait. Then, God willing, he would shed the Americans' blood. He studied the map of Lightning Force's base again. he had studied it a dozen times, but a dozen years of war had taught him that there were no unimportant details when you were planning an attack.

He looked up as Saada Almori entered the room. He still didn't like her. He did not care for Westernized women, and there were times when Saada looked and acted like a naked-faced whore rather than a decent Arab woman. Despite that, he was glad that Colonel Sadiq had sent her. She was highly intelligent and had a subtle mind. She was extremely effective in dealing with their Egyptian allies. Tawfiq was not subtle, but he was an excellent soldier, an outstanding commando leader, and his men would follow him anywhere. Together, he and Saada made an unlikely but highly effective team.

Something had happened. Saada was excited. She held a sheet of paper in her hand. "A message from the Sudan. I have decoded it. We have orders from the Colonel," she said quickly.

"God grant that the news is good," Tawfiq said piously.

"God is great! The revolution in the Sudan is a complete success! The Mahdi's forces have control of the country. Colonel Sadiq now has complete freedom of action."

"What are our orders?"

"They are in a code within a code. I do not understand them. I assume that you will. They are execute Retribution, execute Thunderbolt, prepare for Hellfire."

Tawfiq smiled. His white teeth gleamed through his thick black beard. He threw his arms around Saada and squeezed her hard. Tawfiq was a large, strong man, and it was like being embraced by a bear. Saada thought her ribs would break.

"God is great, Saada, God is great! Now we will see their blood. Now we will make them pay!"

Saada smiled. Tawfiq's joy was contagious. She had not missed the word we. It was good that Tawfiq was beginning to trust her.

"I am glad the orders please you, but there is one other thing you must know. The Americans raided our base north of Dongola. Most of our men there were killed."

Tawfiq's heart nearly stopped beating. "The weapons, did the sons of Satan capture our weapons?"

Saada shook her head. "No, all but one had been removed before the Americans got there. They are on their way to their assigned locations."

"Thank God for that!" Tawfiq said happily. "Very well, we will proceed immediately with Operation Retribution."

"I understand Retribution, and I am happy to hear the order. It is time that Omega Force paid with their blood for their crimes against the Arab Nation. But I do not know Thunderbolt or Hellfire. May I know what they are?"

Tawfiq smiled again. "You do not need to know, Saada. It is not that the colonel does not trust you, but he tells anyone only what they must know. Even I do not know what Hellfire is. Remember, you may be captured. The Egyptian secret police are very efficient, and they are brutal with those who they consider terrorists. But no matter what they do to you, you cannot tell them what you do not know."

Saada shuddered. She was a brave woman and was willing to die for her cause if it came to that, but the thought of being tortured filled her with fear. "Yes, Major, I understand," she said quietly. "Let us proceed with Operation Retribution. Is everything ready?"

"Captain Kawash is completing the installation and checkout of the weapons. He says all will be ready by nightfall. The attack team is ready to be briefed, but there is one problem. The Egyptian commando base is large and there are many buildings. We need information on the exact location of Omega Force. I would rather kill one American than a hundred Egyptians. Can our contact give us more precise information?"

"Not without the risk of being discovered, and our contact is too valuable to us to chance that. However, I think there is a way to get the information. It is risky, but I think I can get the information we need." She paused and smiled coldly. "Yes, I think that plan will work. It is time for me to see our old friends, and greet them one last time before they die."

# 10

Amanda Stuart was bored. She had already checked her helicopter repeatedly. It was ready to go, and to check it again would be meaningless. There was really nothing for her to do but wait. She had not been invited to the debriefing, but she understood that. Since she had not been on the mission to the Sudan, she would have had nothing to contribute. She knew that that was true, but she still felt left out, and that rankled. Amanda liked to feel that she was part of the team. Well, they would call her if they needed her. In the meantime, she would continue to cool her heels in Colonel Khier's office. There was no use wasting her time. She went back to studying the large map of Egypt and the Sudan that decorated one wall. It showed the locations of Sudanese air-defense radars and fighter bases. It was useful information. If she had to fly a mission into the Sudan, the more she knew, the better.

Someone knocked softly on the door. It was Colonel Khier's secretary, a pleasant woman in her late thirties. She smiled shyly. It was obvious that she was not used to women who wore battle dress uniforms and flew helicopters. "Excuse me, Captain Stuart, but there is a call for you from the American Embassy. It is a Dr. Rossi. She says that it is urgent. She must speak to you immediately."

Amanda frowned as she reached for the phone. Why should anyone be calling her from the American Embassy, and how would they know that she was there? Well, there was one way to find out. "Hello, this is Amanda Stuart," she said, which gave away nothing.

"This is Carla Rossi, Captain Stuart, with the cultural attaché's office at the American Embassy. We met a few days ago at the embassy. I'm sorry to have taken so long to get back to you. I'm calling in regard to that special tour of the Sphinx your party was interested in taking. I have arranged things, but someone from your group must sign the application forms today. You are the only one I have been able to contact. Can you come to the embassy and sign them today? It is very urgent. I can send a car for you.''

Amanda was instantly on red alert. Something was up. She hadn't requested any tour of the Sphinx, and when the CIA started calling themselves cultural attachés, it was best to be ready for trouble. She thought carefully before she answered. Carla Rossi was being deliberately obscure. Obviously she wasn't sure that the line was secure. Like most Army people involved in special operations, Amanda had a healthy distrust of the CIA. Still it was obvious that Carla Rossi wasn't calling her to talk about the best places for tourists to shop in Cairo. It must be important, or she would not have risked calling at all.

Amanda wanted more information, but she was not stupid enough to ask for it on an open line. She could try to contact General Sykes and get his approval, but Amanda did not care for officers who passed the buck. She was a captain in the U.S. Army, and one of the things they paid her to do was make decisions. This sounded like something she could handle. "Thank you, Miss Rossi. We appreciate your making the arrangements. I will be glad to come."

"Good, Captain Stuart. The car will be there in thirty minutes. Please come alone and wear civilian clothing. Some Egyptians are upset when they see foreign uniforms in Cairo. Oh, one other thing. I have a request from an Israeli free-lance journalist, a Miss Tamar Rosen. She would like to interview an officer from your group. When I mentioned your name she was very interested. She feels that her readers would be interested in what it is like to be a woman officer in the American Army. She has a deadline to meet. I would really appreciate it if you could take the time to talk to her today."

In for a nickel, in for a dime. "Certainly, Dr. Rossi, I'll be glad to talk to her. I'll be ready in thirty minutes. Tell your driver that I'll be wearing a green dress."

"That won't be necessary. The driver knows you. Thank you, again, Captain Stuart. You don't know how much I appreciate this."

Amanda hung up the phone. Immediately she had sober second thoughts. It was nice to be bold and decisive, but the CIA had gotten her in trouble before. She remembered a particularly unpleasant time in Beirut not long ago. It was too late to back out now, but she had better take every precaution she could. She picked up the phone, called the Omega Force barracks and asked for Sergeant Hall. The big Ranger was on the phone in a few seconds. Amanda explained the situation quickly, but she was careful what she said since the phone line might not be secure.

"So you see," she concluded, "I really can't refuse Dr. Rossi, but I don't like the idea of being in downtown Cairo by myself. I might need some company. I thought perhaps you and Sergeant Blake might tag along and keep an eye on me."

"We'd be glad to, Captain Stuart. There's nothing to do here at the moment. Blake and I would be glad to come along and see the sights. We'll wear civilian clothes and drive an unmarked car."

Amanda smiled. There was something extremely reassuring about the sound of Hall's soft southwestern drawl. He was always quiet and polite, but he was the deadliest man Amanda knew. If she was going into danger, there was no one else she would rather have backing her up. She told Colonel Khier's secretary she was leaving, and went quickly to her quarters. They were spartan, but adequate. She took off her uniform and slipped on her green dress, then looked at herself in the cracked mirror. The green dress went well with her dark red hair, and showed her long legs decently but to advantage. It might be a little fancy for midday Cairo, but it was the only dress she had with her. It would have to do.

She checked her 9 mm SIG-Sauer P228 carefully. One round was chambered and a full 13-round magazine was in place. She slipped the pistol and two spare magazines into her purse. That gave her forty shots. If she needed more than that, she would need a machine gun, not a pistol. She was ready to go, or was she? Her purse concealed her gun quite well, but it wasn't the best place in the world to carry one. It was hard to draw fast from a purse in an emergency, and the first thing a woman could lose in a struggle was her purse.

Amanda opened a compartment in her cosmetics case and took out a small, silver-colored, stainless-steel automatic pistol. It was so small she could cover it with one hand. It looked like a toy, but it was not. It was a Walther TPH .22 automatic, tiny but deadly. Blake had gotten it for her, and Sergeant Hall had taught her to shoot it, drilling her again and again until she could put all seven rounds in the head of a silhouette target at seven yards in three seconds. It was not the kind of gun that would win battles, but it might just be enough to save her life.

She made sure the TPH was loaded and slipped it into its small nylon holster. She pulled down the front of her dress and clipped the holster between the cups of her bra, feeling like a complete fool as she did it, like a teenage girl pretending to be a secret agent, but it worked. When she pulled up the front of her green dress, there was nothing for anyone to see. Someone would have to use a metal detector or get extremely friendly to detect the little automatic.

Amanda studied her image in the mirror. She saw a tall redhead in a dark green dress with a large leather purse over her shoulder. She put on a pair of dark sunglasses. There, she was perfectly disguised as a tourist. There was nothing unusual to attract attention, except from men who liked tall redheads, and she was used to that. She glanced at her watch and saw that she had five minutes to go. She walked rapidly to the gate and showed the guards her pass. She was relieved to see Hall and Blake casually loading gear into a blue Ford. Blake had a large nylon camera bag slung over one shoulder. The bag seemed to be unusually heavy, and he was extremely careful with it. Amanda smiled. Blake must have some very interesting things in that case, possibly even a camera.

A horn honked, and a black Mercedes 190 convertible pulled up behind her. The driver waved cheerfully, and Amanda recognized Miriam Mboro. Amanda smiled and waved back. If she was going into danger, Miriam was the kind of lady to have along. She climbed into the passenger seat and fastened her seat belt as Miriam turned and accelerated smoothly back toward Cairo.

Miriam didn't seem interested in conversation and concentrated on her driving, but Amanda didn't mind. She was enjoying herself. When she was a lanky teenager, she had loved spy stories. It had been exciting to imagine that some day she would be a glamorous secret agent, going on dangerous missions in exotic foreign cities. Now she was driving toward downtown Cairo with a genuine CIA agent. It would be a great adventure, if no one blew her head off.

Her curiosity finally got the better of her. "Is it safe to talk?" she asked.

Miriam nodded. "I had the car scanned before I took it out of the garage. It's clean."

That sounded encouraging. "Where are we going?"

"Downtown Cairo, to the Ramases Hotel. We're meeting Carla Rossi and the Israeli woman in the Sky Lair there. Don't worry, I'm just taking routine antisurveillance precautions. It should be a piece of cake." Miriam smiled wickedly. "Or maybe not. The last time you and I went to a hotel together, the party got kind of rough. That hotel in Khartoum may never be the same."

Amanda laughed. She was not likely to forget. "Let's hope things are a little quieter this time."

"I'll drink to that, a double Scotch and water as soon as we get—" she stared at the rearview mirror and frowned. "I don't mean to sound paranoid, but I think someone's following us."

Amanda wasn't surprised. Miriam was a sharp lady and it would be best not to lie to her. "Is it a blue Ford Escort sedan?"

Miriam smiled wickedly again. "Why Amanda, I'm shocked! I'm afraid you're not the sweet and simple girl I took you for. Who is it?"

It was Amanda's turn to smile. "Call it my insurance policy, Miriam. It's Blake and Hall. I hope you don't mind."

Miriam chuckled softly. "I don't mind. I saw them in action in the Sudan. If there's any trouble, I'll be glad to have them along. Don't tell Carla Rossi though. She'd probably blow a fuse."

"Don't worry, I wasn't planning on telling anyone, but why not? Don't you trust Dr. Rossi?"

"It's not a question of trust. It's just that Rossi and I are different kinds of people. She's an intellectual, a headquarters type. Computers and analysis are her thing, and she does things by the book. I'm a field agent, a wild woman who runs around the Sudan getting shot at and blowing things up. That's not the in thing in the CIA today, particularly for a woman. They only let me do it because my parents came from the southern Sudan and I speak Nuer and Dinka."

She chuckled again. "That, and because they can't find anybody else who's crazy enough to do it. Anyway, watch out for Rossi. She won't like it if she finds out you're not a good little girl who follows instructions to the letter."

Amanda thought that over. She wasn't sure she cared whether Carla Rossi approved of her or not, but it was interesting to learn that the CIA was not one big happy family.

They were slowing down now, driving through northern Cairo. Amanda was fascinated by the sights and sounds around her. It was fascinating to think that there had been a city here for more than six thousand years. She couldn't complain that the Army did not send her to some interesting places. It was unfortunate that she usually saw the sights only from the cockpit of her Blackhawk. It was interesting, but she had no idea where they were since the street signs were in Arabic.

"We're almost there," Miriam said. "This is Ramses Street. The hotel is on the river a little north of here, toward the Sixth of October Bridge. You'll like the Sky Lair. It's the cocktail lounge on the top of the hotel. It's got the best view of the city and the Nile in Cairo. They serve good drinks there, too. It's a little expensive, but we'll let the Agency pick up the tab."

They drove past the Egyptian Museum and turned into the hotel parking lot. Miriam tipped the parking-lot attendant, but Amanda noticed she didn't give him the keys. Miriam did not trust people she did not know. They strolled into the lobby like two old friends meeting for an afternoon cocktail. Amanda was nervous. She was used to carrying weapons when she was in uniform, but she seldom carried them concealed when she wore civilian clothes. Her pistols seemed to weigh a ton, and she was sure everyone was staring at her suspiciously. She glanced around quickly, but no one seemed to be paying any attention, except for a man or two who appreciated attractive women.

They took the elevator up to the Sky Lair. Amanda was impressed by the spectacular view of central Cairo with the Nile winding through it. When the hostess came up to greet them, Miriam spoke to her. "We're meeting Dr. Carla Rossi here. She has reserved a table for four."

The hostess smiled. "Certainly, madam. Dr. Rossi sends word that she has been delayed but will be here shortly. Please follow me."

She led them to a window table and beckoned to a waiter. The Sky Lair's service was excellent, and soon Amanda was sipping a tall vodka and tonic while Miriam attacked her double Scotch and water. Amanda looked casually around her and noticed that everyone in the Sky Lair seemed to be drinking too.

She was puzzled. "I thought Muslims didn't drink, Miriam. Am I wrong? All these people can't be tourists."

Miriam sneered. "They're not supposed to drink. What really happens varies from country to country. You'd never see anything like this in the Sudan, but most Egyptians aren't about to let the Koran interfere with the tourist trade or having a good time."

"You don't seem to like Arabs."

"No, I don't. If you'd been called a filthy, unbelieving black whore as often as I have, you wouldn't like them either." Miriam paused and looked toward the door. "Heads up, here's Dr. Rossi now."

The waiter ushered Carla Rossi to the table. She looked as if she had been working long and hard. Her eyes were red, and her white linen dress showed a few wrinkles. She sat down next to Amanda with a sigh of relief. "I'm sorry to be late. I have been talking to the Tel Aviv station, trying to get a better line on Tamar Rosen."

"What did you find out?" Miriam asked quietly.

Dr. Rossi smiled condescendingly. "Don't be impatient, Miriam. Let me put Captain Stuart in the picture."

Miriam took another sip of her drink and glared out the window. It was obvious that she and Carla Rossi did not like each other. Dr. Rossi smiled winningly at Amanda and continued briskly. "Thank you for coming, Amanda. I may call you Amanda, may I not? This may be very important. Tamar Rosen called the embassy three hours ago and asked to speak to me. She knows who I am and what my real job is. She said that she is an Israeli citizen and a free-lance journalist. She claims to have information concerning impending terrorist actions against Egypt and the United States. Miss Rosen seems to be a bit paranoid. She would not tell me anymore over the phone and she was unwilling to come to the embassy. She says it may be under surveillance and she is afraid she will be killed if the terrorists see her contacting American officials. She agreed to meet me at a location I picked."

She paused as the waiter approached and ordered a glass of dry sherry.

"I wouldn't call her paranoid myself," Miriam said quietly. "If she knows what she claims to know, those are sensible precautions."

"That sounds interesting," Amanda said, "but I don't see how I'm involved."

"Because she says her information involves Omega Force. I thought that was very interesting. Omega Force's existence is supposed to be secret. She wanted to speak to one of its officers. When I mentioned your name, she said you would be quite satisfactory. She seems to know you, or at least to know who you are. Do you know her?"

Amanda shook her head. "I was in Israel a few weeks ago, but I don't remember anyone named Tamar Rosen. I suppose she could have heard about me from some of the Israeli military people I met. It may just be a coincidence that we're both in Egypt now."

Carla Rossi smiled and sipped her sherry. Her expression showed that she did not believe in coincidences.

"What did Tel Aviv say about her?" Miriam Mboro asked.

"There is a Tamar Rosen who is a free-lance journalist. She is not popular with the Israeli government because she has written a number of pieces sympathetic to the Palestinians. She has no known contacts with Arab terrorist groups. She has been in Somalia and the southern Sudan for the last four months, covering United Nations famine relief. That is why I asked you to be here, Miriam. Have you ever heard of her?"

Miriam shook her head. "No, but that doesn't prove anything. There have been a lot of media people in the area in the last year. She could have been one of them."

Carla Rossi shrugged. "So much for that. We will just have to see what she has to say. Speak of the devil, here's our mysterious Miss Rosen now."

Amanda looked up. A tall, dark woman in an elegant blue dress was following the waiter to their table. She was wearing large, dark sunglasses. Amanda stared at her. She was sure she had never met anyone named Tamar Rosen, but there was something tantalizingly familiar about the woman. She was tall and well built, with long, black, glossy hair. The blue dress showed off her excellent figure. Slipping into the seat next to Miriam Mboro, she smiled across the table at Amanda.

Carla Rossi took charge immediately. "Miss Rosen? I am Carla Rossi. This is Mriam Mboro, and this is—"

"I know who that is, Dr. Rossi, Captain Amanda Stuart. How are you, Amanda? You are looking very well. That green dress suits you so much better than those ugly uniforms you wear."

Surprise burned through Amanda. Her hand shot toward her purse. "God Almighty" she gasped. "Saada Almori!"

## 11

Saada Almori took off her sunglasses and set them on the table. She kept both hands in view and was careful to make no sudden moves. Amanda's hand was inside her purse, her fingers curled around the checkered plastic grips of her SIG-Sauer, but she didn't draw her pistol. It might be a little difficult to explain why she was holding a 9 mm automatic in the middle of a crowded lounge.

Carla Rossi stared at Amanda. "Do you know this woman?"

"Damned right I do! Her name is Saada Almori, not Tamar Rosen. Watch out, this may be a trap."

Miriam Mboro's hand moved swiftly to her purse and then pressed something hard against Saada Almori's side. "That's a .38 Special Smith & Wesson," Miriam said, "and it's loaded with hollowpoints. Don't do anything that makes me nervous. It would be a shame to blow big holes in that pretty blue dress."

Saada Almori smiled again. "Tell your black friend to be calm, Amanda. If I were trying to kill you, I would have picked a better place and I would not be here alone."

Carla Rossi stared. She was out of her depth in field operations. This was not at all like the Intelligence analysis she was used to doing. Things were getting out of control. She had never expected to be face-to-face with someone high on the suspected-terrorist list. She tried desperately to think what she should do next.

"Get her purse, Miriam," Amanda said quickly. "She carries a small automatic."

Miriam took Saada's purse with her free hand and casually looked inside. "Twenty-five-caliber Beretta, small but effective," she said with a broad smile. To a casual observer, she looked as if she were chatting with old friends. Despite the fact that Carla Rossi did not like Miriam, she admired her coolness under stress. She was very glad that Miriam was there, but Carla was the senior officer. It was up to her to make the decisions.

Saada Almori sat looking at her calmly, a faint smile on her face. Carla Rossi flushed. She had agreed to the meeting. She hated being made to look like a fool.

"You don't deny being Saada Almori?" she asked sharply.

"Of course not. Tamar Rosen is merely an identity I assume from time to time. I used the name to set up a friendly meeting"

"Friendly meeting? You came here using a false identity and carrying a pistol. You call that friendly?"

Saada smiled wickedly. "Come now, Dr. Rossi, people say you are one of the most intelligent women in the CIA. You would not have come here if I had given you my real name. As for my little pistol, I carry it for personal protection. I am not the only one. I do not think it is her finger that your black friend is pushing into my side. Amanda could be clutching her compact, but I doubt it. And if you will forgive me for saying it, if you are not armed, you are a fool. I have come here to give you vital information. If you are not interested, I will leave and you can enjoy the view."

"Carla," Miriam Mboro said urgently, "We're not safe here. Let's cut out the girl talk and get the hell out of here. We can question her when we're in a safe place. If she knows anything, I'll get it out of her."

Carla Rossi felt a cold chill and knew it hadn't been caused by the air-conditioning. She glanced quickly around the room. The people at the other tables looked harmless, but that didn't mean anything. Miriam was right, they were not safe here. She was the field agent and would know what to do. "You're right, Miriam. What is the threat and what should we do?"

Miriam looked casually around her. She might have been admiring the Sky Lair's furnishings. "It's not likely to be a bomb or guns here. There are too many people, and she's sitting with us. No, if they are going to hit us, it will be as we leave or after we're on the road, but we haven't much choice. The longer we stay here, the more danger we're in. Trouble is, there's only one way out of here—down the elevator and out the lobby. Let's do it now."

Carla Rossi paused for a second but she could think of no alternative. It was a relief to have the decision made for her. "All right, Miriam, this is your kind of game. You call the shots."

Whatever problems Miriam Mboro had, lack of confidence was not one of them. "All right then. Let's go now, calm and cool. We leave a nice tip and we walk out of here with happy smiles on our pretty faces. You and Amanda go first, Carla. Miss Almori and I will be right behind you."

She paused and pushed the muzzle of her little Smith & Wesson into Saada Almori's side until she winced. "Listen to your black friend, lady. I don't like Arabs, I don't like bigots and I don't like you. If you try anything, anything at all, I'll kill you."

Miriam swept the room with a quick glance. "Now's as good a time as any, ladies. Let's go."

They walked toward the elevator. Miriam had her left arm around Saada Almori's waist in what looked like a gesture of affection. They might have been best friends or even lovers. The snub-nosed .38 Smith & Wesson was concealed in a fold of Miriam's brightly colored robe. Amanda felt everyone in the Sky Lair was staring at them, but it was a cosmopolitan place and no one gave them a second glance.

The elevator was empty. They stepped inside and Amanda pushed the button for the ground floor. The doors closed and the elevator started smoothly down the shaft. Amanda discovered she had been holding her breath. Being a glamorous agent was not as much fun as she had imagined. She had been in combat, but this was different. The thought that anyone around her, no matter how harmless they looked, might be going to try to kill her was particularly unnerving.

They reached the lobby without incident and headed for the entrance. Amanda, Carla Rossi and Miriam Mboro smiled and chatted as if they didn't have a care in the world. Saada Almori kept a smile on her face and her mouth shut. Miriam was very convincing. It was obvious that Saada Almori believed every word Miriam had said.

They reached the door. Carla Rossi tipped the smiling door-man, and then they were outside. They moved quickly toward the parking facility in the back of the hotel but the parking-lot attendant didn't seem to be there. They would have to look for their cars. Amanda did not like that. Neither did Miriam Mboro. "Heads up," she hissed. "If anything is going to happen, it's probably going down here." Amanda resisted an overwhelming urge to draw her SIG-Sauer. It might be a little difficult to explain why she was strolling through downtown Cairo with a pistol in her hand.

They came to the last row of cars. They passed a blue Ford Escort sedan. The hood was up, and two men were struggling with some mechanical problem. Amanda recognized Blake and Hall. Blake looked up and grinned at her and winked one bright blue eye as they passed. Amanda felt a surge of relief. At least they were not completely alone. She looked down the row of cars. Thank God, there was Miriam's black Mercedes.

They were almost to the car when four men stepped out from between the cars. They wore khaki shirts and pants and peaked blue military caps. One of them wore the insignia of a captain in the Egyptian armed forces. Soldiers? What were Egyptian soldiers doing here? Carla Rossi stiffened. "Tourist police," she said softly. "Let me handle this."

The four men moved toward them, fanning out in a loose arc. Amanda noticed that the captain was armed with a large automatic in a brown leather holster. He did not draw it, but he didn't need to. Each of the other men had a small, deadly-looking submachine gun slung over his right shoulder, with his right hand on the pistol grip. The guns were no bigger than large pistols and almost looked like toys. There was something familiar about the weapons. Amanda tried to remember a demonstration years ago at Fort Benning. Of course, Czechoslovakian VZ 61 Skorpions. The little guns were chambered for the .32 automatic-pistol cartridge. Shot for shot, they were not as powerful as Amanda's pistol, nor were they particularly accurate, but they could empty their 20-round magazines in less than two seconds. They were not very effective military weapons, but they were a favorite with terrorists and assassins.

Carla Rossi started to step forward but froze when the captain pointed his Skorpion at her chest. "Show me your papers," he snapped.

"There must be some mistake. I am Carla Rossi. I am a member of the United States Embassy staff in Cairo. I—"

The captain slapped her brutally across the face. "Be silent, whore. Speak only when you are spoken to!" He tore her purse from her hand. Stunned, Carla Rossi stood there shocked and trembling. Nothing like this had ever happened to her before. One of the men laughed and said something in Arabic that Amanda did not understand but Miriam Mboro did. "Sudanese," she whispered.

One of the other men pointed at Miriam Mboro and Saada Almori.

The captain looked quickly at Miriam. "Yes, she is the one," he said. He took a metal cylinder from his pocket and began to screw it onto the barrel of his Skorpion. Amanda felt a cold chill. A silencer. What kind of police were these?

He motioned Amanda to one side and for a second she considered drawing her SIG-Sauer, but a Skorpion was unwaveringly trained on her. Although she was good with a pistol, she wasn't going to be able to draw and fire before he could pull his trigger.

The captain stared coldly at Miriam Mboro, who had not moved, though her right hand was still pressed against Saada Almori's side.

"We have looked for you for a long time, you filthy black whore. You have been responsible for the deaths of many true believers in the south. You will pay for that now. I will shoot you in the belly so that you will be a long time dying. I will enjoy listening to you moan. Say a prayer to your false god if—"

Miriam Mboro exploded into action. Her right hand flashed forward and she pulled the trigger on her .38 Smith & Wesson as fast as she could. Three high-velocity hollowpoints tore through the captain's chest and killed him where he stood. Miriam swung her revolver toward another man, but he fired before she could shoot again. As his Skorpion roared into life, half a dozen .32-caliber bullets smashed into Miriam's chest, and she went down. Her Smith & Wesson dropped to the ground as she fell.

Amanda threw herself to the right, instinctively looking for cover, but there was none. Carla Rossi screamed and threw herself on the man who had shot Miriam Mboro, clawing at his face. He swore in Arabic and struck at Carla with his left hand. Another man leapt forward to help him. The three of them swayed back and forth in a tangle of flailing arms and legs. Amanda heard the spiteful crackle of a Skorpion firing a long burst. It missed her by inches, but an invisible hand seemed to grab her purse and tear it away. She hit the ground and rolled, instinctively following her combat training. Another long burst ripped into the ground where she had been a split second before. Full-metal-jacketed .32-caliber bullets ricocheted away, and concrete chips stung Amanda's thighs. The lethal hail of bullets seemed to go on and on, then it stopped abruptly as the Skorpion's 20-round magazine ran dry.

The gunner swore and reached for a fresh magazine. Amanda tore frantically at the front of her dress. It would take him two or three seconds to reload, and that was the only chance she had. Amanda had superb reflexes, which was one of the things that made her a good pilot. Her fingers closed on the black plastic grips of her TPH, and she drew the little Walther and pointed it at the man's face with one fluid motion. He was snarling as he pushed a new magazine into his Skorpion.

The TPH had superb sights. Lining them up, centering the bright orange dot on the front sight on the center of the man's face, she pressed the trigger as fast as she could. The Walther barked again and again. Its .22-caliber bullets were small but deadly when they hit vital spots. The man's face dissolved into a mask of blood. He died where he stood and fell heavily across his weapon. Amanda heard the hammer of her Walther fall with a click on an empty chamber. She had a spare magazine, but it was in her purse. She twisted frantically, trying to find it, but it was out of reach, under the Mercedes.

She heard Carla Rossi scream as the men she was struggling with threw her against the side of the black Mercedes. The man whose face she had clawed was furious. He thrust the barrel of his Skorpion at Carla and pulled the trigger. Amanda could see her jerk and quiver as half a dozen bullets struck her. She slid limply down the side of the car. The man who had shot her swore as blood dripped down the left side of his face. He said something sizzling in Arabic, and aimed at Carla Rossi again. The other man turned toward Amanda, pointing the cold, black muzzle of his Skorpion at her face.

Suddenly, incredibly, Miriam Mboro moved. She had Saada Almori's little .25 Beretta in her hand. She fired from the floor at the man who was threatening Carla Rossi. The little automatic barked repeatedly as Miriam pulled its trigger as fast as she could. The range was less than ten feet, and bullet after bullet struck home. At least one of them hit a vital spot. The Skorpion slipped from his fingers as he fell.

The man who was threatening Amanda was startled by the sound of the pistol firing behind him. He pivoted to swing his Skorpion back toward Miriam Mboro, but Miriam had the advantage. She only had to move her hands, not her body. She fired before the man could bring his Skorpion to bear. Both shots hit, but the little .25 bullets had no stopping power unless they hit a vital spot. The man swayed, but he was still on his feet, and the deadly little Skorpion was still in his hands. Miriam tried to fire again, but the Beretta's hammer clicked futilely on an empty chamber.

Amanda had one last, desperate chance. She got her long legs under her and was about to lunge at the man when someone shouted in a parade-ground bellow, "Down! Stay down!" The voice radiated command authority. Training took hold, and she flattened herself to the ground. She heard a strange ripping, thumping and a soft, repeated hissing sound. The man with the Skorpion shuddered as a burst of superbly aimed 9 mm bullets struck. He fell like a puppet whose strings had been cut. Blake came running forward, a silenced 9 mm submachine gun in his hands, ready to fire, but there was no one left to shoot.

There was a sudden, deafening silence. Amanda began to shake with reaction. The whole fight had taken less than ten seconds. Miriam Mboro staggered painfully to her feet. Scooping up her small .38 Smith & Wesson with one hand. She held her side with the other hand, grimacing with pain.

Amanda moved quickly to help her, astounded that Miriam was still alive. "Are you hurt?" she gasped.

Miriam was not amused. It didn't seem like a smart question to her. "Damned right I hurt!" She pulled open her robe. She was wearing a white vest that covered her from her breasts to her abdomen. Amanda could see the bases of half a dozen .32 automatic bullets embedded in the shiny white material.

"Kevlar soft body armor," Miriam said with a painful smile. "Thank God for Dupont, but I feel like I've taken six hard punches to the ribs. I've been wearing it since Khartoum. I thought I could use a little cheap life insurance. Carla thought it was silly, but I—" Miriam suddenly stopped smiling. "Carla's hit. We've got to help her. There's a first-aid kit in the car. I'll get it."

"Don't touch the car!" Blake snapped. "I think they put something under it. If it's a bomb, it may be fuzed to detonate when the door's opened."

Miriam stopped instantly. She was an experienced agent and knew better than to argue about explosives with a demolition expert. Blake stood up and waved, and Hall started the engine of the blue Ford and drove it forward. He handed Blake his kit bag without a word and began to scan the area around them, his submachine gun ready. Amanda looked around, surprised to see no one coming. She thought the shooting would have drawn a crowd. She had not stopped to think that in the Middle East, smart people don't rush toward the sound of gunfire.

Blake and Miriam Mboro were crouched over Carla Rossi. Half a dozen red stains were spreading over the front of her white linen dress. Blake was tearing open a package of trauma dressings, but he shook his head as he did it. Carla Rossi opened her eyes and looked around her. She looked pale and dazed. Shock was setting in. "I'm sorry, Miriam," she said softly. "I blew it, but I did the best I could. I—" She began to cough, and a thin stream of blood trickled from one corner of her mouth.

Miriam Mboro had seen people shot before. "We've got to get her to a hospital. She needs plasma and a doctor now!"

Carla shuddered and lay still, and Blake shook his head. "It's too late. She's gone. Come on, everybody into the car. We've got to get out of here!''

They piled into the Ford, and Hall revved up the engine.

"We can't just leave Carla here," Amanda protested.

"We can't do anything for her, Captain," Blake explained patiently. He could see that Amanda was still shaken by the sudden burst of violence. "This way it looks like a terrorist attack on an embassy official." It sounded cold-blooded, but Amanda knew he was right. She knew that Carla Rossi would not have wanted sentiment to jeopardize the mission. Hall drove rapidly out of the parking lot and swung south toward Ramses street. He glanced at Amanda. "Where to, Captain?" he asked.

Amanda still felt numb. It was hard for her to think clearly. The embassy? No, it was probably being watched. "Back to the base," she said. Hall nodded and concentrated on his driving, staying with the traffic but moving as fast as he could without attracting attention.

Amanda looked at the other women. Saada Almori sat quietly in one corner of the backseat, looking pale and shaken. Miriam Mboro was checking her Smith & Wesson. She swung out the cylinder and slipped on three fresh cartridges. She stared coldly at Saada Almori.

"Lady," she said grimly, "you've got a lot to answer for, and I'd better believe those answers. If I don't, I'll kill you."

## 12

The debriefing was not going well. Dr. Kaye sat at the center of the table and seethed quietly. He was a study in a cold, contained rage. It would have bothered Amanda much less if he had sworn and pounded his fist on the table. He had finished questioning Blake and Hall. Now he glared ferociously at Amanda. "So Captain Stuart, you received a phone call from Dr. Rossi, put on your party dress and off you went to contact Saada Almori, no plan, no coordination and no backup?"

Amanda Stuart was not easily frightened. She had been with the 101st Air Assault Division in Iraq, and in Lybia and Lebanon with Omega Force. She had seen far more frightening things than Dr. Kaye. "No Doctor, that is not correct. I had no idea the meeting was with Saada Almori. I had no reason to question what Dr. Rossi said, and I requested Sergeant Hall and Sergeant Blake to provide backup."

"They don't seem to have been very effective," Kaye sneered. "If they had acted sooner, Dr. Rossi might not have been killed. I thought Omega Force was more efficient than that."

Amanda flushed angrily. That was completely unfair. Before she could make a hot reply, Miriam Mboro interrupted smoothly. "They reacted as soon as possible, Doctor. The terrorists were correctly dressed in Egyptian police uniforms. Until they spoke and I heard Sudanese accents, I had no idea they weren't the real thing. Even I don't go around shooting policemen in friendly countries on sight. They neutralized all of the terrorists who were still in action in two seconds. I would call that efficient."

Kaye thought for a second. "Perhaps you are right, but this whole affair is pathetic. Dr. Rossi was a brilliant woman. She had a great future with the CIA. Her life has been thrown away for nothing."

General Sykes sighed. Kaye's questions were logical, but he was beating a dead horse. Sykes had learned when he was a young lieutenant in Cambodia that not all missions were successful and that the good guys didn't always win. When things went wrong, you had to accept that and go on from there.

"We're wasting time, Doctor," he said quietly. "From what Miss Mboro and Captain Stuart say, everyone, your people and mine, did the best they could with the information they had at the time. With twenty-twenty hindsight, maybe they could have done better, but I don't think anyone's to blame. I'm as sorry as anyone that Carla Rossi was killed, but let's remember why she went to the meeting in the first place. She thought Tamar Rosen had vital information. Saada Almori wanted the meeting for a reason, and she must have something to say. So let's stop wasting time. Let's get her in here and get it out of her."

Kaye frowned. He did not like to be told what to do, even by general officers, but what Sykes said was logical, and Kaye was nothing if not logical. "You are right, General. Let's talk to Miss Almori. That woman has a lot to answer for, and I intend to see that she does," Kaye said, his voice as cold as ice. "Colonel Khier, send her in."

A guard shoved Saada Almori into the briefing room. She did not look happy. The strip search she had been subjected to had been prolonged and humiliating. She wore a coarse, loose-fitting cotton robe, and her hands were uncomfortably handcuffed behind her. She glared around the room. She did not see any friendly faces. "You have no right to do this to me!" she said angrily. "I am an accredited journalist. I am not subject to military law. I have a Jordanian passport. I demand to see the Jordanian ambassador!"

Colonel Khier smiled at her coldly. "You have no rights. You are a suspected terrorist, implicated in acts against the Egyptian government. You should be glad you are here. My people are as gentle as doves compared to the secret police. I would advise you to answer us quickly and truthfully, or you will find that out for yourself."

"That's a good idea. We ought to let them work on her for a few hours before we question her. I hear they do some very interesting things with electricity," Miriam Mboro said cruelly.

Saada Almori shuddered. "Why are you treating me this way? It is not my fault Carla Rossi is dead. You heard Mboro. The terrorists who attacked us were Sudanese. What do I have to do with Sudanese terrorists?"

Dr. Kaye smiled like a shark about to bite. "That's one of the things we are going to find out, Miss Almori. Now, what was this immensely important information you were going to give Carla Rossi?"

Saada Almori took a deep breath and began to speak slowly and carefully. "As you know, I am a free-lance journalist. I specialize in Middle Eastern affairs. I have recently received information from reliable sources in the Sudan that two major acts of terrorism are about to occur. One will be aimed against the United States, the other against Egypt. Together they will totally discredit the United States in the Middle East, and lead to the overthrow of the Egyptian government."

Dr. Kaye sneered. "Yes, of course, and since you are such a great friend of the United States, and love the Egyptian government, you came to Cairo to warn us. Really, Miss Almori, you must think we are complete idiots!"

Saada Almori flushed. "I despise the United States. It will be a great day when you are driven out of the Middle East forever. I will be happy if the Egyptian government is overthrown. They have sold their souls for American aid. I am here at great personal risk because I want to prevent the loss of vast numbers of innocent lives, but I see that the CIA knows everything, Dr. Kaye. You obviously do not need to hear my information. Release me then, and I will be gone. The disaster will be on your heads, not mine."

Saada paused for a moment to let her words sink in. She glanced quickly around the room. Kaye, General Sykes and Colonel Khier were the key players. It was hard to read Kaye's face. He had his usual superior look on his face, but Sykes and Khier looked concerned. Good, she would build on that.

"Let's hear what she has to say, Doctor," Sykes said quietly. "It may be important."

"Very well, General, as you wish. Tell us your fairy tale, Miss Almori. What is this major act of terror against the United States?"

Saada smiled to herself. Suspicious as the Americans were, they were taking the bait. Now she would tell them just enough to convince them that what she said was true. "Within forty-eight hours an airliner will be hijacked. One or more important American officials will be on board. The hijackers will bring the plane to Egypt. The American officials and their staffs will be publicly executed. The American government will be shown to be powerless, and the Egyptian government discredited. American political opinion will turn against support for Egypt. It will be the end of your alliance."

Sykes sat bolt upright in his chair. Saada had certainly attracted his attention. "Do you know the airline and the flight number?" he asked.

Saada shook her head. "Terrorists do not share that kind of information with even their closest sympathizers. I only know what I have told you. Beyond that it is up to you."

Sykes looked at Kaye. "It sounds plausible, Doctor. Do we believe her?"

Kaye frowned. He did not like what Saada Almori had said. A messy incident in Egypt while he was head of Task Force Sphinx could ruin his prospects for promotion. "That is the wrong question, General. It doesn't matter whether we believe her or not, we simply cannot afford to ignore her." Kaye turned to Miriam. "Mboro, contact Washington on SATCOM immediately. I want a complete and immediate computer search and correlation of all international flights underway or scheduled for the next forty-eight hours. Start with U.S. airlines. Then expand to include all airlines belonging to countries which supported the United States in the Gulf War. Correlate against the travel plans of U.S. government officials, cabinet members, members of Congress, senior military officers and ambassadors. Tell them not to stop with one or two correlations. Have them wring it out completely. We need to know every possibility. Got it?"

Miriam nodded. "Yes, doctor, but this is a tremendous amount of number crunching. It may take a long time. Shall I—"

Kaye smiled coldly. "Tell them this is triple-A priority urgently required to support Task Force Sphinx. All other work has lower priority. If anyone has any complaints, tell them to take them up with the director. Clear?"

Miriam nodded and swept out of the room. She was smiling as she left. She was not assigned to Kaye, and technically it was not her task, but she did not mind. This was the first time in her career with the CIA that she had been able to tell Washington what to do and make it stick.

"Well, General, unless there is some military action you wish to take, I believe that is all that can be done now."

Sykes shook his head. He didn't like Peter Kaye, and he wasn't fond of the CIA, but he had to admit he was impressed. Whether Kaye believed Saada Almori or not, he was certainly taking action. "Let's wait and see what you find out," he said.

"Very well, Mboro is right—the search will take some time. Let's adjourn until we hear from Washington. Colonel Khier, will you ensure that Miss Almori is kept in custody?"

Khier frowned. "One moment, Doctor Kaye. Something seems to be missing. Miss Almori spoke of major acts of terrorism, one of which will be aimed against the United States, the other against Egypt. She said one would lead to the overthrow of the Egyptian government. The hijacking of an airliner and the public execution of an American official on Egyptian soil would be a very unpleasant incident, but airliners have been hijacked and hostages killed before. There would certainly be a great outcry in your media, but the United States and Egypt have been allies for twenty years. I do not think our alliance would be destroyed. Certainly the Egyptian government would not be overthrown. I would like to know what she meant when she said this."

Saada Almori kept her face impassive, inwardly she shrieked with glee. God is great! she thought. He was delivering them into her hands!

Dr. Kaye nodded. "That is a reasonable question. What do you have to say, Miss Almori?"

Saada smiled. "You did not give me a chance to finish, Dr. Kaye. Colonel Khier is absolutely correct. I will be glad to explain, but I believe that this information is very sensitive, what you Americans call top secret. Do you wish everyone in the room to hear it?"

"Everyone here is cleared. Proceed."

"There is a terrorist movement operating in the Sudan. They are supporting the Mahdi. This group was headed by Colonel Sadiq. I do not know who is leading it now, only that they are religious fanatics. They wish to punish the United States and its allies for their crimes against the Arab people. They want to see them struck by the wrath of God."

Dr. Kaye sneered. "Spare us your propaganda, Miss Almori, and tell us something we do not already know. Just how do these terrorists propose to punish us?"

"They have nuclear weapons, at least two of them, perhaps more. They will provide the hellfire that the Mahdi says will strike the Egyptians to punish them for their sins."

Saada paused for a moment and glanced quickly around the room. No one said anything, but she could tell by the expressions on their faces that she had them. They were hanging on every word.

Dr. Kaye broke the silence. "So, Miss Almori, your terrorist friends are about to use nuclear weapons against Egypt, but of course you do not know the targets."

Saada smiled again. Dr. Kaye did not sound quite so confident now. "Oh, but I do, Doctor. That is why I am here. I do not want to see vast numbers of innocent Egyptians die for what their leaders have done. I am taking a great personal risk to warn you, but I must prevent that from happening."

Dr. Kaye stared at her. He would have been much happier if she had demanded a million dollars. If there was anything twenty years in the CIA had taught him, it was to distrust idealists. But everything Saada Almori had said so far was consistent with the CIA's information and what Omega Force had found in the Sudan. Perhaps the terrorists were planning something so horrible that even she could not stomach it.

"Don't keep us in suspense, Miss Almori. What are the targets?"

"There is only one target, Doctor. Both weapons will be used to ensure its total destruction." She paused and stared at him for a moment. "It is the Aswan High Dam."

"What, the dam?" Colonel Khier was on his feet. The Americans were startled. Khier was a tough, experienced soldier. Now, he suddenly seemed to be frightened to death. "God protect us!" He stared at Saada Almori as if she had announced that the world was about to end. "How do you know this? How will the weapons be delivered?"

Saada Almori shrugged. "I do not know how or when the weapons will be delivered. I know the plan because it is very disturbing to many in the movement. They feel as I do. The Egyptian government is corrupt and deserves to be destroyed, but these men are soldiers. They cannot believe that so many people deserve to die, even if the Mahdi says it is God's will."

Khier turned to leave the room. "Learn anything else you can from her. I must contact the brigade commander immediately. The high command must be notified. We must stop this attack at any cost!"

Sykes spoke quickly. "You're way ahead of us, Colonel. Why are you so concerned about this dam? Wouldn't a city be a much more dangerous target than any dam?"

"You do not understand, General. There is no more dangerous target," Khier said quietly. He moved to the large map of Egypt and the Sudan on the wall. "Look, here is the Nile. It crosses the border here, and it flows all the way to the Mediterranean Sea in the north. Here is the Aswan Dam, near the Sudanese border. It is one of the largest dams in the world. It created Lake Nasser, the largest man-made body of water in the world. It controls the flow of the Nile."

Sykes nodded. He understood what Khier had said. It was interesting, but he was not certain what it meant or why Khier thought it was so important.

Khier pointed at the map again. "Look at the Nile. Ninety-five percent of all Egyptians live within the fertile belt within five miles of the banks of the Nile. The rest of the country is desert. This area contains all our large cities, and all of our significant industry and agriculture. If the Aswan Dam is breached, the area will be flooded. There will be nowhere for people to go, nothing for them to eat. Our industry and our agriculture will be ruined. There will be famine and plague. It will be the worst catastrophe in human history."

Dr. Kaye stared at Colonel Khier. "Surely you exaggerate, Colonel. You must be wrong. I don't doubt that the effects would be serious, but they simply could not possibly be as bad as you describe."

Khier shook his head. He wasn't angry, but looked like a man whose worst fears have suddenly been realized. "No, I am not wrong. We have studied this matter very carefully before the dam was built. A major earthquake was an obvious risk. Some people argued that the risk was so great that the dam should never be built, but the potential benefits were so great that we went ahead despite their fears. The dam is huge. All possible safety features are included in its construction, but if it is broken, the Almori woman is right, Egypt will be destroyed."

Sykes was stunned. He had seen a lot of war in the past twenty-five years and some horrible acts of terrorism, but this went beyond anything he had ever imagined—an entire country devastated by one explosion. "Isn't there something you can do?" he asked. "Don't you have some contingency plans? Can you evacuate the danger zone?"

"What contingency plans?" Khier said bitterly. "Evacuation is impossible. There is no place for people to go except into the desert, and they would starve there in days. There is nothing we can do but try to prevent it from occurring. God grant that it does not happen. If it does, it will be as bad as I say."

"It will be worse," Blake said quietly. Everyone stared at him. They had almost forgotten he was there. He had been sitting there quietly, listening to what was said. Blake felt that when colonels and generals were having meetings, the wisest course for sergeants was to be seen and not heard. But his information was essential. As he got slowly to his feet, he was not smiling in his usual way. That was a bad sign.

Colonel Khier stared at him. He wasn't used to being contradicted by sergeants, but he had seen Blake in action and he was willing to listen to anything he had to say. "What do you mean, Sergeant?"

"Its the rate of release, Colonel. Your experts are right. What they've told you is true, but they haven't allowed for the rate of release. I've studied the tactical use of nuclear demolition and I've been involved in nuclear tests in Nevada. I'm absolutely certain that I'm right. The rate of release is extremely critical."

Khier and Sykes looked blank. Tower smiled. He was used to Blake. Blake was being perfectly clear as far as he was concerned, he was simply not allowing for the fact that most people did not understand things that were simple to him.

"Could you explain that, Sergeant?" Tower inquired.

Blake frowned slightly. It didn't appear to him that there was anything to explain, but Tower must have some reason for asking. "What the Egyptian experts say would be true if the dam were broken by an earthquake or by a conventional explosion. The water would pour through the break, but most of the dam would still be there. The release would be gradual. A nuclear explosion will be different. The dam will simply cease to exist. Everything within the fireball will simply cease to exist. Outside the fireball, the blast wave will shatter the structure into small pieces. All the water in Lake Nasser will be released in a few seconds. You won't just get a flood, you'll get a tidal wave hundreds of feet high going straight down the Nile. Millions of people will be killed. Egypt as a nation will be wiped off the face of the earth."

Khier looked like a man who has just been shown his death warrant. Perhaps he had. "Excuse me, but I must go now," he said urgently. "Our high command must be notified. We must get more men and equipment to the dam as soon as possible."

"Certainly, Colonel. Tell your high command they can count on us. We will do anything we can." Kaye said as Khier dashed out the door. Kaye turned to Sykes. "This is extremely serious, General. What can we do and how fast can we do it?"

Sykes thought for a moment. "Not much. Omega Force is not a security force. They wouldn't be any more effective guarding the Aswan Dam than an Egyptian commando company, maybe less. They don't know the country or speak the language. If you can locate the weapons, we can try to take them out. Are you having any luck?''

Kaye shook his head. ''No, not so far. We are using all our assets, but we haven't found any trace of the weapons once they left the base you raided in Sudan. Our people are doing the best they can, but the Mahdi's takeover has disrupted operations in the Sudan.''

Sykes looked at Cray and Tower. He wasn't the kind of general who tried to pass the buck to his subordinates, he simply hoped one of them might have a brilliant idea. First Tower shook his head, then Cray. No luck. They all sat silently for a moment, and Sykes resisted the temptation to swear. It was grindingly frustrating, like trying to fight shadows in the dark. The situation was bad. The enemy had the initiative, and all they could do was react.

Miriam Mboro swept back into the room. ''What's the matter with Colonel Khier?'' she asked. ''I just passed him in the hall. He looks like he's seen a ghost.''

Dr. Kaye wasn't in the mood for polite conversation. ''I will brief you later, Mboro. What have you heard from Washington?''

Miriam grinned. She wasn't the kind of person to tell to do something unless it really had to be done. ''It took a little arguing, but they are giving us absolute priority, and I only had to threaten them with the director twice. Preliminary results will be available in an hour via SATCOM. That's the good news. The bad news is that we may not need it.

''We just got a message from our Khartoum station. Air Zimbabwe flight four has been hijacked en route to Nairobi, with Congresswoman Vera Kline and her staff on board. The plane landed at Khartoum ten minutes ago, and the hijackers are letting all Muslim passengers off the plane. They are demanding that the plane be refueled and flown to Cairo International Airport or they will kill everyone still on board. The Sudanese have agreed. The plane will be landing here in about three hours. The Egyptian government has been informed. There are approximately six hijackers, armed with pistols and light automatic weapons. They say they have a bomb and will blow up the plane if anyone tries to stop them. That's all we know so far.''

Dr. Kaye smiled grimly. "Well, it would appear that some of what Miss Almori told us is true. Let's get ready to give these hijackers a warm reception, General. Will you have Major Cray move Omega Force to the Cairo airport immediately?''

Sykes felt a curious sense of relief. Here was something he knew how to deal with. "Come on, Major,'' he said quickly. "You heard the man, let's go!''

**13**

Cray had set up his command post near the door of a maintenance hangar. Inside, his men were busy checking weapons and equipment. He stood at the edge of the taxi way and took one last look to make absolutely sure that there was nothing which could be seen from outside that would give their presence away. He checked his watch. Three hours till dark. If their estimates were right, the hijacked airliner should be landing in ten minutes.

He stepped back inside the hangar, grateful for the shelter from the brutal afternoon heat beating down on the concrete runways. Tower and Blake were sitting at a table near the door. Both were wearing white coveralls with markings that proclaimed that they were employees of Egyptair, the Egyptian national airline. Tower was listening to a radio, monitoring messages between the control tower and the Air Zimbabwe plane. Blake was hard at work at a portable computer. Its display showed a detailed cutaway drawing of a four-engined airliner.

He glanced around the hangar. Kaye and General Sykes were not there. They had gone to the embassy to try to sort out the political situation, and Cray was glad he wasn't involved in that. It was a hell of a mess. A Zimbabwean plane was going to be on Egyptian soil with an American official and her staff on board. The diplomats and the lawyers could argue for the next twenty years over who should do what and to whom. Cray's job was simpler, but not easy. If the politicians could make up their damned minds, he would storm the airliner and try to rescue the hostages, but it was not an idea that filled him with glee. The history of special-operations hostage-rescue attempts included some very unpleasant failures.

A black Mercedes pulled into the hangar and parked in the back. Colonel Khier got out, followed by Saada Almori and Miriam Mboro. Cray was surprised to see the two women. Khier came over quickly.

"How are your preparations coming, Major?" Khier asked. "Do you have everything you require?"

Cray nodded. "We're all set. I'm keeping everyone inside until the plane lands. I'll put snipers on the roof as soon as I'm sure they're down. I'll select the assault team when we have a better feel for the situation."

"It is well that you are prepared. Stay ready. If anyone is going to do it, it will be your Omega Force."

Cray was relieved to hear it. He didn't doubt that Khier's commandos were good, but he had more faith in his own people than in anyone else. "Any reason for that?" he inquired.

"Zimbabwe cannot do it. They lack troops with the proper training and equipment. My own leaders do not wish to accept the responsibility. We tried two such operations a few years ago, one on Cyprus and one on Malta. Both were failures and there were very heavy casualties. Our politicians do not believe such an operation will be a success. To be frank, if your congresswoman and the other passengers are killed, they wish it to be clear that it was an American failure, not theirs."

Cray smiled bitterly. It seemed that politicians were the same the whole world over. Still, it would have been nice to hear that the decision had been based on immense faith in Omega Force. He was tempted to say something sarcastic, but that would not be fair. Khier did not make national policy. "So it's an all-American operation?"

Khier's teeth flashed in his dark face as he smiled broadly. "Not entirely, my leaders want an Egyptian observer with the assault team. I did not volunteer of course, but I was selected. My superiors are very pleased with me. They feel that I get along marvelously well with Americans. Doubtless I will be promoted if I live through all this."

Cray laughed. It would be hard to dislike Khier. Whatever the Egyptian politicians were up to, Khier was putting his life on the line. "Welcome to the team. Maybe we can both get promoted if we're lucky. One question, what's Saada Almori doing here?''

Khier shrugged. ''God knows, but I do not. Your famous Dr. Kaye asked me to bring her here, but he did not tell me why. He does not confide in lowly Egyptian commando colonels. Do not worry about her. She is under control. The Mboro woman is guarding her.''

Cray nodded. He had more important things to worry about. Tower was signaling, and Cray moved to the table and stood behind him. The radio was buzzing with traffic. Unfortunately the messages were in Arabic. Cray sighed. If he ever had the time, he was going to have to learn the language, but in the meantime, he would have to depend on Tower.

''They're coming in now,'' Tower said quickly. ''The hijackers are making a number of demands. All security forces must stay away from the plane. They want food and water and they want the plane refueled. They demand to speak to the American ambassador. If they don't get what they want, they will begin to kill the passengers, starting with the Americans. The control tower is saying they have to refer this to higher authorities.''

Cray thought for a moment. Khier had made it clear that the Americans were calling the shots, and he was the senior American officer present. ''Call the tower on the secure land line. Tell them to agree to food and water and refueling the plane. That will keep the hijackers happy and it will let us get some people and equipment close to the plane

Cray turned to Blake. ''What have you found out so far?''

Blake pointed to his computer display. ''It's not going to be easy, Major. The plane is a Boeing 707-330B. It's a four-engined low-wing monoplane. Access is limited. There are only two entry doors, one just back of the cockpit and the other aft by the tail. Both are on the left side. The emergency exits are just back of the wings, and the fuel tanks are in the wings. We've also got the passenger manifest. Allowing for the people they let off at Khartoum, there should be about seventy-five people still on board.''

''All right. Start planning for an opposed entry. Assume there are hijackers in the cockpit and in the passenger compartment. Figure out alternate entry plans just in case. Emphasize speed and surprise. We've got to hit them hard and fast and take them out before they can do anything."

That sounded great, but Cray was painfully aware that it was a hell of a lot easier said than done. The hijackers had automatic weapons, and if anything went wrong there could be a bloodbath in seconds.

"They're on the ground and headed this way," Tower said. "The control tower has told them this is the service area where they will be refueled. The hijackers sound a little more relaxed since we seem to be going along with them."

Cray heard the whine of jet engines. He stepped to the hangar door and used his field glasses. The 707 was painted a gleaming white with a band of green, gold, red and black stripes running from the nose to the tail. No doubt about it, he could see Air Zimbabwe painted in black letters on the fuselage.

It was time to go to work. Sergeant Hall and the sniper team were already headed for the roof. Hall was carrying his huge .50-caliber long-range sniper's rifle. The rest of Cray's men were waiting quietly for orders. The 707 slowed and came to a stop about two hundred yards from the hangar. The hijackers were not taking any chances.

Khier checked his equipment and looked at his watch. "Time to go and talk to our friends. I will keep them occupied until the diplomats get here. Who knows, perhaps my silver tongue can persuade them to surrender."

Cray smiled. It was a nice thought, but he would not like to bet a year's pay on it. He watched as Khier walked slowly out to the 707. Khier had a tactical radio slung over his shoulder, and his 9 mm Beretta in its holster by his side. Somehow it didn't seem like much against a terrorist team with bombs and automatic weapons.

The 707's forward entry door swung open as Khier reached the plane, and a man appeared in the door and began to talk to him. Khier had set his radio to transmit, so that they could hear his side of the conversation. Tower listened intently.

"He's telling them who he is, and that high-level government officials are on the way. They want their fuel and supplies right away. They're telling Khier they will kill everybody and destroy the plane if he tries anything." There was nothing surprising in any of that. It passed for polite and reasonable conversation in terrorist circles.

"They want the forward boarding ramp brought out."

Actually that was a good sign. They would not have asked for the ramp unless they wanted to talk. Cray was not surprised. Whatever they intended to do in the end, hijackers always wanted publicity. Now he had to make a decision about who should go out with the ramp. Tower and Blake, of course, as key members of the assault team, but should he go? He was the senior American officer until General Sykes got there, and technically he should stay back and make command decisions. Sykes might not be amused if he found his major out at the plane eyeball-to-eyeball with the terrorists. Then Cray shrugged. He was never going to be chief of staff anyway, and he had to see what was going on if he was going to make the right decisions. He turned to Blake and Tower. "Come on, let's go."

Blake activated the ramp and began to steer it toward the plane. Cray followed, staying to the right of the ramp, trying to look as if he was doing something terribly important. With Tower on the other side, they moved steadily toward the plane. Cray was painfully aware that the man in the 707's door was holding an AK-47 ready for action. If he decided to shoot, there was no cover. One or two bursts, and they would all be dead. However, that would be the last thing the terrorist ever did because Hall would put a .50-caliber bullet through his head a second later. Cray did not find that terribly comforting. He told himself it was not logical for the terrorists to shoot, but his nerves still crawled. He had met a lot of terrorists, and none of them had ever seemed to be particularly logical to him.

Blake positioned the ramp against the plane. A man stepped through the door of the 707 and came down the ramp. He looked deceptively ordinary. Cray would have passed him on any street in the Middle East without a second glance. He was carrying a holstered pistol, but he didn't really need it. Two other men had moved to the top of the ramp with AK-47s in their hands. Cray saw a flicker of movement inside the door. Two more men were there with weapons in their hands. The terrorists obviously knew their business. Unless the assault team could achieve complete surprise, an attack up the ramp would be suicidal. They would have to think of something else.

As the hijacker began to talk to Colonel Khier in Arabic, Cray led Blake and Tower to the 707's nose wheel. Blake produced some tools and they made a show of checking it out. Tower listened to the conversation and translated quickly, keeping his voice low.

"He wants to know what we're doing. Khier is telling him we're conducting standard preflight safety checks before refueling. He seems to be buying that. Now he's giving Khier a list of their demands. They want all political prisoners in Egypt freed and all U.S. military forces withdrawn from the Middle East. They want to speak with the American ambassador. They demand media access so they can speak on radio and television. Khier is saying he does not have the authority to agree to this. He will relay their demands to the proper authorities.

Tower paused, his head bent as he wrote on his clipboard. "We'd better move now. They'll get suspicious if we stay here too long."

They moved to the left main landing gear. Cray stared at the undercarriage and the four big tires as if he knew what he was doing. He did not think he had a brilliant future as an aircraft mechanic. He could see the opening of the well that held the landing gear when it was retracted, but it didn't look promising. Men might climb the undercarriage, but the well didn't offer any access to the passenger compartment. Blake was right. It was not going to be easy.

The conversation by the ramp was growing louder.

"Heads up," Tower said quietly. "Our friend is not happy. They won't hesitate to kill the hostages if they don't get what they want, and they'll start with the Americans. He wants everybody away from the plane. Their demands are nonnegotiable. No one is come back except to give them what they want. Khier says he's leaving. Come on, let's go."

They followed Colonel Khier back to the hangar. Cray was glad to be back inside. He didn't like people glaring at him while they were holding AK-47s. He started for the radio to check with the embassy, but that wasn't going to be necessary.

Dr. Kaye was waiting impatiently at the table. Obviously they were going to get the word from on high directly. From the look on Kaye's face, they were not going to enjoy it.

"There you are, Cray. What is the situation?" Kaye snapped.

"The plane has landed, Doctor. We have taken a look at it while Colonel Khier talked to the terrorists. We are preparing plans to storm the aircraft if necessary. As soon as it gets dark, we will be ready to go. It won't be easy. The hijackers are well armed and appear to be alert. They have made a series of demands, and Colonel Khier can fill you in on that."

Kaye nodded and Colonel Khier began to describe his conversation with the hijacker. Cray also listened intently, aware that he might have missed something when Tower had been translating. Even the smallest point might be critical. Khier was an excellent briefer who stuck to the facts. "I agree with Major Cray," he concluded. "They are alert and it will be very difficult to storm and secure the plane before they kill the passengers. We should do it only if there is no other alternative."

"Thank you, Colonel. An excellent briefing. Now, I would like to ask you one more thing. You are the only one to have talked directly to their leader. Nuances are important in these affairs. What are your impressions? How do you feel about the situation?"

Khier thought for a moment and spoke slowly and carefully. "Their demands are extreme and unrealistic. Freeing all political prisoners in Egypt and withdrawing all U.S. military forces from the Middle East could only be agreed to at the highest levels of both our governments. If they were to agree, they would require weeks, perhaps months, to accomplish. They demand to speak with the American ambassador in person, but it would be very unwise for him to come here. They could easily kill him. Their other demands, food, fuel and media access, are typical. I would recommend that we grant them, but I cannot speak for my government."

Kaye smiled coldly. "You don't have to, Colonel. Your government has decided that the United States must call the shots. If anything goes wrong, it will be our responsibility. Anything else?"

"Yes, the whole situation does not feel right. I have talked with terrorists before, and they are usually nervous and very tense, under great stress when they are in the middle of an operation. That was not the case with this man. He was calm and relaxed, almost peaceful, making his demands like an actor reciting lines from a play. He had the air of a man who knows something that I do not. I almost felt he was playing with me, saying these things only because I expected to hear them. He really seemed to care only about the security of the plane."

Kaye frowned. He dealt in facts, not feelings, but he had asked Khier for his opinion. "What do you conclude from this?" he asked in his flat, precise voice.

"We are missing something, Doctor. We do not know their real purpose, I am certain of that. Perhaps I do not understand the situation completely. I am ignorant of American politics. Is this congresswoman really so important?"

Kaye sneered. "Vera Kline? She is a media darling, a crusader for peace, the environment and feminist causes. She has influence, and her husband has a lot of money. Her latest cause is famine relief in Africa. That's why she's over here. Washington does not want anything to happen to her if it can be prevented. They don't want the bad press, but she is of no real importance. There are dozens like her."

He smiled coldly. "Of course that is not the official position of the Agency, and I would not care to be quoted. Ms. Kline hates the CIA and loathes the military, but we will save her if we can. Do you think they will negotiate?"

"They will talk to you, Doctor, if we can convince them you are an important American official. They may make some concessions, but they will not release the Kline woman. She is their trump card."

"Very well, we will talk to them. It will pass the time while they make up their minds in Washington. In the meantime, complete your preparations, Cray. Assume we will storm the plane."

Cray did not miss the "we," but somehow he doubted that Kaye was volunteering to lead the assault team. "All right. Tell them we will deliver food and water right away. Stall on refueling the plane until after dark. That way the noise will provide cover for the assault team. Aside from that—''

"Dr. Kaye," Miriam Mboro interrupted "there's a call for you from the embassy on the secure phone. Top secret voice line has been established. I told them you were having a meeting, but they say it is extremely urgent."

Kaye picked up the phone with the look of a man who does not suffer fools gladly. "Kaye here. Just what is so important?" He listened intently for thirty seconds. Suddenly he glared at the phone. "Say that again. Your certain? Why wasn't I told this hours ago? What fool decided that? Very well, tell the director I will handle it, but I must have immediate authority to order an attack on the plane. Don't sit there babbling—do it!"

He slammed the receiver down. It was just as well that the secure phone was strongly built; otherwise its printed circuits would have been spread over the hangar floor.

"What a group of miserable incompetents! With people like that on our side, we don't need enemies. I think we have the other piece of the puzzle. The secretary of state is on his way to Cairo. He left Washington four hours ago on *Air Force Two*, and he will be landing here in approximately five hours. The president of Egypt is coming here to meet him. As you can imagine, this place will be crawling with reporters. I don't believe in coincidences. The terrorists obviously intend to do something to embarrass the American and Egyptian governments that will get worldwide attention. My orders are to resolve the situation at any cost before the secretary arrives."

He paused for a moment and stared at Cray. "Get your men ready, Major, the ball is in your court. I expect the authorization to storm the plane within the hour."

**14**

General Sykes came quietly through the back door of the maintenance hangar. He motioned to Amanda Stuart to stop, and stood for a minute, letting his eyes adjust to the light. The hangar was bustling with organized confusion as the assault team and the backup teams checked their weapons and equipment. Every weapon, radio and special-purpose device had to be checked and rechecked. There were no unimportant details prior to an assault on an airliner full of terrorists and their hostages. Sykes watched the men carefully. He saw no signs of low morale. Some of the men looked a little tense, but that was to be expected. Premission nerves were normal when men were about to go in to kill or be killed.

Cray and his officers and senior NCOs were clustered around Blake's computer, staring intently at the display while Blake discussed the fine points of the 330B version of the Boeing 707. Sykes walked quietly across the hangar. No one stopped working, but there was a stir of interest as he passed each group. Something was going to happen if the general was there.

Cray and Tower looked up as Sykes approached and moved quickly to meet him, and reported.

Sykes did not waste any time on polite conversation. "Any change in the situation?"

Cray shook his head. "We've given food and water. We're stalling them on refueling the plane. We've run a phone line to the plane, and Dr. Kaye has talked to them. They've repeated their demands for media access. Kaye has demanded evidence that the hostages are all right before we will consider making any more concessions. They refuse to let anyone on the plane to talk to Congresswoman Kline, and they're not stupid enough to bring her out of the plane. For the moment it's a Mexican standoff.''

"Not for long. Washington doesn't want to take any chances with the secretary of state on the way. We can't have any messy incidents on CNN. They've delegated the authority to us. Kaye makes the decision, but my head's still on the platter. I've got to approve the plan. That way, the good doctor and I will hang together. Since my career is on the line, fill me in. What's your plan?''

Cray pointed to Blake's computer. "It's dictated by the basic layout of the 707. It's an old, narrow body design. There's a single aisle, and most of the passenger compartment has six-abreast seating, three seats on each side of the aisle. There's a small first-class area up front, near the cockpit. The narrow aisle is a major problem. It limits the number of people we can use in the assault party. We plan to enter near the center of the aircraft. There will be two three-man teams. One goes forward toward the nose, the other aft toward the tail. That should minimize the chances of any of our people being hit by friendly fire. Our entry will be preceded by the use of nonlethal, special-purpose grenades, including CS tear gas, and accompanied by diversions outside the plane to distract and confuse the enemy. Backup teams stand by in case they are needed. With luck, we take the terrorists by surprise and neutralize them before they can kill the passengers or blow up the plane.''

Sykes nodded. It sounded like a good plan, but he could see one big problem Cray hadn't covered. "Fine, but how do you get your teams inside the plane? From what you've said, there's only the forward boarding ramp, and that's guarded by men with automatic weapons. You can't take the time to fight your way in, they'll kill the passengers.''

Cray ran his hand through his closely cropped brown hair. Sykes was right. Twenty-five years in the Rangers had taught him the tricks of the trade. "That's the problem all right, General, but Sergeant Blake has a plan.''

Sykes smiled. It seemed Sergeant Blake always had a plan. "All right, Sergeant, how do we do it?''

Blake smiled and held up a long length of triangular metal tubing. "Flexible linear-shaped charges, General. We just make our own doors, and go in without knocking. FLSC uses the same principle as the shaped charges we use in our antitank missiles, but instead of blowing a hole in something we use it as a cutting charge. If we place the flexible tube properly, we can cut a door in the fuselage in less than a second."

Sykes looked skeptical. "You're going to blast a big hole in the side of the fuselage? Doesn't that risk killing some of the passengers?"

Blake sighed. He thought Sykes was the best general officer he had ever known, but his knowledge of technical matters left a great deal to be desired. "No sir," Blake said diplomatically, "I'm not going to blast a hole—I'm going to cut one. It's a completely different type of explosive action. The force of the detonation is confined to the area directly under the tube. Fragmentation will be extremely limited. Of course the metal section we cut will be driven inside the plane with considerable force, and if anyone is sitting in the seats directly in line with the charge, they may be killed or injured. But other than that, the danger area will be limited." Sykes smiled. He was not going to argue demolition techniques with Blake. "All right, Sergeant, I'll take your word for it, FLSC it is."

Sykes thought for a minute. The essence of a successful attack on a hijacked airliner was surprise and speed. Unless the assault teams could deal with the terrorists immediately, they would massacre the passengers. Cray's plan seemed good, but it would all depend on the speed and force of the execution.

"I'll buy it. Work on the assumption that we'll do it that way. Now, let's fill Kaye in and see if he will go along with it."

Cray sighed. It wasn't a happy sound. He did not think Kaye was a military genius.

"I know, Major, and I feel the same way, but we have to face the facts. With the secretary of state and a congresswoman involved, the decisions can't be purely military."

Cray shrugged. He didn't like it, but that didn't matter. He didn't make national policy; he just carried it out. "All right, General, I understand. I'll get Dr. Kaye. It will be clearer if he can see the computer display while we brief him."

Cray escorted Dr. Kaye to the computer and repeated the briefing he had given General Sykes, speaking slowly and carefully. Kaye listened intently, thinking about every word. Cray didn't like the man, but he had to admit that Kaye was extremely intelligent and he had a lot of experience in the Middle East. His comments might actually be useful.

Kaye thought for a moment after Cray had finished. "Thank you, Major. I am not a military expert, of course, but your plan seems well thought out. However, there does seem to be a weak point. Your Intelligence is poor. You have no knowledge of the situation inside the aircraft, how many terrorists there are, and where they and the hostages are located inside the plane. It seems to me that this information is essential."

Cray didn't like Kaye's superior tone when he was merely stating the obvious. "You're right, Doctor. We certainly would like to have that information, but I don't see how we can get it."

Kaye smiled coldly. He seemed to be enjoying himself. "Perhaps I can help you, Cray. After all, Intelligence is my business. I have just been on the phone talking to our friends again, and they are growing very insistent about getting their message to the media. They have threatened to kill one of the American hostages unless we concede this point. I have suggested a compromise. We will allow two Third World journalists to board the plane. They will record the hijacker's message and confirm that the hostages are unharmed."

Cray frowned and shook his head. "I don't see how that will work. Even if you can find some cooperative journalists, they won't know what to look for unless we tell them our plan. We're sure as hell not going to do that, and if we did, I don't see how they can get us information fast enough to be of any use."

"I think I have the solution to that problem. Miss Mboro, please bring your equipment over here."

Miriam Mboro joined the group. She had a large nylon carrying bag slung over her shoulder. Kaye opened the bag and placed its contents on the table with the air of a magician about to perform a trick. His smile broadened. "You gentlemen are not the only ones with high-technology devices. Look at this, I think you will find it very interesting. It looks like a video Camcorder, and it is. It will record video and sound. There is nothing unusual about that, but it has a few other functions. The Agency has modified it to include a miniaturized TV cam-

era and transmitter. The unit can thus transmit real time im-
agery and sound. These are miniature receivers. They are small
and light enough to easily be carried in one hand. The picture
is black-and-white and the range is only a few thousand yards,
but with this unit inside the plane, our problems are
solved.Show the gentlemen, Miriam.''

Miriam lifted the Camcorder to her shoulder and scanned the
group. "Smile, gentlemen, you're on TV," she said cheerfully.

Cray watched the monitors. He was impressed. The screens
were small, but the pictures were clear. He could easily identify people and objects. "All right, I'm sold," he said. "Now,
how do we get it on the plane, and who operates it?''

"As you can see, Miriam can operate it. As for getting it on
the plane, the hijackers have requested media access, including TV. Miriam's cover is that she is a journalist in the Sudan.
Here she is with her equipment, ready to give them what they
want. They will welcome her with open arms.''

Cray frowned. He almost said he didn't like the idea of
sending a young woman into danger, but he thought better of
it. If he implied Miriam Mboro was a delicate creature who required protection from strong men, she would probably do him
great bodily harm on the spot. "It sounds like it will work,
Doctor, but you promised them more than one journalist. Who
do you want to go with her, one of us?''

Kaye chuckled dryly. "Hardly, Major. None of you look like
Third World journalists, even in civilian clothes, but we have
the perfect person here—Saada Almori.''

Cray was stunned. "Saada Almori? That's crazy. For all we
know, she's one of them. She may tell them everything she
knows the minute she's on the plane.''

"Really, Major, what can she tell them? Merely that there are
soldiers nearby. They would be remarkably stupid if they had
not deduced that. Remember, she doesn't know your plan''

"I can think of one thing she can tell them," Tower said
quickly. "She knows that Miriam Mboro is with the CIA.
Suppose she tells them that and they blow Miriam's head off.''

"I don't think that will happen. We have analyzed the situation. We don't think it is likely that Saada Almori would have
had contact with the hijacking team prior to their mission. In

the event we are wrong, it is unlikely that they will kill her immediately. She would be another valuable hostage. At any rate, we are prepared to accept the risk.''

Tower felt that Kaye, as usual, was being remarkably generous with other people's lives. He looked inquiringly at Miriam Mboro.

''It's all right,'' she said calmly. ''I think Dr. Kaye's analysis is correct. I'm willing to go.''

Tower shrugged. There was no more to say. It was up to Miriam, and she would not have been a CIA field agent if she were afraid to take chances.

''Very well, then,'' Kaye said briskly, ''come with me, Miriam. Let's recruit Miss Almori.''

Kaye and Miriam Mboro moved toward the table where Saada Almori sat quietly. Tower had not been invited, but he followed them anyway. The idea still made him uneasy, and he wanted to see Saada Almori's reaction to Kaye's plan.

Saada looked up as they approached. Tower noticed that she was pale and tense. Something was making her nervous. As Dr. Kaye began to outline the sanitized version of his plan, she didn't seem enthused. The more Kaye talked, the unhappier she seemed.

''You want me to go on board a hijacked airliner? You are putting me in danger,'' she said angrily. ''Why should I do this for you Americans? You have never been friends of mine. Why should I take risks for you?''

''I am surprised that you are not eager to go,'' Kaye said smoothly. ''You have always claimed to be a journalist who just happens to have excellent contacts with terrorist groups. If this is true, we are offering you a major scoop. Your face will be on television all over the world. If you want another incentive, consider this. You are implicated in the death of Carla Rossi. You swear that you are innocent, but that may be difficult to prove. You may spend a long time in an Egyptian jail before you are released, if ever.''

Saada Almori winced. She knew that her life as a suspected terrorist in an Egyptian prison would be very unpleasant.

''We need to be sure that the hostages, particularly Congresswoman Kline, are alive and unharmed, before proceeding with any further negotiations. Let's be frank. You know that Miss Mboro works for the U.S. government. If you do what I ask and help her verify the hostages are safe, we will be suitably grateful. There will be no charges against you, and you will be free to leave Egypt as soon as this situation is resolved.''

Saada thought for a moment, and shrugged her shoulders. "You leave me no choice. I will go. What will happen is in the hands of God.''

## 15

Tower crouched in the dark on the right wing of the 707 and made one last check of the assault team. Everyone was in position, almost invisible in their nonreflective black uniforms, body armor, M40 gas masks and the special raid hoods that protected their eyes and ears. The team had discarded their rifles and machine guns. The high-powered ammunition they fired had far too much penetration to be used inside an airliner. Most of them carried silenced 9 mm Heckler & Koch MP-5 submachine guns. Tower's own weapon, a large, black Benelli Super 90 12-gauge semiautomatic shotgun, was unusual. He knew the choice was controversial. Many antiterrorist experts considered shotguns unsuitable rescue-team weapons because of their limited magazine capacity and marginal accuracy if a pinpoint shot close to hostages was required.

Tower knew all that, but he was leading the team that would fight its way forward toward the 707's nose. He needed to stop any hijackers he shot instantly. He had seen men continue to fight after being hit with several 9 mm bullets. Each of the eight shells in the Benelli held twelve heavy lead buckshot delivered in a single massive blast. That should instantly disable any man who ever lived, if any precision shooting had to be done and Hall and Blake would be right behind him with their MP-5s.

Kaye was putting on a good show, and there was a bustle of activity in front of the main hangar door. Floodlights illuminated the area. Police vehicles and ambulances were standing by, the refueling vehicles were parked under the airliner's left wing, and mechanics were beginning to refuel the left wing tanks. The sights and sounds should attract the hijacker's attention and cover the actions of the assault team.

Blake finished placing the cutting charge against the 707's side. Tower watched as Blake looked quickly through one of the windows, then gave the thumbs-up signal. No one was sitting in the seats in line with the charge, and he was ready to fire.

Tower spoke softly in to the radio microphone attached to his hood. "Blue Team ready."

Sykes replied instantly. "Roger, Blue Leader. Stand by. They seem to be buying it. Mboro and Almori are going on board now."

Tower acknowledged and took a deep breath to steady his nerves. They were about to try one of the most difficult anti-terrorist operations in the book, and he would be the first man through the door. It was at times like this that he had trouble remembering why he had wanted to be a Green Beret. He pointed at Hall and Colonel Khier, and they moved forward, holding grenades in their hands. The special flash-bang grenades were designed not to be lethal, but they were extremely unpleasant to be near when they went off. Tower turned on his miniature TV monitor, hoping it worked. Although Kaye had assured him the TV signal would not be blocked by the plane's fuselage, but Kaye wasn't betting his life on it.

At first all Tower saw was static. Then the small screen cleared and he could hear Saada Almori talking. The pictures were not perfect, but they were clear enough. Miriam was panning the camera. They were standing just inside the forward door, talking to the leader of the hijackers. He was speaking rapidly, explaining the justice of his cause and the many crimes of the United States government. Now they were moving toward the rear of the plane, into the first-class compartment. Miriam pointed her camera at two women sitting side by side. The woman next to the window was Vera Kline. Tower recognized her from the pictures Kaye had shown him. He didn't recognize the other woman. The congresswoman looked unhappy, but she didn't appear to have been harmed.

Miriam swung the camera around. There were four armed men in the first-class compartment. The door into the cockpit was closed. At least one terrorist must be in there. The others must be watching the passengers in the tourist-class compartment or in the back of the plane, but there was no way to be sure. Miriam could not wander around the plane without arousing suspicion.

Tower decided that he knew as much as he was likely to know. Any further delay would simply increase the chances the team might be discovered. He spoke into his microphone.

"Eagle, Blue Leader. Recommend go."

Sykes agreed. "Roger, Blue Leader. Go!"

Tower took a deep breath. This was it. "Blue Team, on my count, three, two, one, go!"

Blake fired the cutting charge. The big 707 shook and shuddered as the exploding FLSC cut a six-by-four-foot section neatly from the side of the fuselage and hurled it inward.

"Grenades!"

Khier and Hall hurled their special grenades through the opening. Tower took three long strides and was inside the plane. He fought the urge to run and kept looking straight ahead. If he snagged his uniform or equipment on the wreckage of the seats, it could be fatal. He reached the aisle and crouched low behind the back of the seat in front of him. Three seconds gone. The passenger compartment became a close approximation of hell as it was suddenly lit by intensely bright flashes and shaken by incredibly loud noises from the detonation of the exploding flash and stun grenades. Tower's earphones filtered out most of the sound of the blasts, but even so, the blasts of sound were stunning. Any unprotected person near the blasts must be dazed and disoriented.

Now he had to move, before they could recover. Tower lunged out into the aisle, the Benelli ready in his hands. A man was standing in the aisle ten feet in front of him. He seemed dazed and stared wildly at Tower. In his black raid uniform, gas mask and hood, Tower looked like a demon fresh from hell. Passenger? No! Tower saw a big automatic pistol in the man's right hand. Tower pulled the trigger, and the big Benelli bucked and roared. Twelve buckshot struck the hijacker in the chest, delivering over a ton of energy in one simultaneous terrible blow. The man went down as if he had been struck by a sledgehammer.

Tower could see people in the seats ahead as he moved rapidly forward. Some of them were shouting and screaming.

Others sat dazed, pale with shock. Incredibly some were trying to get out of their seats. He shouted "Down! Stay down!"
at the top of his lungs and shoved people down as he moved
forward with Hall and Blake close behind him. Thin gray
smoke from the grenades was beginning to fill the passenger
compartment. He fervently hoped that none of the passengers
panicked and came out into the aisle. It would be terribly easy
to make a mistake and shoot the wrong target.

A man's head and shoulder suddenly appeared around the
back of a seat ahead. For a fraction of a second Tower hesitated. Then he saw the flickering yellow muzzle-flash as the
man fired a 9 mm automatic and felt a smashing blow in the
center of his chest, like a hard left jab from a heavyweight
boxer. He pulled the trigger of his shotgun instinctively and sent
a swarm of buckshot streaking toward the man. His face
snapped back, dissolved in a mask of blood, but he still had the
automatic in his hand. Tower fired again, and the blast of
buckshot dropped the man across the arm of his seat. The big
automatic slipped from his hand as he fell.

Tower could still move his arms and legs. His body armor
must have stopped the bullet. He was grateful for Kevlar, but
he had to keep going. The entrance to the first-class compartment was twenty feet ahead. Tower waited for a second, but
luck wasn't with him. The hijackers were using their heads, not
rushing out into the aisle to shoot it out but staying put with
their weapons covering the door. The first man to stick his head
inside would get his head blown off.

Tower was brave, but he was not suicidal. He dropped to one
knee, pointed his shotgun at the entrance and shouted, "Grenade!" Blake pulled the pin and threw a grenade through the
entrance. Tower saw the bright flash and felt the shock wave
from the blast as the grenade exploded. The effects within the
small first-class compartment were much worse. No one was
going to stay inside and wait for more grenades. Two men
staggered through the entrance, one after the other, their
AK-47s blazing in their hands.

Tower fired. The heavy buckshot load struck the hijacker and
hurled him backward. He was dying as he fell, but his finger
tightened on his AK-47's trigger, and it roared into life in a

sustained, ripping burst. A dozen steel-jacketed .30-caliber bullets tore into the fuselage above Tower's head. He ducked instinctively as he was showered with shards of broken plastics and bits of flying metal. The second hijacker snapped his AK-47 to his shoulder, ready to fire an aimed burst, but Sergeant Hall fired first. Hall did not trust 9 mm weapons. To him, any weapon smaller than .44-caliber was effeminate. He made up for his present lack of power with precision and put a 4-round burst through the hijacker's head.

Tower rushed forward, staying low. He took a chance and lunged through the first-class compartment entrance door. The leader of the hijackers was still on his feet. He had pulled Congresswoman Kline from her seat and was holding a 9 mm Browning automatic to her head. No one could shoot without taking a serious chance of hitting her. Miriam Mboro was standing right behind him. He evidently did not consider her to be a threat, and that was his mistake. With one smooth motion, she smashed her Camcorder into the back of the man's head.

The leader staggered, trying to bring his Browning to bear. Miriam grabbed his shooting hand in the classic disarming grip and twisted his hand back and up, trying to break his wrist or tear the pistol from his hand. They swayed back and forth, struggling for the gun, too close together for Tower to risk a shot. He saw the muzzle-flash as the terrorist pulled the Browning's trigger twice. The bullets struck the woman next to Congresswoman Kline in the face. But Miriam hung on grimly. She had learned her unarmed combat in a rough school. She drove a hard edge-of-the-foot kick to the man's right shin, trying to break his ankle.

She did not quite succeed, but she broke the terrorist's balance. Instinctively he threw his left leg to one side to keep from falling. Tower was not interested in fair fights—at this point, it was a luxury they couldn't afford. He thrust the muzzle of the Benelli against the man's leg and pulled the trigger. The buckshot did not have time to spread and tore into the man's thigh like a single huge projectile. The shock was terrible, and Miriam, fighting for her life, managed to twist the Browning from the hijacker's hands. With the reflexes that come from years of practice, she grasped the pistol in her right hand, thrust it into the hijacker's face and pulled the trigger. She fired again and again until the Browning's side locked open on its empty magazine. The terrorist slumped to the floor and lay still.

Miriam stood over him, shaking from nervous reaction and holding the empty pistol in her hand. Congresswoman Kline was screaming at the top of her lungs, but Tower didn't blame her. Pistol shots at point-blank range were messy. She and Miriam were spattered with the terrorist leader's blood. Miriam stared at Tower for a second. She could not recognize him in his raid equipment, but she knew he must be from Omega Force.

She pointed at the closed cockpit door. "Look out!" she yelled. "One of them's in there!" Tower swung his shotgun up as the door was suddenly thrust partway open. Tower saw a man with something in his hand. Even before his mind consciously registered that it was a grenade, he pulled the trigger of the Benelli again and again. The repeated impact of the heavy buckshot drove the man back into the cockpit. The grenade fell at his feet, but Tower could see the safety handle fly free as it fell from his hand. The fuze was burning. Tower dived forward desperately, slammed the cockpit door closed and threw himself to the floor of the first-class compartment.

He heard a dull boom as the grenade detonated, and then a second, much larger blast rocked the cabin. The plane shook, and thin white smoke began to drift out from under the buckled cockpit door. Acting almost by reflex, he shoved fresh shells into the Benelli's tubular magazine and tried desperately to think. It seemed to him that he had been fighting his way through the 707 for hours. Actually it had been less than sixty seconds since Blake had fired the cutting charge. He had to get the passengers off now, and quickly. If the plane was on fire, he could have panic on his hands.

He looked at Miriam and pointed to Congresswoman Kline and the rest of the first-class passengers. "Get them out of here!"

Miriam didn't move. She stared at him blankly, and Tower realized she couldn't hear him. Miriam had no ear protection and was temporarily deafened by the blasts from the flash and

stun grenades. He pointed at the passengers and motioned toward the door. When Miriam nodded and began to usher the
dazed passengers out, Tower gave a thumbs-up signal. She had
done a damned good job. He did not know if the CIA gave its
agents medals, but if they did, Miriam deserved one.

It was time to do something about the cockpit. Blake had
grabbed a large fire extinguisher from the cabin wall, and Hall
was pointing his submachine gun at the door. Tower heaved the
door open, staying carefully to one side. He didn't think anybody could be left alive in there, but the penalty for being
wrong could be high. Hall stared for a second, then lowered his
submachine gun. There was no one there to shoot. Five bodies
filled the cockpit. Three wore uniforms, the pilot, copilot and
the flight engineer. The other two were hijackers. The wind-
shields and controls were riddled with fragments and shattered
by the blast.

Some of the control panels were emitting blue-white sparks
and thin, acrid smoke. Stepping forward, Blake sprayed them
with the fire extinguisher. Just then, Tower realized there was
a voice in his ear. It was Sykes.

"Blue Leader, what is your situation?"

Tower looked back down the aisle. No one was shooting, and
the passengers in tourist class were streaming out the emergency exit. Someone in a black raid suit gave Tower the thumbs-
up gesture. Tower spoke quickly into his headset. "Eagle, this
is Blue Leader. The terrorists have been neutralized, and we are
securing the aircraft. Passengers are being evacuated now.
Congresswoman Kline is alive. Sorry to report the woman passenger sitting next to her and cockpit crew are dead. There may
be others."

"Roger, Blue Leader. Damned good work! We see smoke
from the nose of the aircraft. Do you require assistance?"

Tower glanced into the cockpit. Blake had the fire out and
was rapidly checking things out. There was no use slowing him
down by asking questions.

"Negative, Eagle. Keep everyone away from the plane. The
fire is out, but the situation is still hazardous. Blake is checking for bombs and booby traps."

"Roger, Blue Leader. We will stand by." Blake emerged from the cockpit and shook his head. "It's a hell of a mess in there, Captain. They had a small explosive charge rigged under the instrument panels. Between that and the hand grenade, there's not much left. The plane cannot be flown or taxied. If we want to move it, it will have to be towed."

"No other explosives? Remember, they threatened to destroy the plane completely."

Blake nodded. "That's right, Captain. The charge in the cockpit blew hell out of the cockpit, but it was far too small to destroy the plane. Any good explosives man would realize that. Unless they were bluffing, there must be another bomb with a much bigger charge. We'd better check the luggage racks and the baggage compartment."

Blake paused for a moment. "There's one other thing we'd better think about, Captain. We may have overlooked something. Maybe you should ask General Sykes to evacuate the airport."

Tower stared at Blake blankly. "Why should I do that?"

"Nothing says it has to be a conventional bomb, Captain. It may be a nuclear weapon."

## 16

Tower and General Sykes moved carefully through the 707's forward baggage compartment. It was not a pleasant place. Under the floor of the passenger compartment and designed to carry baggage and cargo, it would have given anyone with claustrophobia immediate hysterics. Blake had been close-mouthed on the radio, but Tower had a dismal feeling he knew what Blake had found. He would have had no reason to ask Sykes to come on board the plane if all he had found was a simple conventional bomb.

They reached the back of the compartment where Blake was kneeling by a dull gray cylinder about four feet long and two feet in diameter. Tower recognized the thing instantly. It still reminded him of a hot-water heater lying on its side. As far as he could tell, it was identical to the weapon they had brought back from the Sudan. Blake was moving one of his small black boxes slowly over the surface of the cylinder, being very careful not to touch it. He was frowning as he worked, occasionally speaking softly into his telephone headset. That didn't make Tower feel any better. Blake was usually cheerful, no matter what, and if the situation was serious enough to make Blake frown, then it must be serious indeed.

Blake didn't waste time on military protocol. He knew that what his officers needed was information, not a snappy salute. "I've completed my preliminary checks. There are indications of low-level electrical activity, and I can detect low-level radioactivity through the case. I conclude that the weapon is live and that it is armed."

Tower felt a cold knot in his stomach. He did not find it reassuring to be standing three feet away from a nuclear weapon that may be about to detonate.

"Exactly what do you mean by armed, Blake?" Sykes asked quietly. "Do you mean that it's ready to go off?" Tower admired Sykes's coolness. He might be scared to death, but if he was, it did not show.

Blake shook his head. "No, sir. You have to be very careful with nuclear weapons. Most of ours have what we call an arming, fuzing and firing system. When the weapon is not armed, it is basically inert and safe to handle and transport. In theory, it's impossible for the weapon to detonate when it's not armed. Fuzing is the next step, when certain preset conditions are met, all safety features are disabled, and the weapon is ready to be fired. The firing command is the final step. It's sent by the fuze when something initiates fuze action. That can be done in many different ways—contact, time, pressure. That is determined by the fuze designer. This weapon is definitely armed, and it may be fuzed. There could be a timer counting down to a preset detonation time. I would have to open it up to determine that."

"What happens if it goes off?"

Blake flashed his old smile. "We won't have a worry in the world. The plane and anyone on it will literally be blown to atoms. I can't be sure of the exact yield, but I estimate that this half of the airport will be destroyed or severely damaged. I recommend that the entire airport be evacuated, if that's possible."

Sykes thought long and hard. "What can we do about it? Can we get it out of here, move it to a safe area, or disable or disarm it?"

It was Blake's turn to think long and hard. "I'm afraid this is a bad situation, General," he said finally. "I think we've been outmaneuvered from start to finish. I think this whole thing, Saada Almori's tip-off, Congresswoman Kline and the hijacking itself, was just a diversion to get the weapon here to Cairo International. If they had tried to send it on a military aircraft from the Sudan, it would probably have been detected and engaged by the Egyptian air-defense system. The odds are it would have been shot down. This way, we were expecting a hijacking, and our first priority was to rescue the hostages. So the plane was cleared to land here without any question. That's all

they wanted. They didn't give a damn about anything else—
they just wanted to be sure their bomb got here.''

Sykes nodded. As usual, what Blake said made sense to him.
"You're probably right, Sergeant, but whether that was their
plan or not, how does it change anything? The bomb is here,
and we've got to deal with it.''

"If I'm right, it means the bomb is going to be extremely
difficult to deal with. I've examined it carefully from the outside. I don't see any signs that it can be detonated by an external command. There are no wires or antennae to receive a
command, and we found no control devices on the bodies of
the hijackers. That weapon was set to follow a precise sequence of events before it was loaded on the 707 at Khartoum.
No, all signs are that the weapon is self-contained. It has a
programmed set of instructions, and it's sitting there, following them to the letter.''

Sykes saw one big problem with that. "What about the hijackers? If they had no control over the bomb, then they were
just sitting there on top of it, waiting for it to go off. They
didn't stand a chance in hell. They were certain to be killed.''

"You're right, General," Tower said softly, "but they didn't
care. They were holy martyrs. They wanted to die for their
faith. Remember, Colonel Khier said they seemed peaceful,
almost calm, when he talked to them. You can see why. Once
they landed here with the bomb, they had accomplished their
mission. When they'd done that, they were ready to die. They
thought they were going straight to paradise.''

"And we have to consider this, General," Blake said somberly. "We're up against some very intelligent people. They
wouldn't want to take the chance we would succeed in rescuing
hostages, find the weapon and disarm it before it went off. They
will have booby-trapped the bomb every way they can think of,
and there won't be anti-intrusion devices designed just to kill
me. If I make a mistake, the weapon will detonate.''

"Is there anything else we can do? Can you rig some charges
of your own and damage the damn thing so that it can't go nuclear?''

Blake shook his head. "No, we don't want to try that because of the way nuclear weapons work. Mechanically they are

extremely complex, but the basic principles are simple. They all use fissionable material, uranium 235 or plutonium 239. Either one can only exist in pieces below a certain weight called the critical mass. Above the critical mass, you're going to have nuclear fission and a nuclear explosion. A nuclear warhead has two or more subcritical masses. When the weapon is fired, conventional high-explosive charges drive them together. For a fraction of a second, you have one critical mass, then a nuclear explosion. If I explode charges on the outside of the weapon, they will set off the explosives in the bomb, and we'll have a nuclear detonation. The precise timing may be disrupted. If that happens, the bomb will go low order. That means the power of the explosion will be less than the design level, but it will still be a nuclear explosion, equal to several thousand tons of TNT."

"How much time do we have?"

"There's no way to tell, but I would guess it's set to go a few minutes after the secretary of state arrives. If his plane's on schedule, that's less than an hour from now."

Sykes resisted the temptation to swear. They were damned if they did and damned if they didn't, but there was really only one choice. They could divert the secretary's plane, but there were thousands of people in the airport. There was no way they could be evacuated in an hour.

"I don't like it, Blake, but I think we have to try to disarm it. Are you willing to give it a try?"

Blake flashed his old grin. "Yes, sir, somebody has to do it, and I guess I'm somebody."

Sykes felt a quiet sense of pride. One of the reasons he had stayed in the Army for twenty-five years was to serve with men like Blake. "All right, then, let's go. Do you need anything? Any help or special equipment?"

Blake's smile broadened, and he smiled wickedly at Tower as he spoke. "I've got all the equipment I need, General, but I will need one man to help me, and it would be extremely helpful if that man could read Arabic."

Tower swallowed hard. The last place in the world he wanted to be was next to an atomic bomb that might be about to explode, but he had never been the kind of officer who abandoned his men when they were in danger. He was not about to start now.

He tried to match Blake's grin. "I've always wanted to see the insides of an atomic bomb. I volunteer."

"One more thing, General," Blake said quietly. "I can't wait, but I recommend you move all our people out of the hangar and get them as far away as possible. Get them at least five miles away if you can. They ought to be fairly safe at that distance."

There was nothing more to be decided. It was time to do it. Sykes was proud of them both, and he would have liked to have said something splendid, ringing words that would inspire them, but he was not very good at making speeches. "I'll take care of it. Good luck" was all he said as he turned and left Blake and Tower alone with the dull gray cylinder.

Blake stared at the bomb for a few seconds, then smiled at Tower. "Well, let's get started, Captain. It's not going to get any easier. I've connected the phone line to the SATCOM in the hangar. Anything we say will be transmitted and recorded. We're probably going to encounter these weapons again. I will describe everything I do before I do it, and if I make a mistake, they will need to know what I did wrong."

Tower nodded. Like most of Blake's ideas, it was perfectly logical, but Tower did not find it very comforting.

Blake set his phone headset for continuous transmission and began to speak. His voice changed. He spoke in precise, emotionless tones, like a professor lecturing a class on some obscure point of physics.

"I am Master Sergeant Robert A. Blake, United States Army. Captain David Tower is assisting me. I am about to attempt to disarm the nuclear weapon discovered aboard Air Zimbabwe flight four at Cairo International Airport. From the outside, the weapon appears to be identical to the one captured by Omega Force in the Sudan. External scans indicate electrical activity and the presence of radioactive material inside the weapon case. I am proceeding on the assumption that this is a live nuclear weapon and that it is armed.

"There is an access panel approximately twelve inches long and eight inches high in the top of the weapon's case. I will now attempt to open this panel. I am now checking the panel and the surrounding area with a multimeter. I do not detect any signs of electrical activity. The panel is held in place by ten screws. I will now start to remove the screws.''

Blake took a long-handled screwdriver. Tower found himself holding his breath as Blake began to remove the screws, one by one.

"I have removed the retaining screws. The panel appears to be designed to be lifted straight upward. I am now lifting the panel approximately one quarter of an inch. I am now examining the underside of the panel and the structure below it. I do not see any device attached to the panel or any wires running from it. I am lifting off the panel now."

He lifted the panel. Nothing happened, and Tower took a deep breath. Blake shone a flashlight inside the weapon case. The inside of the case was filled with complex objects, metal tubes and spheres, black boxes and electrical wires and cables running everywhere like an electronic spiderweb.

Tower had no idea what any of it was. He hoped to God Blake did. "Can you tell what we're up against?" he asked quickly.

"Disturbance."

Tower looked blank.

Blake smiled. "It's the first thing you learn when you take a bomb-disarming course. There are only three ways to detonate a bomb. There are thousands of variations, but there are only remote control, timed control or disturbance. We can rule out remote control, and a timer can only fire the weapon at a preset time. That's no good against an attempt to disarm it. What we're up against is devices that sense changes when we do something, motion detection, making or breaking an electrical circuit, or a simple mechanical thing, pushing or pulling on something, or breaking a trip wire. There can be more than one, and any one can fire the bomb. I've got to find them all and neutralize them without setting one off."

Blake resumed his examination. Everything seemed to be taking him forever. Tower resisted the temptation to tell him he must hurry. Distracting Blake or making him nervous could be a quick way of committing suicide.

At last Blake nodded and spoke into his headset again. "I have examined the interior of the weapon. It is basically the same as the weapon captured in the Sudan, but a number of small components appear to have been added. All are connected to the arming, fuzing and firing system assembly. I will now attempt to disarm the weapon, proceeding in what appears to be a logical sequence."

Tower noticed that Blake was sweating. For that matter, he was, too. The 707's designers had not wasted air-conditioning on the baggage compartment, but the heat was not the only reason. Tower wondered if he would feel anything if the bomb went off or if he would simply cease to exist so fast that he would never know it had happened.

"The first component is an ambient-pressure-sensing switch. It has been activated. It sensed the drop in air pressure after the plane took off and armed the weapon. I am now disconnecting this switch. The next component is a motion sensor. It will activate if the bomb is moved or tipped. It is connected to the arming, fuzing and firing assembly. I do not detect any power in the wires. I am cutting them now."

Tower discovered he had been holding his breath again. But they were still there, so Blake must have been right.

"I now have access to the arming, fuzing and firing assembly. I will examine it now."

Blake leaned forward and delicately touched the black box he called the arming, fuzing and firing assembly with the two slender probes from his multimeter. He looked at the small red letters and numbers on the meters display and nodded to himself.

"I detect steady electrical activity, including a regular pulse at precise, one-second intervals. I conclude that this is from the timing device. It is activated and is counting down toward detonation."

Blake took a small mirror mounted on a plastic shaft from his tool kit and carefully scanned the black box, top, bottom and sides. Tower saw a dim, flickering, red light reflected in the mirror.

"There is a four-digit visual display," Blake continued coolly. "It reads 7:20 and is changing at one-second intervals. I conclude that the bomb will detonate in approximately seven minutes and twenty seconds.''

Tower stared at the flickering red numbers as they changed second by second, eighteen, seventeen, sixteen. The effect was almost hypnotic, but at the same time it was coldly terrifying. His nerves screamed at him to run or hide, but there was no place to hide and no time to run far enough away to be safe if the damned thing detonated.

''I do not see any other devices connected to the arming, fuzing and firing assembly, but there may be anti-intrusion devices inside it. There is a high-voltage cable leading from the assembly. I am tracing it now. It connects to the closed end of a large, metallic, tubular device. From disassembly of the previous weapon, I know that this is a gun-type weapon, a relatively primitive and inefficient design similar to the weapon used at Hiroshima. My next action will be based on that.

''The gun contains a subcritical mass. When the firing command is given, the gun fires this mass into the stationary target mass, critical mass is achieved, and a nuclear explosion occurs. I intend to prevent the gun from firing. The cable leading from the arming, fuzing and firing assembly to the gun is a high-voltage cable, so the detonators which fire the conventional explosives in the gun must be electrical. I assume that the system is set to fire if the cable is disturbed. This will happen very rapidly, but not instantaneously. I intend to sever the cable before the high-voltage pulse can be generated and reach the detonators in the gun. I cannot use a mechanical device. Human reflexes are too slow. I intend to use a flexible, linear-shaped charge to cut the cable.''

Tower shuddered. Was Blake really going to set off an explosive charge inside a nuclear weapon? Somehow that did not seem like a very good idea to Tower at all.

Blake noticed the look on Tower's face and smiled again. ''I realize that there is a certain amount of risk in this approach, but I believe it is justifiable. The detonating velocity of the FLSC is over twenty thousand feet per second. It should cut the cable before the firing pulse can reach the detonators. The conventional explosives in the gun assembly will be of a highly insensitive, shock-resistant type for safety during weapon transportation and handling. There is a low probability that they will detonate.''

Blake clicked off his phone headset. He looked at Tower inquiringly. ''Is that all right with you, Captain? I think the chances are seventy or eighty percent it will work. If not, it will be a low-order detonation. Damage to the airport will be reduced significantly, and a lot less people will be killed. What do you say?''

Tower thought hard. If he said yes, he was betting his life on Blake's skill and knowledge, but what the hell, he had done that when he volunteered to stay. ''All right, let's do it!''

Blake clicked his headset on and drew a short length of FLSC from his tool kit. Quickly but carefully he began to wind it around the firing cable. ''I am now installing the FLSC. I am now attaching the detonators. Estimate ready to fire in thirty seconds.''

Tower stared, fascinated, at the small red numbers: three-thirty, twenty-nine, twenty-eight. He had known he was risking his life when he volunteered for Omega Force, but he had never thought it might end like this, a cold, impersonal struggle with a deadly machine in the guts of a grounded airliner. He glanced at Blake as he coolly attached his firing wires to either end of the FLSC. If this was the end, he was in damned good company.

Blake connected the other ends of his firing wires to his miniature blasting machine.

Tower thought briefly of swearing or praying, but he had no time for either.

''I am now going to fire the FLSC. Three, two, one, fire!''

Tower heard a sharp cracking noise and saw a yellow flash as the FLSC fired. The case of the weapon vibrated, blue-white sparks flickered briefly, and the acrid smell of burnt explosives and ozone filled the air. Then there was a deafening silence, and he glanced at Blake. He was beaming, feeling the tremendous high that came from successfully disarming a big bomb and knowing you were still alive.

''The weapon is successfully disarmed. Send in the removal crew,'' Blake said.

Tower felt a great wave of elation. He clapped Blake on the shoulder. "Good work! Damned good work. I'm going to put you in for a medal. If there's anything else I can do for you, just let me know."

Blake flashed his old grin. "Thanks, Captain, I appreciate that. There *is* one thing. Do you suppose they have a bottle of Jack Daniel's at this airport? I could sure as hell use a drink!"

## 17

Tower slipped quietly into the main terminal waiting area. The scene resembled a three-ring circus, with people from the media clustered around the dazed passengers from the hijacked 707 like sharks around a school of fish. Tower had changed from his black raid suit to his normal battle dress uniform. The area swarmed with Egyptian security police and heavily armed Egyptian soldiers, and no one paid any attention to him. He appeared to be just another soldier in a camouflage uniform.

A group of reporters were gathered around Colonel Khier. Tower smiled at Khier as the colonel spoke earnestly into the cameras. "An outstanding example of American-Egyptian co-operation. The joint assault force secured the aircraft, neutralized the terrorists and rescued the majority of the hostages. It is unfortunate that the terrorists killed three passengers and the flight crew. However, the operation must be regarded as a complete success."

The reporters began to shout questions, and Tower was glad Khier had to deal with them. Tower would rather deal with terrorists. At least he was allowed to shoot them.

Another group of reporters was clustered around Congresswoman Kline. She looked pale and shaken in her blood-spattered white silk suit. Amanda Stuart was also standing at the edge of the group, still wearing her dark green dress. The tall redhead's face was flushed and angry. Vera Kline glared at Tower as he joined the group. That was strange. She could not identify Tower as part of the assault group, which was just as well. Omega Force officially didn't exist, and U.S. policy prohibited the identification and photography of members of hostage-rescue teams. Perhaps Ms. Kline simply did not like Green Berets.

"It was horrible, horrible! Like some awful nightmare! There were explosions, and then these men in black burst into the plane! There was no attempt to negotiate. They simply started shooting left and right! My assistant was killed at my side. This is her blood on my suit! It was all unnecessary...nobody had to die! The whole situation could have been resolved peacefully. There will be a congressional investigation when I get back to Washington. The irresponsible macho militarists responsible for this will be made to pay!"

Tower took Amanda's hand and pulled her away. Amanda was so angry she was shaking. "That goddamned ungrateful bitch! That..."

Tower was amazed. Her command of the English language was superb, and she had learned some interesting words during her military career. Tower shrugged. He didn't like what Vera Kline had said, but he was a soldier. Gratitude had never been part of the contract.

Then they proceeded to attend a meeting General Sykes had called in the airport security office. Tower looked around as they entered the office. Sykes, Cray and Dr. Kaye were sitting at a conference table, and Sykes motioned for them to be seated.

"Your team did an excellent job, Tower," Kaye said, "and I intend to say so in my report. Now that we are all here, let's plan our next move."

"Before we do that, Doctor," Tower said quickly, "I'd like to say that Miriam Mboro did a hell of a good job on the plane. If it hadn't been for her, Congresswoman Kline would have been killed."

"I'm not sure that that would have been any great loss," Kaye said coldly, "but Miriam did do an excellent job. I will mention that in my report."

"Where is Miriam?" Tower asked. "I'd like to tell her that personally."

"Miriam is busy at the moment, Captain. She is keeping an eye on Saada Almori."

Kaye had that look that so many Intelligence people seemed to have—*I know something you don't know and you probably aren't cleared to find out.* Tower had always found that attitude extremely annoying, but he wanted an answer. "All right, Doctor, where is Saada Almori?"

Kaye glanced at his watch. "At the moment she is enjoying an excellent view of the Nile. She is on board Egyptair flight twenty-six flying south to Luxor."

Tower was stunned. "You mean she just walked out of here and hopped on an airplane? Why the hell didn't somebody stop her?"

"No one had any reason to stop her. She's a respectable journalist, just saved from a desperate situation by heroic American-Egyptian special forces. She was escorted to the central terminal area with the other people from the 707. She slipped away as soon as she could, made a phone call and then bought a ticket to Luxor under the name of Tamar Rosen."

"You mean you let her escape?"

"Of course we did, Tower. Credit us with some intelligence! Miss Almori is a very clever young woman, but not quite as clever as she thinks. At the moment she is of no particular importance, but her friends are, and she can lead us to them. We have two people on the plane watching her and two others who will follow her at Luxor. She has reserved a car at the airport there, and that car will have some special equipment installed before she arrives. We will be able to follow her anywhere, day or night."

Amanda Stuart frowned. Egyptian geography was not her strong suit. "Where is Luxor? Is there anything important there, anything that might be a terrorist target?"

"Luxor is approximately three hundred miles to the south of Cairo on the Nile. It is a city of ninety thousand people. As to what is there, Luxor is one of the biggest tourist attractions in Egypt. It is located on the site of the ancient capital city of Thebes. Some of the most famous and best preserved temples and tombs are there."

Tower was puzzled. That was all very interesting, but he didn't think Saada Almori had developed a sudden passion for ancient Egyptian tombs. "Why would she go there, Doctor?"

"Luxor's airport is a very busy place, swarming with tourists at this time of year. She won't attract any attention there. She will look like just one more tourist in the crowd. I think there is also another reason. Luxor is the last city with a major airport north of Aswan. The city of Aswan and the dam itself are about one hundred twenty-five miles to the south. At the moment Aswan is swarming with Egyptian troops and security police. I don't think that Miss Almori's friends are there, but they must be within striking distance. Almost certainly they're somewhere between Luxor and Aswan, and I'm sure she knows where.''

Kaye paused for a moment and stared around the room. ''I have a message from Washington. They are extremely pleased with what we have done so far. That is gratifying, but it will mean absolutely nothing if the terrorists destroy the Aswan Dam. Our experts confirm what Sergeant Blake said. It will be a catastrophe of immense proportions. Millions of people will die, and we must prevent that at all costs. You gentlemen are the military experts. What are your recommendations?''

Sykes thought for a moment while he stared at a map of Egypt on the wall. ''The best way is to stop them before they get started. If Miriam can locate their base, we should raid it immediately and destroy them before they can move the weapons. I recommend we move Omega Force to the south immediately to be ready to do that. If they get their attack under way before we can hit them, that's a harder nut to crack. We have to try and think how they'll attempt it. Blake says the weapon will have to be detonated very close to the dam—ideally in direct contact with it. I don't think they'll try bringing it in on the ground. They'd have to use a truck to move something that heavy. Khier tells me there's only one road that goes to the dam, and it's crawling with Egyptian soldiers who have orders to shoot first and ask questions later. That leaves a boat on the river or some kind of low-flying aircraft, probably at night. I'm not sure I see anything we can do about that.''

Amanda Stuart had been sitting quietly. She was not sure whether Kaye included her in his ''you gentlemen,'' but she didn't care. She was not there because of her good looks or her charming personality. She was a highly competent professional officer, and this was in her area of expertise.

''Excuse me, General, but I think there's a lot we can do about it. I recommend we use our helicopter. Remember, it's a special-ops MH-60K, not an ordinary Blackhawk. Its night-vision equipment is ten years ahead of anything the Egyptians have, and it's got the external store-support system installed. With the ESSS, I can carry a full load of rocket pods and missiles. I can blow hell out of any boat, and I'll have something to say to a helicopter or even a light plane."

Sykes smiled. He liked junior officers who could think and show initiative.

"That's good thinking, Stuart, we'll do that. Any other ideas? All right, then, let's do it. Cray, contact the Air Force and set up some C-130s to take us south. Stuart, check out the Blackhawk and get ready to go. Tower, you go with Captain Stuart. Ask Colonel Khier to accompany you and clear things with the Egyptian commander in the Aswan area. Let's get moving. Now!"

Cray looked at his officers and grinned. "You heard the man. Let's go!"

SAADA ALMORI DROVE slowly down the bumpy dirt road. She was completely miserable. It was ten degrees hotter here in the south, well over a hundred degrees, and the air-conditioning on the Ford Escort she had rented in Luxor was not working. Her blue dress was soaked with sweat, and her long black hair was a filthy mess. Saada snarled and condemned the designer of the air conditioner to the hottest fires of hell. She told herself that she was a soldier of the Arab Nation and soldiers must suffer and make sacrifices, but that didn't make her feel any better.

She slowed down as she approached a cluster of dusty buildings. Tawfiq would have guards posted, even if she couldn't see them. It would not do to be shot to death by a friendly but nervous sentry. A man came out of the largest building and casually signaled Saada to stop. He didn't appear to be armed, but she had no doubt that several men were staring at her over the sights of their AK-47s. She got out of the car slowly, careful to keep her hands away from her purse. She relaxed when she saw the man's face clearly. She could not remember his name, but he was one of Tawfiq's sergeants. Quickly she asked him to take her to Major Tawfiq. He nodded and motioned for Saada to follow him into the building.

The inside of the building was one large room. It was a little cooler, and she took off her sunglasses and looked around. Jamal Tawfiq was sitting at a small wooden table, studying a map and some photographs. At Saada's approach he looked up, smiled and greeted her formally. "God is great! Peace be upon you, Saada."

"Peace and God's blessing be upon you, Jamal," Saada replied politely. She smiled to herself. She had not been certain how Tawfiq would react when he saw her. He might blame her if the mission in Cairo had failed. That would not be fair, but if a scapegoat were needed, she was the obvious choice. But Tawfiq did not seem to be angry. He appeared to be genuinely glad to see her as he motioned to her to be seated.

"You do not look as if you have had an easy time, Saada. Have some tea. Tell me, what happened to you in Cairo?"

"I made contact with the CIA as we had planned. They took me to that son of Satan, Kaye, and the leaders of their damned Omega Force. I told them the cover story, that the Aswan Dam was our target, and I told them that the hijacking would occur, to convince them I was telling the truth. It worked well, up to a point. When they learned that the airliner had been hijacked with an American Congresswoman on board, they believed me.

"They decided to send their Omega Force to the airport as we thought they would. Kaye insisted I go along. I am not sure why, perhaps it was a test. However, I said nothing—I went."

She paused and stared at Tawfiq. "I expected to be killed when the bomb exploded, but that did not matter. I am as willing to die for our cause as any man."

Tawfiq nodded. He believed her.

"Bashir's group captured the airliner without incident, and it landed at Cairo International Airport. Kaye insisted I go on board in my role as a journalist. I am not sure why. Perhaps so that he could get the Mboro woman on board for some reason I do not understand. We went and were interviewing Bashir and his hostages. Suddenly the plane was stormed. The attackers were men dressed in black and they carried unusual weapons. I am sure it was Omega Force, may they burn in hell! Our people fought bravely, but they were killed. There was a great deal of confusion after the attack. They ordered the passengers to leave the plane, and I went with them. When we reached the main terminal I slipped away. I felt you must know what had happened, so I flew to Luxor. The rest you know. But tell me, I have heard nothing. Did our bomb explode?"

"I am afraid not. It is long past the time it was set to go off, and we have heard nothing. I do not believe the Egyptians could have kept it a secret. Somehow the sons of Satan must have found our bomb and disarmed it."

Saada had been afraid of this, but that did not make it easier for her to accept. She resisted the temptation to swear or cry. She would be ashamed if she did either in front of Tawfiq. "So, they have won again," she said bitterly.

"Perhaps not," Tawfiq said quietly. "We still have one weapon left. Kawash is checking it out now. If God is willing, we will strike them a blow they will never forget."

Despite her fatigue and disappointment, Saada felt a thrill of hope. Tawfiq had lived only for revenge since his family had died in the bombing of Iraq. He was not brilliant, but he was totally dedicated to the cause, and he was a superb soldier. If he thought they still might win, there must be a chance that they could.

"God is great! What is the target?"

Tawfiq smiled and handed her a photograph. It was not a pleasant smile. "The dam," he said simply.

"The dam? But the Aswan Dam was never a real target? That was only a lie to deceive them."

"That was what the colonel wished you to believe, Saada. It was not that he did not trust you, but you were going into the hands of the enemy. They might have tortured you. You are a strong woman, but in the end you would have told them everything you knew. It was best that you believed the dam was not a target. They could not make you tell what you did not know."

Saada was stunned. "The devastation will be awful! It may be far worse than we think. Their man, Blake, is a weapons expert. He said that if the dam is destroyed, there will not be a flood but a tidal wave three hundred feet high! Millions of Egyptians will die. Should we do such a thing?"

Tawfiq shrugged. "The Egyptians are a corrupt people, not true Arabs, and they deserve to be punished. They betrayed us. They sent more troops to fight against us in Kuwait than any other country except the United States. And I have my orders. I will attack. What happens after we destroy the dam is in God's hands, not mine."

Saada's doubts vanished. Tawfiq was right. He was a fanatic, but so was she. "God is great! Let us do it! I will go with you."

"You are a brave woman, Saada, but you are not a helicopter pilot or a weapons expert. Those of us who go are not likely to come back. You must live to carry on our work if we fail."

He paused for a moment and looked at his map. "This American, Blake, may be right. Take your car and get as far away from the Nile as you can."

He paused for a moment and smiled. "Go with God, Saada. I do not think we will meet again."

TWELVE HUNDRED YARDS away Miriam Mboro was sweating in her desert camouflage smock. She crawled carefully to the top of a small ridge and took out her field glasses, then scanned the small group of buildings slowly. Good, her tracker had not lied. The white Ford Escort that Saada Almori had rented was parked near the largest building. She searched the surrounding area carefully. The defenses were well camouflaged, but they were there. She could see at least two machine guns well dug in, and there were probably more. Miriam was brave, but she was not a fool. This was far more than she could handle. She turned on her radio.

"Eagle, this is Hawk. The songbird is in her nest. Better come loaded for bear—she has a lot of friends."

18

The four Air Force C-130s flew steadily southward, following the Nile. Cray checked his watch. Everything was taking longer than it should. It had taken time to get the C-130s to Cairo International, time to load Omega Force's men and equipment and still more time to get the Egyptian air-defense command clearance to fly planes into the sensitive Aswan area. He wanted to be in Aswan before dark so that he could coordinate with the local Egyptian commanders. It looked as if they would make it, but not by much. But worrying was not going to make the C-130 go any faster, he decided, and spread out his maps on a folding aluminum table and began to commit the Aswan area to memory.

He caught a flicker of motion out of the corner of his eye. General Sykes was coming slowly down the aisle. He seemed to be in no hurry, stopping now and then to speak briefly with some of the men he knew. He was checking morale, of course, but he genuinely cared about the men under his command. Cray admired Sykes. He thought he was the best general officer he knew. He hoped he could do as well when he was a general. Then Cray smiled at himself. He was not a West Pointer, and he had spent most of his career in the Army in exotic units doing strange things, not the traditional things Army brass preferred. He would be lucky if he made colonel before he retired!

Dr. Kaye was following Sykes closely. In his wrinkled dark gray suit, he looked singularly out of place in the aluminum and nylon webbing of the cargo compartment. Sykes and Kaye slipped into the folding web seats on either side of Cray and looked at his map.

"Any change in the situation?" Cray asked.

"Not much," Syke replied. "We got another message from Miriam Mboro. Saada Almori got back in her car and drove north toward Luxor. She went by herself, and nothing was loaded in her car. Miriam decided to continue to keep the place Saada visited under surveillance, but one of the other CIA people picked up the tail. Halfway to Luxor she turned off at a place called Idfu and headed for the Red Sea coast. Nobody knows why, but I don't think it matters. Whoever she went to see is still there."

Cray pointed at the map. "From what Miriam says, she is here, about ten miles north of Kom Ombo. That's a farming town on the Nile. There's nothing important there that I can see, but it's only fifty miles from the dam, and it's outside the Aswan security area. I think it's their base."

"Assuming you are right, gentlemen, just what do you propose to do about it?" Kaye inquired.

Cray scowled. That was not an easy question. "We don't have enough information to make a decent plan, Doctor. All we really know is that Saada Almori went there, and Miriam says the place is heavily guarded. We don't know who's there or if the nuclear weapons are there. Do you think Miriam could get more information?"

Kaye shook his head. "I think that would be most unwise. Miriam will try if we ask her. She is much too venturesome for her own good. But she would have to get inside the buildings to find out more. If she tries that during daylight, the odds are she will be detected. If she is killed or captured, that will alert the terrorists."

Cray had to agree. Kaye spoke with all the warmth and humanity of a chess master discussing the possible loss of a pawn, but he was right. Any attempt to reconnoiter the area on foot in broad daylight would not be brave; it would be suicidal. He looked at his map again. "Then it looks like the best plan is to go on to Aswan, land there and wait for dark. If Colonel Khier can get us some Egyptian military helicopters, we can send in a reconnaissance team or conduct a raid. What do you think General?"

Sykes looked at the map and nodded. "That sounds good to me, if—"

He stopped and looked up. An Air Force sergeant was coming rapidly down the aisle. The sergeant threw Sykes a quick salute. "Excuse me, sir, there's a radio message for you on tactical channel three, correct frequency and using call sign Hawk. She says it's extremely urgent."

Sykes didn't waste time asking questions. He followed the sergeant toward the C-130's nose, motioning to Cray and Dr. Kaye to follow him. They moved to the front of the cargo compartment and stepped up onto the flight deck. The systems engineer was manning the radio. He flicked a switch, and Miriam Mboro's voice came from the speaker.

Miriam was not happy. "Eagle, this is Hawk. What the hell is going on? Two helicopters are circling the area at low altitude. They look like Alouette IIs, and they have Egyptian military markings. Do you have an operation under way you haven't told me about? If so, what the hell do you want me to do?"

Sykes stared hard at Kaye. He would not have put it past Kaye to be doing all sorts of things without telling them, but Kaye looked surprised and shook his head. He either knew nothing or he was a remarkably good actor.

Sykes spoke quickly into the microphone. "Hawk, this is Eagle. Negative! I say again, negative! We know of no operation under way in your area. Have they seen you?"

"I don't believe so, Eagle. They are continuing to circle the area, but I'm fairly well concealed. What are your instructions?"

"Remain under cover. Maintain surveillance. Report any change in the situation immediately. Do you understand?"

"Roger, Eagle, understood. Hawk out."

Kaye looked suspicious. "Could the Egyptians be up to something? I am not sure we can trust them completely."

Sykes wondered if there was anyone in the world Kaye trusted completely. "Damned if I know, Doctor, but I doubt it. They need our support badly. I don't see what they could hope to gain by double-crossing us."

"It doesn't have to be the Egyptian government," Cray said. "We know there's an Egyptian fundamentalist movement. Some of them may be in the military. Maybe some of them are helping the terrorists."

Miriam Mboro's voice suddenly crackled in the speaker. "Eagle, both helicopters have landed near the main building. Two men in military uniforms have gotten out and are entering the building."

"Roger, Hawk. Maintain surveillance."

"What is an Alouette II, Major?" Kaye asked quickly. "What are its capabilities?"

"It's a light utility helicopter. Some of them are armed, but they're mostly used in the light transport role."

"Could one of them carry one of the terrorist's nuclear weapons?"

Cray thought for a second. "I don't remember the specifications, but they have a crew of two and can carry up to six passengers. Blake says their weapons weigh about four hundred pounds. Sure, they could do it!"

"Damn it, that's it!" Sykes snapped. "They can go in low at night and place the weapons right against the dam!"

Kaye looked doubtful. "Surely the Egyptians must have defenses, General! Can't they shoot them down?"

"I don't think so. Khier told me the Egyptians have Soviet SAM-6 air-defense missiles to protect the dam. They're not bad, but they're ineffective against targets flying below two hundred feet. A good helicopter pilot can go in at a hundred. They'll never lay a finger on them!"

"Then there is only one thing to do, gentlemen," Kaye said quickly. "We cannot wait. This may be our last chance. How is up to you, but we must attack immediately!"

CRAY WAITED TENSELY as the C-130's pilot throttled back and started down. The past fifteen minutes had been a nightmare of organized confusion as his men struggled into their chutes, checked their equipment and prepared to jump. He didn't like the plan. A daylight attack without reconnaissance or rehearsal could be a recipe for disaster. Unfortunately he had no choice. He had rejected a flyover. Surprise was critical. Seeing even one aircraft with American markings would be enough to alert the enemy. He had to depend on Miriam Mboro's description of the target area. Although Cray trusted Miriam, she was not a trained soldier. She might have missed some critical detail. Well, he expected he would find out when he hit the ground.

General Sykes came down the aisle, and Cray looked at him inquiringly.

"Any luck, General?"

Sykes shook his head. "Not a damned bit! I must have talked to half a dozen different headquarters, but I can't get anybody to move fast. Hell, we'll probably get an armored division and a wing of fighters next Sunday, but we're on our own for the next hour or two!"

Cray was not happy, but he was not surprised. Security was a two-edged sword. To anyone who didn't know the real situation, a sudden request for support from an obscure unit was not likely to get first priority no matter what Sykes said. Special operations are not all fun and games.

"No use waiting, then, General. We'd better go. We're running out of time!"

"It's your call, Major. What's your plan?"

"Drop as close as we can and hit them with everything we've got as fast as we can. I don't want to try and jump directly on the objective. There's no cover, and Miriam says there are several dug-in machine guns. They could cut us to pieces while we're landing. I thought about surrounding the place, but we just don't have enough men for that. Miriam says there are some fences and dry irrigation ditches about four hundred yards to the west, along the approach road. That'll give us some cover. I'll put the landing zone just to the west of there. First and Third platoons attack as soon as we can get them organized. Second Platoon is the reserve. The support group is with them. They will have the heavy weapons. Blake's in charge of that."

Sykes saw nothing to criticize. It was a simple and straightforward plan. Nothing fancy, but that kind of plan was often best. He could see one possible problem. "Everything is coming in from the west. The east side isn't covered. Suppose they all bug out that way?"

"There's no road and no place for them to go except out into the desert. If they try that, they'll die out there even if we don't hunt them down."

"All right, it sounds good. Let's do it!"

Cray felt the tension start to build as he stood up and gave a hand signal to Sergeant Hall. He would act as the jump master. Hall had made more jumps than anyone else in Omega Force, and he kept his head if things got bad.

The steady whine of the C-130's four turbo prop engines changed as the pilot throttled back and leveled off. Sergeant Hall came slowly down the aisle. "Get ready!" Hall's voice rang through the troop compartment, loud and clear over the whine of the plane's engines. Cray felt a cold knot in his stomach. He was not fond of parachute jumping, but he did it because it was part of his job.

All eyes were on Hall now. He gestured upward with both hands.

"Jump party! Stand...up!"

The assault team heaved themselves to their feet, each man fighting the drag of the one hundred ten pounds of his two parachutes, weapons and combat equipment. Cray could feel the shoulder straps of his parachute harness cutting into his shoulders.

"Check equipment!" Hall shouted.

Cray checked his equipment and the equipment of the man to his right. The four-minute-warning light was on. Each man gave the thumbs-up signal. Hall nodded and pointed toward the tail door.

Slowly and carefully they moved toward the aft door. They would jump at three-second intervals. Cray would be one of the first men out. Two-minute warning. They were standing in two long lines, facing aft toward the C-130's tail door. The red warning lights came on, and the tail door was lowered and locked open in the horizontal position. Cray heard the high-pitched whine of hydraulic motors and the howl of the outside air rushing by as he stared out the door. All he could see was sand flashing by below while the C-130 headed east at one hundred twenty knots and four hundred feet.

One-minute warning. Cray looked back and made a thumbs-up gesture to his team. Each man returned the gesture with his own thumbs-up signal. No one was having equipment problems. They were all ready to go.

The thirty-second-warning light came on, and there was a sudden change in the roar of the engines as the Air Force pilot throttled back. He was holding the C-130 as close to its stalling speed as he could to reduce the strength of the airflow around the big plane's fuselage. When he was satisfied, he would push the ten-second-warning light. The big plane began to shake and vibrate as its speed dropped to within a few knots of stalling. The ten-second-warning light came on.

"Standby!" Hall shouted. That was the last warning before the jump. Cray felt a surge of adrenaline flood his body. There was nothing left for him to do now but worry. It was a simple jump, no oxygen masks or special equipment, but forty-five men had to clear the plane in sixty seconds. Something could always go wrong. But there was no more time for thinking, the go light was on.

Cray heard Hall screaming, "Go! Go! Go!" Suddenly the men ahead of him were moving. Cray took four quick strides along the ramp and dived through the open door. Instantly he was falling. It was like jumping into a hurricane. He waited tensely for the tug of his nylon static line as it opened his main chute. When it came, it was a bone-jarring jolt. Cray felt an immense surge of relief. His chute was open! He looked up quickly. Men were pouring out of the C-130s. The sky was full of parachutes.

He looked down. Miriam had done a good job of describing the area. As far as Cray could tell, they were in the right place. Now, if they could only get down and get organized before the enemy could react. But no such luck. Cray heard the rattle of a machine gun opening fire, then another and another. Green tracers streaked upward, clawing at him and his men. Every weapon seemed to be firing straight at him. He knew that only a lucky shot could hit falling parachutists; the real danger would come when they hit the ground. Somehow that didn't make him feel better.

Drops from four hundred feet did not take long. It was already time to think about landing. At one hundred feet, Cray pulled the release and felt his equipment rucksack drop away to dangle below him. The ground came rushing up, and he hit and rolled to break his fall. He pulled his quick-release handles and slipped out of his parachute harness. Quickly he reached for the nylon weapons case under his left arm and pulled out his rifle. He stayed low. He could hear the steady crackle of machine guns as the defenders continued to fire. Cover! He needed cover! The irrigation ditch was twenty feet away. Instantly, instinctively, Cray stayed down and rolled for the ditch. He landed with a thump. The ditch was dry and dusty, but he didn't care. It seemed like the most beautiful place in the world as he heard steel-jacketed machine-gun bullets tear into the ground above him.

He looked to the left and right. His men were piling into the ditch. Cray heard the snarling crackle of M-16A2 rifles and SAW light machine guns as they opened up. He risked a quick look toward the buildings. The light was fading, but he could still see clearly. There were half a dozen bodies in camouflage uniforms sprawled on the ground, caught in the deadly cross fire as they landed. Miriam had been right! There was no cover within four hundred yards of the cluster of buildings. At least six machine guns were firing steadily. They were well placed and well dug in. The flat open area in front of him was a killing ground. To try to attack across it during daylight would be suicidal, but he couldn't wait for dark. He had to do something now.

He had only one card to play. He pushed the button on his tactical radio. "Omega Four, this is Omega Six. We are under heavy machine gun and rifle fire. I need the mortars now!"

Cray heard the reassuring sound of Blake's voice. "Roger, Omega Six. Completing emplacement now. Give me target coordinates. Ready to fire in two minutes."

TAWFIQ WAS STUDYING his map when he heard the sound of engines. For a second he wondered if it was their helicopters showing up, a few minutes early, but he realized that the sound was wrong. Then, he heard his machine guns firing. He picked up his AK-47 and ran for the door. His men were shouting and pointing at the sky, and he stared upward. Paratroopers, dozens of them, were dropping from the sky. He snapped up his field glasses. The planes were Lockheed C-130s. He could see white stars on their wings. Americans! Many Americans! The rest of his men were pouring out of the buildings and forming a firing line, but he was outnumbered at least three to one.

He stared intently as the Americans hit the ground. They were dropping four hundred yards away, taking cover in an irrigation ditch. A few landed long and were cut down by his machine guns, but most of them made it to the ditch, and Tawfiq could see a flickering line of yellow muzzle-flashes as they opened fire. The situation was not good, but Tawfiq was an experienced soldier and he didn't panic. He had six belt-fed .30-caliber machine guns and plenty of ammunition. Although he could not drive the Americans from the ditch, they would have no cover if they left it to attack. The cross fire would cut them to pieces. Surely he could hold them for ten or fifteen minutes, and that should be enough.

He beckoned to one of his sergeants. ''Tell Captain Kawash that we are under attack, but we are holding them. Tell him to be prepared to move the weapon.''

He swept the American position with his field glasses. They were firing steadily, but he saw no sign of movement. That was curious since they couldn't hope to win sitting in the ditch. He didn't think the American commander was a fool. He was waiting for something, but what? He did not have long to wait.

Tawfiq heard an odd sound. It came again. He knew instantly what it was, tube noise. Enemy mortars firing. Every experienced infantryman knew and hated that sound. ''Take cover! Take cover!'' he shouted, but it was really not necessary. His men were combat veterans. There was nothing to do now but pray. The mortar bombs were shooting upward on high, arcing trajectories and then dropping down from above at steep angles. It would take them twenty or thirty seconds to reach their targets.

Tawfiq waited tensely. A pair of mortar bombs burst forty yards in front of him. Gray-white smoke began to billow upward. Two more bombs burst, and then two more. The explosions moved closer and closer as the enemy adjusted their fire. Tawfiq heard the deadly whine of steel fragments shrieking by. The Americans were mixing high-explosive fragmentation bombs with their smoke.

They were shifting their fire left and right, screening their position from Tawfiq's gunners. Already, parts of their position were obscured. That was their plan. His men, dug in and fairly well protected, couldn't be blasted from their positions other than a few that might be killed by an unlucky direct hit. The smoke was the key. As soon as his gunners were blinded, the Americans would attack. There was nothing to do but fight and die.

Over the sounds of battle, Tawfiq heard engines and the distinctive sound of helicopter blades. The Americans hadn't won yet. He dashed back into the main building and snatched up two grenades, then ran to the back of the building. Kawash was standing by the weapon, which was ready on its transport dolly.

Kawash looked pale but determined. "I have installed the command circuits, Major. I can detonate the weapon now if you give the order."

Tawfiq felt a surge of pride. He had no family left since the Gulf War, but men like Kawash were his brothers. "No, we must still carry out the mission. The helicopters are here. Throw these smoke grenades behind the building. That is the signal. As soon as the helicopters land, load the weapon, take off and carry out the mission."

Kawash understood but he hesitated. "How will you and the rest of our men escape?"

Tawfiq smiled. It was not a pleasant smile. "We will not. The Americans will attack at any moment. I will buy you a few minutes, and I will see their blood before I die. Now, go with God, Kawash! Go with God!"

CRAY STARED INTENTLY through his field glasses as the 81 mm mortar bombs rained down on the enemy position. Blake had moved forward to the ditch and was acting as the forward observer, placing his rounds with a surgeon's skill. The cluster of buildings was nearly obscured by clouds of gray-white smoke. Blake was carefully keeping the impact points of the high-explosive bombs away from the buildings, and Cray agreed with that. He remembered Blake's words about low-order nuclear detonations. He wasn't sure what would happen if he were four hundred yards away from a nuclear weapon when it detonated low order, and he did not want to find out.

Blake was yelling over the steady noise of small-arms fire. "Major, we're firing the last smoke bombs now! Impact in thirty seconds."

Cray didn't want to go out there. He had seen all too often what a burst of machine-gun bullets could do to the human body. Still, they had not twisted his arm when he took command of Omega Force, and leading attacks was what they paid him for. He took one last look through his field glasses. A breeze was beginning to blow as the sun went down. The smoke would not last forever. Hall was crouched three feet to his left.

Cray swung his left arm forward and pointed at the enemy. "Go!"

Hall blew his whistle. Its shrill tones cut through the crackle of rifle and machine-gun fire. Cray rolled out of the ditch and started forward, yelling "Come on, men, let's go!" The attack order echoed up and down the ditch as the squad leaders repeated it. Cray's men were combat veterans. They didn't waste their breath on cheering. Silent and deadly, they moved toward the enemy to kill or be killed.

Three hundred yards! The enemy machine gunners were still firing, but they were shooting blind. Here and there a man went down, but the attack went forward. Two hundred yards! The mortars were still firing, pouring thirty-two rounds per minute into the smoke in a final barrage. One hundred yards! Blake ordered the mortars to cease fire. The attacking line reached the edge of the smoke and charged forward. Cray was blinded by the thick, billowing smoke, and the acrid smell filled his lungs.

The enemy knew they were coming and poured out almost continuous streams of machine-gun fire. Cray fought the temptation to throw himself down, and urged himself forward.

Suddenly they were through the smoke. Twenty yards away, Cray saw a machine-gun team firing madly at the oncoming Americans. He snapped his rifle up and fired burst after burst. His aim was good, but the light .223 bullets from his M-16A2 failed to penetrate the sandbags around the gun. Hall also fired two quick shots, but the machine gun hadn't been silenced. Blake had an M-203 grenade launcher clipped under the barrel of his rifle. He aimed quickly and pulled the trigger. The 40 mm grenade sailed through the air, struck and detonated. The machine gun was abruptly silent. One of the defenders threw a hand grenade, and he felt the deadly, high-velocity fragments tear into his body armor.

Cray was filled with the strange mixture of fear and fury that close combat brings. He went toward the door of the main building. Four or five men were defending it, led by a large man with a black beard. The muzzles of their lethal AK-47s were swinging toward Cray, Blake and Hall. Cray blasted them with every shot left in his 30-round magazine. Blake was firing, too. Three of the men fell, then Cray's M-16A2 locked open with a click on the empty magazine. Blake also stopped firing. His rifle must be empty, too.

Cray reached desperately for a fresh magazine, thinking that he wasn't going to live long enough to reload. Then he heard the roar of a .50-caliber semiautomatic rifle as Hall fired three fast shots. The two men staggered and fell, but the leader pulled the trigger of his AK-47 as he fell. Something struck Cray's left leg and smashed it out from under him. It was like being kicked by a giant, and he fell heavily. He felt no pain, but his leg was numb and would not respond when he tried to get up. Blake and Hall were crouching over him. Hall was tearing open a trauma dressing.

Cray tried hard to think. The sound of firing had died away. They must have taken the position. There had been fewer defenders than he had estimated, but they had fought to the end, sacrificing themselves for something. Suddenly he heard the sound of engines and the noise of rotors. Helicopters taking off!

"Find out what the hell's going on, Blake," he gasped.

Blake nodded and dived through the building door. For a moment there was silence, then the snarling rattle of an M-16A2 firing on full automatic as Blake emptied his magazine, then silence again. Blake emerged from the building and moved quickly to Cray's side.

"There were four Mi-8 helicopters, Major. They were taking off when I got to the back door. They are flying south, staying low."

"Were there any nuclear weapons in the building?"

Cray knew from the look on Blake's face that he was not going to like the answer.

"No, Major, but I found checkout equipment. It's identical to the equipment we found in Sudan, and there are traces of residual radioactivity next to the equipment. They must have had one weapon there, and there's only one place it can have gone. It's got to be on one of those helicopters."

Cray was beginning to feel cold and drowsy. Shock was setting in. A medic had appeared at his side and was rolling up Cray's sleeve, but Cray motioned for him to wait. There was one thing he still had to do. He forced himself to speak clearly. "Blake, get on the radio to General Sykes. Tell him what happened. Ask him to alert Captain Tower and Colonel Khier. Four helicopters headed south, toward the dam. One or more nuclear weapons on board."

"Roger, Major, right away."

Cray heard a horrible choking laugh. He glanced to the left and found himself looking into the fierce, bearded face of the man who had shot him. Somehow the face was familiar. He had seen it in Intelligence files. Then recognition dawned. It was Jamal Tawfiq. Cray had fought Tawfiq half a dozen times, but he had never met him face-to-face. Now they were both lying wounded in a godforsaken hole in Egypt. That was hilarious in a way, but Cray did not feel like laughing.

Tawfiq's face was pale with pain and shock, but he grinned like a wounded wolf. "God is great!" he gasped. "You think you have won, but you have failed!"

Then he collapsed, either unconscious or dead. It didn't matter to Cray. The numbness in his leg was gone, and it began to throb with pain. He felt the prick of a needle in his arm. He was having trouble thinking, but it didn't matter. He had done the best he could. It was up to Tower and Amanda Stuart now.

## 19

Amanda Stuart sat tensely at the controls of her MH-60K Blackhawk. The dull black helicopter was armed, refueled and ready to go. There was nothing to do now but wait, and Amanda hated waiting. Tower was sitting in the copilot's seat beside her, monitoring the communications control panel. A green light began to flash, indicating an incoming message. Tower listened intently for a minute and then answered in Arabic. Amanda could tell by the look on his face that something was up. She checked her instrument displays and poised her hand over the starting switches.

"Let's go!" Tower snapped.

She pushed the engine starter switches and felt the Blackhawk shudder as the twin turbine engines began to whine. The whine deepened to a howl as she went to full power and lifted the Blackhawk into the air. Almost instantly the lights of the Egyptian airstrip vanished into the dark. She checked her displays. Both engines were running smoothly. They were skimming over the surface of Lake Nasser at two hundred feet, headed for the dam. The lake was immense, the largest manmade body of water in the world. It was hard to imagine what would happen if all that water were suddenly released into the Nile.

Amanda concentrated on her flying. She kept her eyes on the multifunctional display, or the MFD, which converted the data from the MH-60K's infrared sensors into a clear picture of the scene ahead. She and Tower were wearing aviators' night-vision goggles, which let them see left and right out of the cockpit windows. She kept her running lights on. The Egyptian army had placed a dozen ZSU-23-4 automatic cannon along the dam as a last-ditch defence. She did not want to alarm their gunners.

They passed over the dam. It was huge, an immense structure of steel and concrete, with a four-lane road running along its top. It stretched for two miles in an arc across the river. It looked indestructible, but nothing could stand up to a direct hit with a nuclear weapon. Suddenly they shot over the top of the dam, and instantly the scene changed. The surface of the river was five hundred feet below. Eight miles away, up river, she could see the lights of the city of Aswan. Two hundred thousand people lived there. Colonel Khier had said it was an interesting place to visit. Amanda hoped it would still be there an hour from now.

She took the Blackhawk down. If the opposition knew anything about helicopter tactics, they would come in low and fast. She leveled off at a hundred feet and looked at Tower. He was finishing his checks and arming the weapons systems. A row of green lights on the weapons control console came on. The Blackhawk was carrying a dual Stinger missile launcher and 2.75-inch multiple-rocket launchers under each stubby ESSS wing. They were ready to fire. Amanda checked the .50-caliber machine gun she controlled. It was loaded and on safe. They were as ready as they would ever be. Now it was time for tactics.

"We probably ought to intercept them as far north as possible. Shall I take her up the river?" Amanda asked.

Tower was not sure. He was an outstanding infantry officer, but air-to-air helicopter combat tactics were not his strong suit. "What happens if they go out into the desert and come in behind us?"

Amanda shook her head. "I don't think they'll do that. They don't have any way of knowing we're here, and they'll want to catch the Egyptians by surprise. It will be much harder for radar to pick them up if they stay low and fly along the river. That's what I'd do if I were trying to attack the dam."

"All right, you're the expert. Take us up the river. Now, Blake says they're flying Mi-8 Hips. What are their capabilities?"

Amanda thought for a moment. She knew a lot about Hips. They were the standard air-assault helicopter of the Russian army, and widely used throughout the world. What did she know about them that was important now?

"They're bigger than a Blackhawk, but slower. They have a top speed at sea level of about one hundred sixty miles per hour. We can do one eighty-five, and we ought to be able to outmaneuver them. Some of them have been modified to carry night-vision equipment. These probably have it, but it won't be as good as ours. With any luck, we ought to see them before they see us."

"What about weapons?"

"They aren't gunships, but they're armed for the air-assault role. They have a 12.7 mm heavy machine gun in the nose. That has about the same range and power as one of our .50 calibers. They carry 57 mm rocket launchers and missiles. Some of them have been modified to carry SA-7 air-to-air missiles. We have to figure they will be able to shoot back."

Tower nodded grimly. This was not the best news he had ever heard, but at least he knew the facts. He looked down. They were passing over Aswan, and he could see the lights of cars moving in the streets below. People were busy going about their business, doing whatever was done in Aswan on Friday night, oblivious to the fact that they might be about to die. Tower could not imagine a wall of water three hundred feet high sweeping through the city. But if it happened, he knew that not a trace of Aswan or its people would be left. Nothing at all.

Amanda kept her eyes on the MFD, scanning the night ahead. Suddenly she stiffened. Something was moving toward them at the limit of the sensor's resolution. One—no, two—objects flying south. "Multiple targets, probably helicopters, dead ahead and closing fast!" she snapped.

Tower spoke quickly into his headset, listened for a moment and nodded. "Colonel Khier confirms that there are no Egyptian helicopters or aircraft flying at low altitude in the area. Weapons free!"

Amanda was staring at the MFD. The images were getting larger and clearer as they closed on the targets ahead at a combined speed of three hundred miles per hour. The targets were definitely helicopters with rounded bodies and long, slender tail booms. They were certainly Hips, and behind them she could see two more, about two thousand yards behind the leaders. It was decision time.

"Blake said there's only one weapon," Amanda said quickly. "One of the rear two is probably carrying it. Do you want me to try to get around the front pair and attack the two in back?"

Tower shook his head. "Negative! We haven't got the time, and there's a chance one of the front two is carrying the weapon. We've got to take them all out if we can. We'll use the Stingers and blast our way through!"

"Roger, let them have it!"

Tower aimed at the right-hand Hip, centering its image in the range ring. He pressed the tracker-activation switch and heard a steady tone as the Stinger's tracker activated. The Hips were coming on steadily, showing no sign that they were aware of the Blackhawk. Amanda was right. Their night-vision equipment was not as good as hers. The steady tone in Tower's headset suddenly changed pitch. Lock on! Instantly Tower pressed the firing switch. The Stinger's solid-propellant rocket motor ignited, and it flashed toward the Hip at fifteen hundred miles per hour.

Only one Stinger could be launched at a time. Tower centered the range ring on the second Hip and activated another Stinger. Amanda poised her fingers over her countermeasures switches. If the enemy had not known they were there before, they sure as hell knew now! Tower fired and sent the second Stinger on its way. The first Stinger struck the right-hand Hip on the nose and exploded in a flash of yellow fire. Its seven-pound warhead was too small to blow the Hip to pieces, but the big helicopter staggered and began to belch orange flames and smoke.

The second Stinger shot toward the target. Its infrared heat-seeking guidance unit saw the flames from the burning Hip as a superb target. The missile turned and struck it in the rotor assembly. The Hip's rotor blades disintegrated into fragments, and it dropped like a stone into the water below.

Amanda saw a bright flash in the MFD. A missile shot from the second Hip and flashed toward the Blackhawk, trailing a plume of fire. Instantly Amanda pushed her infrared countermeasures switch. The Blackhawk's ALQ-144 jammer began to emit immensely bright flashes of infrared light, and infrared decoy flares ejected from their launcher and began to burn behind her helicopter. The enemy missile was a Russian SA-7. It was an old design, and its guidance unit lacked the advanced technology of an American Stinger. Blinded and confused, it lost lock on the Blackhawk and streaked harmlessly by, chasing a decoy flare.

Tower fired again. The Stinger raced toward the Hip at twice the speed of sound. Amanda could see flashes of light around the Hip as its pilot desperately launched decoy flares, but the Stinger's advanced guidance unit was not deceived. The missile struck the Hip's cockpit and detonated. The pilot and co-pilot died instantly, and the aircraft nosed over and smashed into the river at one hundred forty miles per hour, vanishing in a huge cloud of spray.

They were racing toward the second pair of Hips at three hundred miles per hour. One of them was pulling ahead of the other, its bulbous nose pointed straight at her. Amanda saw rapidly blinking yellow flashes, and green tracers streaked by the Blackhawk as the Hip's 12.7 mm machine gun opened fire. The range was too long for accurate machine-gun fire, but it wouldn't be for long.

Amanda thought furiously. To turn or dive would merely give the Hip a better shot, but she had to do something. The Blackhawk had no armor, and a nose-to-nose gun duel would probably be fatal to both helicopters. Suddenly she had the answer. The rockets! The 2.75-inch rockets had originally been designed for air-to-air combat. Her hand shot to the weapons console, and she threw the firing switches. The Blackhawk's stubby ESSS wings were wreathed in fire as the 19-round rocket launchers blazed into life, sending showers of rockets streaking at the Hip. The rockets were not guided, but they were like the lethal blast from a giant shotgun. Amanda watched, fascinated, as half a dozen rockets struck in six seconds and their high-explosive warheads reduced the Hip to a shattered, burning hulk. It exploded in a ball of orange fire and thick gray smoke.

Amanda almost succumbed to target fixation. She was flying straight toward the expanding ball of fire, but at the last desperate moment she reacted. The Blackhawk shuddered and vibrated as she pulled it into a hard left turn. She was losing altitude. The engines howled as she went to full emergency power and tried to level out twenty feet above the water. Now she was flying straight and level, but almost touching the dark water streaking by just below the Blackhawk's belly.

Carefully she went up to a hundred feet and checked her displays. One engine was running rough, vibrating and down several hundred rpm. Amanda found that she was shaking with tension. To fly into the water at this speed would be like hitting a solid wall. Tower was shouting something and pointed at the MFD. Amanda stared, horrified. There was nothing to see but the river ahead. The fourth Hip had gotten by them. Amanda yanked the Blackhawk into a turn that would have given its designers heart failure. Now they were headed south, back toward the dam, desperately looking for the helicopter. Then they spotted it, dead ahead and flying all out fifty feet above the river.

Amanda kept her engines at full power, ignoring a warning light that began to flash. Number-two engine was not happy with life. In a normal peacetime training flight, Amanda would have declared an emergency and landed immediately, but this was not peacetime. They were flying toward the dam at three miles per minute, but the Blackhawk was only forty miles an hour faster than the Hip. They were gaining on it, but too damned slowly!!

They had one Stinger left. Tower centered the image of the Hip in the range ring. It was too far ahead! They were racing over Aswan now, the lights of the city flashing by in a blur below. Amanda could see the dam ahead in the distance, stretching across the river like a huge wall. It was now or never. Tower pressed the tracker-activation switch and heard a steady tone as the last Stinger's tracker activated. The sound in his headset suddenly changed pitch. Lock on! The Stinger had the target. Tower pressed the firing switch. The Stinger's solid-propellant rocket motor fired, and it shot after the Hip.

The MFD exploded in brilliant flashes of light as the Hip's pilot activated his pulse jammer and fired decoy flares. The slender, lethal missile raced toward the Hip. Its guidance unit saw and rejected the false targets. Amanda saw a bright yellow flash as it struck the Hip on the rear cargo door, just below the long, slender tail boom. The Hip shuddered and lost speed, but it was still flying. Amanda swore bitterly. She had one weapon left, the .50-caliber machine gun, but she had to get closer to use it, and every second brought them closer to the dam.

She stared at the Hip through her sights, two thousand yards, fifteen hundred. She pressed the trigger, and the Blackhawk vibrated as the big .50 caliber roared into life. Red tracers clawed at the Hip. She saw winking yellow flashes as metal struck metal and the armor-piercing incendiary bullets tore into the rear fuselage. Flame and smoke began to trail behind the Hip, but the damned thing still flew! Amanda steadied her sights and got ready to fire another burst.

CAPTAIN KAWASH SAT in the copilot's seat of the Hip. The cockpit was full of smoke, and his pilot was wounded, but the great gray wall of the dam was only a few thousand yards ahead. He heard the shriek of tearing metal as a burst of machine-gun bullets struck the rear of the helicopter. The fire alarm began to sound. Kawash knew he was about to die, but then, he had known he would not survive the mission before he took off. He didn't care. He would die a holy martyr. Now, if only the bomb were not damaged. He pressed a switch on the control box in this hand and waited tensely. God is great! he thought as the ready light went on. He pushed the first button. Armed! Then the second. Fuzed! His finger was poised over the fire button. They would crash directly into the dam if they could. If not, he would fire the bomb as he died.

AMANDA STUART LINED UP her sights again. They were running out of time. She had four hundred rounds left for the .50

caliber. She would fire them all in one last attack. Suddenly she heard a sound that froze her blood. The survivability system was beeping insistently. Antiaircraft fire-control radars were operating nearby, trying to lock on. The warning panel display read "multiple gun-dish radars—Soviet ZSU-23-4s." They were flying into a hornet's nest. The Egyptian antiaircraft gunners on the dam were trying to lock on and engage, but there was no way they could tell one helicopter from another in the dark. That would not stop them from firing at anything flying toward the dam. Too much was at stake.

Tower was shouting, "Break! Break! The Egyptians are going to fire! Get us out of here!"

Amanda pulled the Blackhawk into the hardest right-hand turn she dared. The dull black helicopter shuddered, but it held together. She glanced out the side window. The Hip was still headed for the dam, trailing flames. The darkness exploded in fountains of green tracers as thousands of 23 mm cannon shells clawed at the Hip. It nosed over, went down and smashed into the Nile in a cloud of spray.

Amanda saw an intensely bright, yellow-white point of light where the Hip had been a fraction of a second before. The point of light expanded rapidly into a glowing ball of unbearable intensity. The Blackhawk's cockpit was illuminated by the incredible brightness. Amanda's eyes were dazzled, and now the cockpit seemed to be filled with bright green spots. For a fraction of a second, a small piece of the sun seemed to have appeared on the river's surface. A huge dome of spray and foam heaved upward.

A giant hand seemed to strike the Blackhawk and tilt it crazily. The engines surged and lost power as they ingested spray. Amanda struggled with her controls, flying more by instinct than by thought. She thought she was flying level, but she could not see the MFD or her other displays. She blinked, desperately trying to clear her eyes, but her vision was blurred, and the world seemed to be full of glowing green spots.

"Jesus Christ," Tower said reverently, "the damned thing went low order, but the dam's still there!"

That was the least of Amanda's worries. "Dave, you've got to help me!" she announced desperately. "I've got flash blindness! I can't see!"

Tower froze for a second. He did not know how to fly a helicopter. They were flying through the dark at low altitude, and it sounded like the engines were getting ready to quit. If he panicked, they were dead.

"What can I do?"

"What does the MFD show?"

"We're drifting toward the riverbank." Tower knew it was important to speak calmly and clearly, but he wanted to yell. "The radar altimeter says forty feet, thirty. We're tilting to the right. Level off if you can. That's better. Can you—"

The number-two engine flamed out as a turbine rotor failed, and the Blackhawk tilted to the right. Amanda fought the controls and tried to level off. The Blackhawk struck and skidded along the ground on its belly for fifty feet. The shriek of tearing metal died away, and for a moment everything was still. Tower was dazed by the impact. The power was out. The cockpit was illuminated only by the emergency lights. He struggled to remain conscious. He could hear the ominous crackle of short circuits and smelled fuel. He realized that they had to get out. He released his harness and struggled out of his seat.

"Come on, Amanda, we've got to get the hell out of here!" he gasped.

There was no answer. Amanda was still in her seat, slumped unconscious in her flight harness. Tower smelled smoke and heard the crackle of flames behind him. He reached for the quick-release toggle to free Amanda from her harness, but the release was jammed! The smell of smoke was getting stronger. Tower drew his Randall knife and slashed at the tough nylon webbing. At last it gave, and he opened the pilot's door, grabbed Amanda under the arms and dragged her outside.

It took every ounce of strength he had left. There was a sharp pain in his right leg, and he was beginning to get dizzy. The temptation to drop to the ground and lie there was almost irresistible, but the crackle of flames was getting louder. Deserately he dragged Amanda's limp body away from the urning Blackhawk. He managed to make ten yards, then venty. Keep going, his mind shrieked, goddamn it, keep going! Somehow he was at forty yards, fifty! The pain in his leg amed into agony. He collapsed next to Amanda and lay still. lesh and blood could do no more. There was a flash of light nd blast of heat as the Blackhawk exploded in a ball of fire.

**20**

Major Jack Cray lay in the hospital bed feeling restless. The Egyptian military hospital was not luxurious, but he couldn' complain. Colonel Khier had spread the word that Cray had done marvelous but top secret things for Egypt, and the Egyptian doctors and nurses were treating their mysterious American patient like royalty. The doctors told him his leg would be as good as new in a few weeks. Cray wasn't used to lying in bed doing nothing, and he was bored. He tried to concentrate on the news magazine in his hands. It did not make pleasant reading. The world was experiencing its usual crises, famines and civil wars.

Cray heard a knock on the door and looked up as General Sykes came in. For once Sykes appeared relaxed and at ease. He looked at Cray lying in state, and smiled. "How's the hero?"

Cray snorted disrespectfully. He was proud of what Omega Force had done, but he did not feel that being shot in the leg made him a hero, even though he would get another Purple Heart. "What's going on, General?" he asked.

"Not much. The crisis seems to be winding down. You and your people did a damned good job. Washington and Cairo are happy. They're not very happy in Khartoum, though. It seems a lot of people in the Sudan are getting skeptical since the Mahdi hasn't been able to produce the miracles he promised. Dr. Kaye doesn't think his government is going to last very long. Miriam Mboro asked me to say hello and tell you she's sorry she can't come see you. She's gone back to the Sudan to organize opposition to the Mahdi."

Cray smiled. If Miriam Mboro was after him, the Mahdi was in a lot of trouble.

"But I didn't come here to brief you on the international situation, Major. There are a few administrative details we have to take care of."

Cray stopped smiling. He was an outstanding combat soldier, but he knew that his paperwork left a great deal to be desired.

The door swung open. Amanda Stuart and Dave Tower came in, followed by Blake and Hall. Amanda was wearing dark sunglasses and Tower was limping, but Cray was relieved to see that they both seemed to be all right. He noticed that everyone was smiling. They seemed to know something he didn't.

"If Captain Stuart will give me a hand?" Sykes directed.

Amanda went to the closet, took out Cray's uniform and laid it on the bed. She unpinned the two gold oak leaves that showed his rank and handed them to Sykes.

"I wouldn't want you to be out of uniform when you leave the hospital," Sykes said. He handed Cray two silver oak leaves. "Here, pin these on. Congratulations, Colonel!"

Everyone shook Cray's hand. They all knew he had wanted that promotion for a long time. Mercifully no one demanded that he make a speech.

Sykes looked at the two gold oak leaves in his hand. "We can't let these go to waste, and a colonel can't have a captain for an executive officer." He handed the gold oak leaves to Tower. "Colonel Cray doesn't need these anymore. Pin them on. Congratulations, Major Tower!"

Everyone congratulated Tower, then Sykes beckoned to Sergeant Hall. "I think we're about to break a few hospital rules. Better establish perimeter security, Sergeant." Hall smiled and stood by the door, while Blake opened his camera bag and produced a bottle of Jack Daniel's, some plastic cups, and poured the drinks.

"Time for some medicinal whiskey," Sykes commanded. "Rules or no rules, we've got to wet down those new oak leaves. It's bad luck if we don't."

No one said no. Soldiers seldom argued with generals.

"One drink is all you invalids get," Sykes announced, glancing at his watch. "Time to go. Colonel Cray's doctor will be here in five minutes, and we don't want an international incident."

There was a last round of congratulations and the party broke up. Sykes stayed behind as the others left. "One last thing, Jack," he said. "I'm recommending Stuart, Tower, Blake and Hall for the Distinguished Service Cross. I hope they get it. They sure as hell deserve it!"

Cray agreed. They certainly did. Everything seemed to be taken care of, but he was curious. "What happened to the opposition, if that's not top secret?"

"Tawfiq's in a military hospital. They're patching him up while they decide whether to shoot him or give him a life sentence. Saada Almori's disappeared. She must have gotten out of the country. The CIA can't find any trace of Colonel Sadiq. He's just disappeared. If he's still alive, they'll run him down, sooner or later."

Cray nodded. "Well, I guess it's over."

Sykes took the last sip of his drink. His face was somber. "No, it's not over. We've won another battle, but the war is still going on. The world is a dangerous place, and it's getting more dangerous all the time. It doesn't really matter whether Sadiq's alive or dead, there are still a lot of fanatics in the world. Better hurry up and get well. Until the age of miracles arrives and peace breaks out, they're going to need people like you and me."

**Inner-city hell just found a new savior—**

JAKE STRAIT
BOGEYMAN

## by FRANK RICH

Jake Strait is hired to infiltrate a religious sect in Book 3: **DAY OF JUDGMENT**. Hired to turn the sect's team of bumbling soldiers into a hit squad, he plans to lead the attack against the city's criminal subculture.

Jake Strait is a licensed enforcer in a future world gone mad—a world where suburbs are guarded and farmlands are garrisoned around a city of evil.

A struggle for survival in
a savage new world.

# JAMES AXLER

# DEATH LANDS®

## Deep Empire

The crystal waters of the Florida Keys have turned into a death
zone. Ryan Cawdor, along with his band of warrior survivalists,
has found a slice of heaven in this ocean hell—or has he?

Welcome to the Deathlands, and the future nobody planned for.

The Peacekeepers are dispatched
to shut down the fighting
with brute force in...

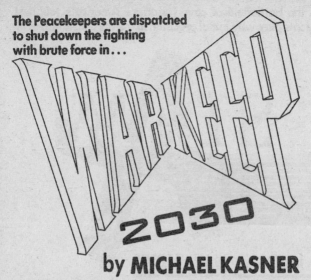

# 2030

## by MICHAEL KASNER

In Book 3: FINGER OF GOD, the Peacekeepers are up
against a ruthless and bloodthirsty enemy, with the specter
of nuclear holocaust looming on the horizon.

Armed with all the tactical advantages of modern technology, battle hard and ready when the free world is threatened—the Peacekeepers are the baddest grunts on the
planet.

**In the battlefield of covert warfare America's toughest agents play with lethal precision in the third installment of**

# SLAM

## by DAN MATTHEWS

In Book 3: SHADOW WARRIORS, hostile Middle East leaders are using the drug pipeline to raise cash for a devastating nuclear arsenal and the SLAM commando unit is ordered to dismantle the pipeline, piece by piece.

In the aftermath of a
brutal apocalypse,
a perilous quest for survival.

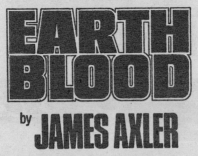

# EARTH BLOOD
by **JAMES AXLER**

The popular author of DEATHLANDS® brings you an action-
packed new postapocalyptic survival series. Earth is laid to
waste by a devastating blight that destroys the world's food
supply. Returning from a deep-space mission, the crew of the
Aquila crash-land in the Nevada desert to find that the world
they knew no longer exists. Now they must set out on an
odyssey to find surviving family members and the key to
future survival.

In this ravaged new world, no one knows who is friend or
foe ... and their quest will test the limits of endurance and
the will to live.

Available in November at your favorite retail outlet.

GOLD
EAGLE ®

EB1